LIFE'S
-A-
PITCH

By

JC Williams

You can subscribe to J C Williams' mailing list and view all his other books at:

www.authorjcwilliams.com

Cover design by JC Williams

Interior formatting, proofreading & editing by Dave Scott

ISBN: 9798838661630

First printing July 2022

Other Books by JC Williams

The Flip of a Coin

The Lonely Heart Attack Club
The Lonely Heart Attack Club: Wrinkly Olympics
The Lonely Heart Attack Club: Project VIP

The Seaside Detective Agency
The Seaside Detective Agency: The Case of the Brazen Burglar

Frank 'n' Stan's Bucket List #1: TT Races
Frank 'n' Stan's Bucket List #2: TT Races
Frank 'n' Stan's Bucket List #3: Isle 'Le Mans' TT
Frank 'n' Stan's Bucket List #4: Bride of Frank 'n' Stan
Frank 'n' Stan's Bucket List #5: Isle of Man TT Aces

The Bookshop by the Beach

The Crafternoon Sewcial Club
The Crafternoon Sewcial Club: Sewing Bee

Cabbage Von Dagel

Hamish McScabbard

Deputy Gabe Rashford: Showdown at Buzzards Creek

Luke 'n' Conor's Hundred-to-One Club

Chapter One

Folks often know it's a balmy summer's eve when the neighbourhood's precious tranquillity is shattered by the incessant throb of two-stroke lawnmower engines. From the moment the first pull cord ignites an engine into a spluttering frenzy, hacking and wheezing into life like a habitual smoker rising from a long nap, curtains around the estate are soon twitching with inquisitive residents (the male of the species, more often than not) drawn to the commotion like moths to the flame. And soon, all thoughts of a relaxing evening in front of the telly are shattered. Steadily, falling victim to peer pressure or an overwhelming sense of one-upmanship, one by one, they emerge, waddling like ducks towards their garden sheds, offering their fellow gardeners a cordial nod of the head while preparing themselves to contribute to the overall racket.

Benjamin (Ben) Parker, living at Number 17, was one such chap. He pressed his nose up against his front window, running his eyes over the state of his lawn which, sadly, was overdue a trim by at least three weeks. He stood there, staring forlornly. Already primed for action, as it should happen, wearing his blue shorts and scruffy t-shirt, along with his battered gardening trainers waiting patiently by the door, he was fully willing and prepared to join his fellows in battle. *Once more unto the breach*, he'd ordinarily be saying right about this time. Only there was one slight problem...

"You still haven't got your lawnmower back from the neighbour, have you?" Ruby remarked, looking up from her school reading assignment whilst lounging on the sofa.

"No. No, I haven't," said Ben, crestfallen. He lingered at the window, assessing the situation. "Perhaps... perhaps the grass will keep for another week?" he mused, turning to Ruby for her opinion, hopeful she might agree.

Ruby swung her legs ninety degrees, raising herself up into a seated position as she spun round. "I dunno. Isn't it time you went and got your property back?" she put forth. "The grass *is* getting a bit long over here, I should think."

Ben sighed. "Yes. Yes, I suppose you're right," he said, working to convince himself of this as he spoke. He returned his attention to the world outside, and in particular the house opposite, where his lawnmower currently resided. "Oh. I think he might actually be finished with it today," he observed, narrowing his eyes for a moment to verify that he was indeed seeing what he believed he was seeing. "Yes. Yes, it looks like he's just finished up. Well that didn't take him long, did it?"

Despite the neighbour apparently being done with the mower today and it thus being ripe for the picking, Ruby couldn't help but notice her dad had remained at the window, fixed to the spot. Ruby placed her book on the sofa beside her, rising to her feet. "Dad. Just *go and ask him for it*," she said, joining her dad by the window, positioning herself slightly behind so that she could knead his shoulders like bread dough. "If you stand here in front of the window much longer, you're going to frighten the neighbourhood children, yeah? So just march over there, right now, and tell him you *need* to use the mower. Tell him you need it back."

"I'll do it!" replied Ben, feeling motivated, and walking over towards the door and reaching for his gardening trainers. "Yes! I'll do just that. Right now. Right this instant!"

Ruby observed as her dad marched confidently across the road. Well, at least until he reached about the halfway point, whereupon he came to an abrupt halt, looking back and now appearing uncertain of his actions. He seemed to be vulnerable, like a child poised on the edge of the diving board, hoping for their mum's approval. *"Go for it,"* Ruby said, mouthing the words, and holding a thumb in the air to spur him on, which appeared to do the trick.

Austin Fletcher had the largest house on the development, a fact he was delighted to remind people of at any given opportunity. It was surprising that someone with such a prestigious (and prodigious) property hadn't replaced their lawnmower the moment their old one had found its way to scrap heaven. But then he was probably not in any kind of rush at all, considering he'd had full use of Ben's for at least a month, with Ben's mower being in Austin's possession that entire time.

Ruby remained at the window, grinding her teeth and somewhat nervous on her dad's behalf. It broke her heart seeing him like this, so timid at times and lacking in confidence. Of course, being a worldly-wise fifteen-year-old, she could quite easily have marched over to reclaim their property herself, but her dad needed to do this. He needed a victory of sorts.

She watched her dad cautiously approach, finger raised like a pupil trying to attract the teacher's attention. There, standing by *their* lawnmower, Austin wiped the sweat from his forehead, surveying his handiwork while barely noticing as Ben crossed the lawn. As Ben drew up alongside him, Austin finally couldn't help but notice him. When he did, he slapped Ben on the upper arm heartily. There was some pointing going on from each of them at this stage, with the both of them indicating sections of the lawn that may or may not have been satisfactorily completed, and then attention drawn to the mower itself, with the pair crouching down to inspect it and presumably discuss its merits and such.

To the casual observer, they might well have seemed like old buddies who were meeting up to share a beer or two on a warm summer's eve. That would, however, be something of a stretch. It wasn't that Austin was a *complete* rotter, necessarily. He just had the innate ability to condescend, making those he came into contact with feel inadequate with his arrogant bluster. Whether this was deliberate was anyone's guess, but Austin's demeanour was often the straw that could break the camel's back if you were already feeling self-conscious and lacking confidence. And Ben was, at present, experiencing both of these unfortunate attributes due to being on the receiving end of several considerable setbacks of late. For that reason, Ruby was very pleased to see her dad wheeling their petrol mower back towards their house a moment or two later.

In itself, it wasn't a momentous event, but Ruby knew the niggling issue of the mower had been playing on her father's mind. So, in securing its tidy return, she hoped this small victory would give him a much-needed boost in self-assurance, restoring some of his old convictions in the process.

Ruby stood in the front doorway, ready to welcome the returning hero. "Way to go, Pops," she offered, walking down the steps to greet him as he approached. "That lawn isn't going to know what's hit it," she added, tipping her head in the direction of the grass.

But Ben didn't stop beside his overgrown grass. Instead, he pressed on, taking a detour towards the garden shed in back. "There's a slight issue," he said over his shoulder.

"Which is...?" asked Ruby, now following closely behind.

Ben stepped inside his wooden shed, reaching for and retrieving a metallic toolbox. "Houston, we have a problem," he joked, from inside the darkened confines of the shed, his echoed voice sounding slightly ominous. But he attempted to put a positive spin on things as he re-emerged. "Ah, it's just as well that Dr Ben Parker's skills are called up today," he suggested, giving himself a new occupation as he dropped down on one knee to begin the delicate operation at hand. "Gives me a chance to break out and make use of my collection of surgical instruments, which is always nice," he said, holding up a spanner and smiling brightly.

"Oh?" replied Ruby.

"Yes, indeed," Ben answered, setting to work. "So Austin was just telling me he's ordered a new car," Ben added, by way of small talk. "Apparently, it cost eighty thousand pounds, which is quite a lot," he said, wrestling with a stubborn bolt.

"Dad?" Ruby said softly, not wishing to interrupt him, but curious as to what the current situation might be. "Dad, what's wrong with the lawnmower?"

"Smoke coming out of the engine, from what Austin was telling me," Ben offered, letting out a half-laugh. "He'd barely started in on his grass when, boom, the engine seized, according to him. But, no matter, I was thinking about maybe upgrading the old girl with a new model at some point in the future anyway. Particularly if I can't get this one fixed, of course."

"Well if that nitwit has so much dosh to throw around, buying a car for eighty flippin' grand, I hope he's putting his hand in his pocket to contribute towards your new mower? After all, he's been making full use of this one for quite a while now," Ruby interjected. "And what's with those stupid, canary-yellow shorts he was wearing, by the way? They were so bright, they were practically blinding me from all the way over here," she remarked.

Ben lowered his spanner, unable to resist another smile. "Those shorts *were* quite offensive," he agreed with a laugh.

"And if those tacky shorts weren't bad enough, the fact he wasn't wearing any top with them wasn't helping matters any, either," Ruby added. "He's got all that bloody money to spend but somehow can't afford a shirt to wear?"

"Oh, that was intentional, I think," Ben answered. "To show off his physique. When he'd finished telling me about his flashy new car, he swiftly moved on, making a point to mention how fabulous he looked, just in case I hadn't noticed. He stood there jiggling his bronzed pectoral muscles the whole time we spoke, without even breaking eye contact. It was a little unnerving, to be honest."

"I doubt that's really muscle," Ruby scoffed. "They're chest implants, I expect. Something people with entirely too much money on their hands do. It's crazy. And as for that bronzing? Cremated on a sunbed, I'd wager."

"That's a thing? Pectoral implants?" Ben asked, perplexed. "Men can do that?"

"Sure. If they've got the money and want to look like a bloody plonker," Ruby advised.

Ben tilted his head, giving the thought some consideration. "I dunno, I may have to look into those implants," he joked, cupping his presently paltry chest. "And don't forget my birthday's coming up. I'm sure I'll be a hit with the ladies if you should buy me a pair of those yellow beauties like he's wearing," he added gamely.

Ruby placed an arm across her father's shoulders. "It's good to see you smile, Dad," she said, patting his back, and then reaching for a tin of WD-40. "And if we do manage to get this mower up and running today, that plonker's got another thing coming if he thinks he's borrowing it again, yeah?"

"Agreed," Ben said, agreeing.

Ruby lifted the sofa cushions, hoping her missing book had slipped down the side as it was nowhere else to be found. "Dad, have you seen that book I was—"

"I placed it there, on top of the fireplace," Ben called back from the kitchen, with impressive mindreading skills, knowing precisely which book his daughter was looking for.

Ruby's friend and trusty school walking companion, Ella, pointed to the clock hanging just above the mantle. "If the shop sells out of sausage baps by the time we get there this morning, I'm blaming you," she gently chided her mate, as Ruby successfully located her book after this moderate delay.

"Ella, you could have some wonderful Scottish porridge if you like," Ben said, calling out from the kitchen as he nursed his steaming bowl of oats like Goldilocks, waiting for the temperature to be just right. "It comes complete with a delicious dollop of lovely local honey as well," he advised.

"Thanks, Mr Parker, it's tempting. But Tuesday is sausage bap day at the shop along the way," Ella hungrily explained, giving her tum a rub for good measure, even though Ben couldn't currently see her. Then, giving her friend Ruby a gentle shove towards the door, "See you soon, Mr Parker," Ella called over her shoulder.

"Have a good day, girls," Ben told them, wandering out from the kitchen to see them off, porridge bowl in hand. "And, Ella, enjoy your breakfast bap."

Ruby turned, remembering something she'd just remembered she wanted to say. "And what is it you'll be doing today, Dad?" she said, in a tone suggesting she already knew what the correct answer to this question ought to be.

"Today...?" Ben asked, with a bit of porridge millimetres from his lips. "As in, *today*, today?" he asked, considering Ruby's question for a moment, before blowing a stream of air over a spoonful of his breakfast. "I expect I'll need to check my Filofax," he advised.

Ruby playfully rolled her eyes. "Dad, you're probably the only person since the late eighties to still use a Filofax," she said with a groan. "But to save you digging out that brick, the answer is that you're going to phone around the recruitment companies," she informed him.

"Ah. Right, right. Now I remember," Ben answered, playing off as if he'd completely forgotten until just this very second, thanks to her helpful suggestion.

Ruby blew her father a goodbye kiss, and then turned once again to her friend. "Come on, Ella, let's get a move on, shall we? Sheesh, I'm always waiting for you!" she teased.

"Ruby," Ella whispered a moment later, even though they were well clear of the house by now. She glanced over her shoulder, like she wanted to say something but didn't know quite how to put it. "It doesn't matter. Never mind," she added a moment later.

"What is it, Ella? Out with it," Ruby insisted.

"Your dad..." Ella said warily, not wanting to cause offence.

"Yeah?"

"Well, has he permed his hair?"

Ruby grinned as she noticed Ella's deadly serious expression. "Permed?" she asked. "No, they're ringlets," she explained. "They make an appearance if he's long overdue a haircut."

"Oh, I thought it was maybe some sort of intentional style choice, or..."

"No, no, nothing like that," Ruby said with a laugh. "Remind me another time and I'll dig out some of his old baby pictures for you to look at. They're adorable. And apparently, with his mop of brunette curls in full swing, most people mistook him for a girl until he was about three."

Ella still looked serious, though, like there was something more on her mind. "He's okay, though? I mean, what with your mum and everything?" she asked, appearing to be worried, perhaps, that the unusual emergence of curls was perhaps a sign that Ben was not taking proper care of himself.

"A work in progress," Ruby suggested, trying to downplay the gravity of the current situation. "There's been a few smiles of late, which is an improvement."

But Ruby's optimistic assessment was considerably wide of the mark because her dad wasn't okay by any stretch of the imagination. He was emotionally wounded and damaged goods. Of course, Ruby had no desire to see anybody suffer like her dad, but it was just so unfair that it should happen to him, she couldn't help but feel. He hardly deserved it, she thought, as he was the sort of person who would do anything for anyone. He was one of the kindest, most charitable persons you could ever hope to meet, nearly to a fault, was her considered opinion.

Losing his wife, career, and financial security all within the span of a few months had taken a considerable toll on Ben. Previously, he was the first to arrive at your party and the last to leave. The life and soul of any social occasion. He was an eager beaver as well, always the first to throw his hand up when a volunteer was needed, for instance. Often, he'd no idea what he was offering his services for, but it didn't matter, not really. Ben was delighted to be asked. And if it was making baked goods for a fundraiser or packing shopping bags at the supermarket for charity, he was always the first in. *An opportunity to meet nice people and do good things,* was his usual reply when asked if he was available for this thing or that.

Right now, however, he was a mere shadow of his former self — anxious, unmotivated, irritable at times, which was quite unlike him, and even leaving the house for him was now a struggle. Overall, he was reasonably helpless, Ruby observed. As a result, she'd stepped up to the plate, with her almost adopting the role of the parent in their household. Though Ruby didn't mind. It was her dad, after all, and she'd do anything to help him navigate his way through the unfortunate potholes in life's highway.

A few minutes later and Ella was exiting the shop, nearly tripping on the step due to having her nose pressed inside her breakfast bag. "That smells *a-ma-zing*," she declared, reaching inside. "You're sure I can't tempt you with a nibble?" she asked, but it was obviously a half-hearted offer she earnestly hoped would be declined.

Ruby shook her head. "No, but thanks. I've still not recovered from when they gave me undercooked sausages that one time," she said, gagging. Although this information didn't appear to offend Ella's appetite, judging by the speed at which she was wolfing her breakfast bap down.

The two of them filtered in with the horde of pupils wearily trudging their way to school for another day of enlightenment. "Do you remember that careers evening we went to the other week?" Ruby asked.

Ella couldn't speak, her cheeks still stuffed at the moment, with her looking like a squirrel storing a mouthful of nuts. "Mmhmm," she offered over the noise of those chatting around them, and then raising a finger as a placeholder.

Ruby waited patiently, allowing her ravenous companion to finish polishing off her chow.

"I do," Ella eventually replied, as they entered the school grounds. "Why, have you been duly inspired? Your future career now mapped out?"

"You've got ketchup all over your chin," Ruby helpfully offered, pointing to the offending area, skipping over Ella's question for a moment. "There was a chap there from a recruitment company," Ruby continued, back on topic. "Jim... John... Geoff...?" she threw out there, searching for the name on the tip of her tongue.

"Giles!" Ella offered, rubbing a moistened thumb on her soiled chin. "Giles from *Love Mondays*," she added, the name of his company still fresh in her mind.

"Yes! That's him. Giles."

Ella thrust her chin forward. "Am I good?"

"You're all clean," Ruby confirmed, inspecting her friend's face. "Anyway, I think I might give Giles a ring," she pondered aloud. "He did say to give him a call, *anytime*, so..."

"What, right now? I'm not sure he'll be able to hook you up with a new job before the school bell rings," Ella joked. "Although he did seem to know what he was talking about."

Ruby smiled, nodding to the lad kindly holding the door open for them. "Not for me, silly," she said, her attention back to Ella.

"Then who? Your dad?" Ella wondered.

"Exactly! He's been threatening to begin job hunting for weeks. So, *technically*, I'm not interfering if I make an appointment for him with a recruitment agent. That's not overstepping the mark, is it?"

"You're being helpful, Ruby, relieving him of that administrative burden," Ella offered, settling the doubt in her friend's mind. "Besides, what's the worst that's going to happen?"

"Right. I'm going to do it, then," Ruby confidently declared. "If nothing else comes from it, at least it'll get him out of the house for a while."

"You should also get your dad an appointment with Chloe," Ella put forth. "Do you remember her? The lady I was speaking with at the careers evening?"

"I will," Ruby responded, pleased with the suggestion and making a mental note to do precisely as recommended. "She's also a recruitment agent, is she?"

"No. Chloe's the *hairdresser*, Ruby," Ella saw fit to remind her.

"And I mention this because your dad *really* needs to sort that mop out before he starts jobhunting."

Chapter Two

Ben fidgeted on the burgundy leather armchair, releasing a squeaking noise each time he shifted his weight from one side of his derrière to the other. Next to him, the water dispenser unexpectedly gurgled into life, belching up a sudden burst of air bubbles from the depths of its reservoir.

"That wasn't me," Ben joked when the lady behind the reception desk glanced in his direction over the rim of her glasses. "The water dispenser. Just there," he explained, snitching on his rowdy neighbour.

"Ah. It does that on occasion," the woman replied with an amiable grin. "By the way, please do help yourself."

Ben was parched, but after a brisk walk in the warm weather to get there, he could feel a worrisome sweat patch had formed on the rear of his blue polo shirt. As such, he was reluctant to stand and put his back to her. "I'm fine, for now," he said, deciding it was best to stay put, hoping the fabric would dry out in time for his meeting.

Of course, he'd had the option to drive to his appointment, and could easily have done so, but to do that would have been criminal on such a beautiful day on the Isle of Man, he had felt. Before his recent setbacks, in fact, Ben had adored nothing more than hiking around this charming little island in the middle of the Irish Sea. Home was Castletown, a picturesque seaside town in the island's south, boasting a pretty harbour at its heart and a splendid medieval castle, Castle Rushen.

Before today, it'd been weeks since Ben ventured into the town centre. It wasn't that he didn't want to go, necessarily. Rather, it was more that he couldn't face bumping into people who'd want to offer him their best wishes, tilting their heads when they asked him the inevitable *"How are things, Benjamin? Are you coping okay?"* and such. This was meant with good intentions from most, of course. Though there were also plenty of folks, nosey buggers, who simply wanted to get the inside track on the town gossip. Either way, it was something he had chosen to avoid.

And as he sat in the reception area, surveying his surroundings, he felt a small wave of optimism wash over him. Something that'd been absent from his life for some good while. It was only a twenty-minute walk he'd accomplished today, but it was something. He was out and about, amongst the people, and here he was now doing something important as well, overcoming his anxiety. Perhaps there was a flicker of light at the end of the tunnel? He hoped so.

Ben twiddled his tie with his left hand as he waited, trying to recall the last time he'd actually worn one. It must have been months, possibly years, he reckoned, as it had taken him four whole attempts to remember how to tie the bloody thing. Under duress, he'd taken Ruby's advice from the previous day and refrained from wearing his Simpsons tie, proud as he was of it, resplendent with images of Homer drinking Duff Beer all the way down the front. Instead, he'd opted for a slightly more understated affair, a tartan check number that Ruby assured him was perfect for a business appointment. Unfortunately, Ben hadn't been able to find a formal shirt anywhere. He'd stripped the contents of his wardrobe, but nothing. So, with no other options on the table, he'd opted for his smartest polo shirt, hoping that would do the trick. It was an unusual combination, polo shirt and tartan tie, he had to admit, and one he suspected his daughter would likely disapprove of had she seen it. Still, at least he would make a lasting impression, he reasoned during the enjoyable walk there.

Soon enough, a pleasant-looking blond-haired chap stepped out from behind one of the doors, running his eyes around the reception area for his next appointment, an act which didn't take long. "Benjamin, I presume?" he asked, flashing his pearly whites. "I'm Giles."

Ben jumped up, concerned by the sound of damp fabric peeling off his leather chair. "At your service," he replied brightly, accepting the hand thrust in his direction.

"Marvellous. If you'd like to come through to my office," Giles said, leading the way. "Did you manage to complete the questionnaire?" he asked, looking over his shoulder.

Ben held up a plastic clipboard, questionnaire attached. "Yes, all done," he was pleased to report. Then, feeling a welcome breeze caress his cheek, he suddenly halted, angling his sweaty back towards the oscillating fan sitting atop a sideboard. Then, taking slow, sideways steps, Ben plucked the rear of his polo shirt like a harpstring, tugging the shirt away from his skin. "Ahhh," he moaned in delight, grateful for the cooling air.

"Ahem, everything okay there, Ben?"

"What's that? Oh, yes. Fine," Ben replied, dropping his eyes to the clipboard in his hand. "I was just..." he began. "Ehm, revisiting my answer to question six," he lied, still mirroring the trajectory of the moving fan so they manoeuvred like dancing partners.

Once seated in Giles' office, Ben offered a nervous smile while the answers to his questionnaire were being reviewed.

"A-ha! I *knew* I recognised your face," Giles exclaimed a moment later, glancing over his desk. "I sometimes popped into your bakery for those amazing cookie sandwiches with icing in the middle."

"Ah," Ben said, nodding along. "Yes, Bread Pitt, my bakery. That was my little baby for, oh, seven years or so. You probably struggled to place the face, as I've dropped a few pounds, and plus the hair's a little longer now. So, I'm a little bit like a malnourished Micky Flanagan at the moment, as you can see."

"Bread Pitt," Giles said, chuckling to himself. "Always made me laugh, by the way. Very creative."

Giles read through the rest of the questionnaire, making noises of encouragement as he went along. "Wonderful. That's just what we need, then," he announced once he'd finished digesting the information, laying the clipboard down. "So. I see you're eager to explore job opportunities," he said, leaning forward. "The good news is that the market, at present, is rather buoyant."

Ben, who'd thankfully cooled down by now, smiled in response. "Yes. Excellent," he said, raising his thumb in appreciation. "Since the bakery closed, I've been between employment," he confessed. "I'd been meaning to start the ball rolling, but what with one thing and another. Fortunately, my daughter took the bull by the horns and made this appointment for me."

"So, you've worked in the bakery for seven years, as you've said," Giles put forth. "Do you mind me asking why you decided to close the business down?"

Ben sighed. "I had a run of unfortunate luck," he confided. "Everything started to unravel when I lost my wife to unhealthy eating."

Giles's jaw dropped. "Oh, my. How terrible," he said, adopting a genuine, sympathetic expression after picking his jaw back up. "I'm very sorry to hear that, Ben. It must have been a particularly challenging time for you," he offered gravely.

"Oh, no, not like that," Ben said, backtracking immediately. "When I say I lost my wife, I didn't mean *lost*, lost," he clarified. "After working in a bakery for so long, you see, she was worried about carrying a little extra luggage. So much so that she hired a dietician to develop a healthy eating plan. Unfortunately, one thing led to another, and she ended up getting more from him than just his *expert opinion*, if you take my meaning," he added with a resigned what-can-you-do sort of shrug. "And that's when things started to go the shape of the pear, and before you know it, I was putting up the closed sign on the business for the final time."

Giles didn't really know what more he could do other than offer another sympathetic smile. "It sounds like you've been through the mill, Ben. But hopefully, we can find an employment opportunity that'll be the perfect match for your skillset."

That positive sentiment raised Ben's spirits. After all, he knew he needed to dust himself down and put himself out there. Also, the allure of watching daytime television had long since waned, and the meagre contents of his savings account were evaporating faster than the sweat patch on his back. The challenge now, however, was finding something that was actually suitable.

"So, to be clear, you're not eager on any sort of office work at all, Ben?" Giles asked, glancing back down to the answers Ben had provided on the questionnaire, with Giles hiding his concern over this relevant bit of info behind a faltering smile. "You should know that this will really limit your options," he advised.

"It's the sitting down all day," Ben suggested, pointing a finger towards his lower back. "Sciatica," he explained with a grimace.

Giles tapped away on his keyboard, making a note accordingly. Then, scrolling down his list of available inventory, "What about retail?" he asked. "With your experience, you'd be ideally suited."

"Hmm, I think I'd like to dip my toe into something completely different, Giles. You know, something away from retail," Ben told him.

"But not office work?" Giles asked rhetorically, before swiftly moving on. "What about driving for a courier company?" he said, looking up from the computer screen.

"Sciatica," Ben indicated again, using the same finger to point to his lower back.

Twenty minutes or so later and Giles could scroll no further, all of his current listings exhausted. Unfortunately, nothing so far appeared to quite hit the spot. For example, the opportunity at the florists wouldn't work owing to a sensitivity to pollen, it was revealed, and a distinct fear of heights put paid to the scaffolding role, and so on.

"I'll let you know if anything exciting comes in," Giles suggested after they'd finished, escorting Ben towards the door. "But the truth is that most of the positions we receive are often office-based," he confided. "From what you're saying, Ben, the bakery sounded like your dream job and was something you were good at. You wouldn't look to go down that route again?"

"I think it's time for a fresh start," Ben said, offering his extended hand. "I sincerely appreciate your efforts, Giles. And, hopefully, hear from you soon?"

"Hopefully. And it's been a pleasure," Giles said, holding open the door. "Ben," Giles added, before Ben should be on his way. "I wasn't going to say anything, but..." he continued, the two of them stepping out into the hallway.

"Is it about the damp patch?" Ben asked, craning his neck for a view over his shoulder. "Or the whole polo shirt and tie combination?"

"What? No?" Giles replied with a laugh. "Although the polo shirt and tie are a first on me," he confided. "But what I was going to say is that a friend of mine went through something similar to you. And it took him a while to get through it. But he did, eventually. Get through it, I mean."

"I appreciate that, Giles."

"For what it's worth, my mate really benefited from the fresh air. You know, getting out into the great outdoors. He started cycling, went camping, and even bought a fishing rod. Anyway, I hope I've not overstepped the mark or anything?"

Ben reflected on this as they made their way through the reception area and over towards the lift, Giles happy to see Ben off. Ben had certainly enjoyed his walk earlier, and was pleased to be out of doors again after his several-month, self-imposed hibernation. "I think I'll do that," he replied, buoyed by the prospect of Giles' fine suggestion. "I'm going to head home and dig the old mountain bike out of the garage, for starters," he said, just as the lift doors opened. "Thanks again, Giles. And fingers crossed the ideal job opportunity crops up."

Ben didn't actually own a bike. Not since he was a kid. But as he and Giles had been having such a pleasant, man-to-man chat, he felt it wasn't the best time to mention that fact. Regardless, he was compelled by the idea of cycling the entire length of his walk home. He didn't fancy the whole notion of wearing skin-tight Lycra, necessarily, crouched over a racing-style bike. But the thought of a leisurely cycle around the winding country roads, on the other hand, was most palatable. However, instead of jumping in feet-first and spending cash on a potentially friv-olous whim, especially given the current status of his finances, he first wanted to make sure he could comfortably ride one. The only bicycle in the household at present belonged to Ruby, her Christmas gift from several years back. And so, just now, after he'd made his way home, he was determined to dig it out.

Cursing the state of the garage, Ben took a mental note to tip half of the contents, most of which hadn't been used in years. He could just catch a glimpse of Ruby's bike which natu-rally, in typical fashion, was parked all the way at the very back, requiring some effort on his part to retrieve. And indeed, after twenty minutes or so, fishing rods, a grass strimmer, garden furniture, rusting BBQ, Christmas decorations, and countless other items were now sitting in front of the house on the drive-way. In fact, several cars slowed as a result, possibly thinking it was a garage sale and hopeful of picking up some lovely bar-gains.

Eventually, a suitable path was cleared, allowing Ruby's bike to be successfully extricated. It was possibly the first time it would be on tarmac since Boxing Day, two years earlier. And sure, the frame size was more suited to a young girl, but it'd do, for now, just to give him a steer as to whether it was a hobby he'd like to progress or not. First, though, Ben had to stop him-self from immediately jumping aboard, conscious of the very same health and safety warnings he was always eager to drill into Ruby. Aware that a collision was always a genuine possi-bility, Ben opted to play things safe by wisely adopting the ap-propriate headgear before his debut jaunt. The fact that the helmet was pink didn't bother him too much, and neither did the words *"Sassy Lady"* displayed across the front in gold glitter.

At the end of the day, he reasoned, you only had one head. "Right, then," Ben said, playfully dinging the bell. "Lookout, roads, I'm coming your way," he announced, slowly freewheeling down the slight gradient of the driveway.

Immediately, his little face erupted into a tremendous cheesy grin. Even though he was only travelling at a snail's pace, and his knees were smacking against the handlebars each time he pedalled, Ben was having a blast burning up the road. He even took a mental note to record a short video of his exploits, confident that Ruby would have a laugh at his expense when she came home from school.

Recalling the correct protocol from his cycling proficiency test, Ben stretched out his right arm upon reaching the end of the street. With a cautionary glance over his shoulder, he performed a faultless U-turn, now heading back the route he'd just ridden. And confidence was high by this point, so much so he was now out of the saddle, pumping his legs furiously.

Ms Riddle, out for a stroll with BoBo, her beloved French poodle, performed a double-take. "What on earth are you up to, Ben?" she said with a laugh, cheering him on.

"Practising for the Tour de France!" Ben shouted over his shoulder, giving his bell another cheery ding as he pedalled along, his teeth dry from smiling so much.

However, Ben's attention was soon taken by the sound of thunder approaching from behind. It was a vehicle of some sort, growling to an extent that it was in danger of loosening Ben's fillings. "What the...?" he said, struggling to glance behind without veering into the kerb. But the vehicle didn't pass, just sitting there, inches away from his rear wheel. "Go around me!" Ben instructed, waving his arm frantically. "I'm on a girl's bike! I can't go any faster!"

But the throaty roar remained positioned behind him, and distractingly so. "Go around!" Ben suggested again, but all he received in response was the sound of an aggressively revving engine, scaring the bejesus out of him, the front wheel of his bicycle now wobbling because he was so terribly flustered. "*Right!*

I'll just pull over, then, shall I?" Ben decided, thrusting his left arm out to signal his intentions.

With one foot soon resting on the kerb, Ben readied himself to issue a stern glare, but the vehicle didn't pass, merely pulling up alongside, engine idling like an angry bull. For a moment, he was concerned he'd somehow antagonised the driver. And sat astride a girl's bike, wearing a *Sassy Lady* helmet, no less, Ben wasn't in any way prepared for a potential road-rage incident.

Ben wasn't especially into cars, necessarily, but even he could see that this one was something to behold. He didn't have a clue what make and model it was. All he knew was that it was bright red, with a spoiler, and wouldn't have looked entirely out of place at a drive-by shooting, he thought unnervingly.

"Can I help? Ben asked, leaning down to look through the now-opened passenger-side window. Then, recognising the driver, Ben removed his helmet. "Ah. I didn't know that was you, Austin," he said, relaxing a bit, and casting an admiring eye over the car's interior. "Oh, you can really appreciate the new car smell, can't you?" he added, as his nostrils took in the scent.

"Don't put your fingers on the bodywork!" Austin barked from the driver's seat. "I've only just picked her up, so I don't want greasy handprints all over the glimmering paint," he warned, as if he were speaking to a toddler.

Ben retracted his arm. "Understood," he replied, for some reason accompanying this with a smart salute. "And the new car *is* rather splendid, I must say," he offered.

"I know," Austin replied, chin in the air. "She goes like the clappers, and the women love it," he insisted, patting his hand on the steering wheel. "Anyway," he added, dabbing his foot on the accelerator to rev the engine, "I thought I'd stop and show you what an eighty-grand sportscar looks like."

"Uh, thanks for that...?" Ben answered. And then, with the unexpected interlude apparently concluding, Ben watched as Austin adjusted his expensive-looking sunglasses.

"I'll leave you to play on your girl's bike," Austin told him, before roaring off towards his house only a short distance ahead.

"It's not mine...!" Ben called out in protest, brandishing his pink helmet, but Austin had already buggered off, and Ben didn't have the inclination to pedal after him.

Once safely back inside, Ben settled onto the sofa with bruised kneecaps and a slightly dented ego. But he wasn't going to let Austin rain on his parade. Nossir. After all, he'd had a thoroughly enjoyable day so far. And while the modest frame on Ruby's bike wasn't ideal, his pleasant exertion around the neighbourhood certainly whetted his appetite for more.

Ben fired up his laptop, a steaming mug of tea he'd prepared now by his side, eager to explore the local classified ads for a steed more suited to his size and stature. But unfortunately, his knowledge of mountain bikes wasn't all that much better than his knowledge of cars. As such, the detailed descriptions in the various posts meant little to him. Meaning that his final decision would likely as not be based more on price than anything else, and also, just as crucially, colour.

Sadly, after extensive scrolling, nothing presented itself as being worthy of a personal inspection. In typical fashion, those bikes that Ben did like were significantly out of his price range, and those more reasonably priced looked as if they were about ready for the scrap heap. He wouldn't be put off just yet, but reckoned a bit more research might perhaps be in order before taking the plunge on such a purchase, leaving it for another day.

Ben reached up to close his laptop, mindful of the Penguin biscuit lying next to his cuppa that required his attention. But before he closed the computer over, he caught a glimpse of another classified, something else this time, not a bike. "Hell-o, what do we have here?" he said, sliding the laptop along his thighs for a closer view, reading through the details in the listing and liking what he was seeing. He narrowed one eye, looking up towards the ceiling with a 'will I, won't I' type of expression on his face, weighing the various pros and cons in his mind. "Ah, what the heck," he decided, figuring you only live once. It definitely wasn't the purchase he'd originally intended, but it just may have been an even better thing.

His chocolate Penguin biscuit would need to 'chill' a while longer, so to speak, as Ben stretched for his mobile, dialling the number provided in the listing. "Hi, is that Gerry?" he asked when the call connected. "Great," he said, upon receiving the requisite confirmation. "I was just calling about your advert on Facebook, and wondered if your item was still available?" he enquired. "Oh, that's terrific news. Would it be possible to come round and view it?" he said, and then, "Oh, that's brilliant. I can pop round this afternoon?"

Ben placed the laptop on the sofa with his free hand, jumping up to locate a pen and paper. He quickly found the unopened envelope from his electricity bill, but a pen proved more elusive. "Won't be a moment," he said into the phone, moving around the living room, shifting this and opening that, though without any success. "Ah," he said, mission accomplished and pleased with himself until he realised he'd actually picked up Ruby's eyeliner pencil. No matter. He'd work with what he had. "Ready when you are," he said, writing the address down and blunting Ruby's pencil. "That's brilliant, Gerry. I'll see you very soon!"

Chapter Three

I t's not too, you know...?" Ruby asked of Ella, running a careful hand over her hair as they walked and talked.

"Garish?" Ella suggested, though not entirely serious. However, she could see the doubt written on her friend's face. "Ruby, if you'd gone for a shocking pink, like a *My Little Pony* colour," she assured her, "then I reckon that might be considered, by some, as garish. But you're more *pink lemonade*, I think, which is slightly more understated and subtle. I really like it."

"Thanks, Ella. And your own hair looks fab-u-lous."

"I know. It does, doesn't it?" a modest Ella agreed. "I just hope that Rob is as equally impressed," she said, crossing her fingers. At this point, Ella veered off towards the lane to her right, parting ways with her friend for the time being. "I'll swing by your house at seven!" she said, walking backwards and blowing a kiss as she made her way along. "Don't forget, we're getting pizza there!"

Already delayed by her hair appointment, Ruby picked up the pace. Not only because she was heading back out in less than two hours, but also because she was eager to speak to her dad. His appointment at the recruitment agency had been on her mind for most of the day, though exchanging messages while in school was nigh on impossible. Fortunately, her dad hadn't appeared overly aggrieved when she'd confessed to making the appointment on his behalf. However, a small part of her suspected he would have talked himself out of it given half the chance, finding some reason or other why he couldn't attend. Still, he'd seemed broadly on board with the idea, which left her feeling fairly positive.

"What's all this?" Ruby muttered to herself, spotting the bits and bobs currently scattered across their driveway. Concerned they were in the process of being burgled, she retrieved her mobile from her pocket, ready to phone the police should it prove necessary. "Dad?" she called out from the pavement, wondering if he was inside the garage. With no response, she ventured forward with caution, scanning for any sign of forced entry or broken glass around the house, of which there was none, at least as near as she could tell. "Aww," she offered with a nostalgic smile, noting her old bike lying there on the grass. "Wait, what's that smell?" she asked out loud, sniffing the air, suddenly convinced she could detect the scent of something burning.

Ruby walked up to the house, pressing her nose against the living room window to peer inside for a closer look. And whilst there was no sign of her father just yet, she could at least see nothing out of place inside, with everything appearing as it should.

"Dad?" she said again, stepping over the threshold, but there was still no response. "Dad!" she shouted up the stairwell. "Dad, are you up—" she started to say, but she was *certain* now that she could indeed smell smoke, though it was difficult to ascertain its precise origin. Fearing it would be a call to the fire brigade rather than the police she'd need to make, Ruby darted towards the kitchen, concerned something burning in the oven might be the culprit. And it was then she discovered both the guilty party and the source of the smell that she'd been smelling.

She couldn't help but laugh, setting her schoolbag down on the kitchen table. "What are you doing?" she said, mouthing the words through the patio glass.

Standing outside in the rear garden, Ben motioned for Ruby to join him, which Ruby duly obliged. "Welcome home," he told her, prodding the campfire with an old broom handle. "Oh, and your hair looks smashing! I quite like it."

Ruby could be forgiven for appearing somewhat surprised. After all, she'd left a man that morning who'd rarely ventured outside the house for weeks, and for whom changing out of his pyjamas into something more approaching daytime attire had remained a daunting challenge. Yet there he was now, dressed in his finest khaki, toasting marshmallows on a fire pit he'd crafted by laying out a circle of surplus paving bricks. Oh, and the small matter of the tent, of all things, as well, standing proudly behind him. And this wasn't just any old tent, either. This was a jolly *big* tent.

"Were the circus having a clearance sale?" Ruby joked, walking past her father and poking her head inside the canvas flap. "No trapeze artists?" she enquired with an air of disappointment as her head re-emerged.

"They're just on their break with the lion tamers. They've been working all afternoon," Ben advised, glancing over his shoulder at her. "Marshmallow?"

For Ruby, this was the best welcome home from school she could remember. And while she didn't have the faintest idea what was going on, she was overjoyed to see her dear dad with that cheeky sparkle back in his eye. She came up behind him, draping her arms around his neck like a scarf. "I'd love a marshmallow, Dad," she said, pecking him on the cheek.

The two of them sat around the fire on fabric camping chairs, staring into the crackling flames while enjoying a lightly toasted marshmallow or three.

"So," Ruby said eventually, shooting a brief look at the tent. "You've quite a bit to fill me in on."

"I do?" Ben teased.

"Just a bit, yes. You can start with your meeting with Giles and explain why the garage looks like it's been hit by a tornado, and I'm intrigued to know about the Big Top right there behind us."

Ben took a sip of his tea, made using water boiled over the open fire. "I've had a flippin' good day, Ruby, I won't lie," he said.

"Giles found something suitable for you?"

"Nah, nothing. Giles didn't say it out loud, but we both knew he thought I was pretty much a lost cause," Ben told her, remaining remarkably upbeat considering.

"That *does* sound encouraging," Ruby suggested with a touch of sarcasm present in her voice.

Ben proceeded to fill Ruby in on his enjoyable day, sparing none of the finer details, including more information than she needed to know about his impressive sweat patch. She was rather amused at the mental image of him wearing a polo shirt with a tie, but recommended a visit to Marksies for a nice white dress shirt nonetheless.

"... And that's when Giles planted the seed about venturing into the great outdoors," Ben concluded, smiling contentedly.

"And when you also decided to go for a ride on a girl's bike?" an amused Ruby enquired.

"Exactly," Ben replied. "And got me searching for my own. Unfortunately, I couldn't find a suitable bike in my price range, but that's when *this* little beauty presented itself to me instead," he said, offering his unexpected new purchase a loving glance. "Honestly, Ruby, it must have been fate, or what have you. True, it was a *completely* different item than what I'd initially been looking for. But it was in fantastic condition, only mildly used, and the fellow selling it was offering it at such a reasonable price, so how could I resist? And, true, I know it may be a bit on the large side, but I figured you'd want some space when we go camping, yeah? And in this one, you've practically got your own *room*, am I right?"

"I think I could squeeze in a four-poster bed if I wanted," Ruby speculated.

Ben leaned over, scooping up his daughter's hand. "Ruby, I know camping's never really been your thing, and it's probably not the coolest of activities for a teenager with pink hair to do with her dad. But we can go fishing, hiking, eat burgers until they come out of our ears, and—"

"It's fine, you had me at burgers," Ruby offered, squeezing his hand. "And I can't think of a better way of spending a weekend than with you, Pop. Only if you don't snore, that is."

"I'll buy those nose plugs, Ruby," Ben promised, jumping to his feet to fetch another log. "Anyway, for tonight's entertainment, I've bought a tub of that ice cream you like, we've got a full bundle of logs for the fire, and we can find a nice little film to stream on the laptop whilst relaxing in our new tent," he suggested, rubbing his hands at the prospect of a night spent amidst the great outdoors, even if their trial run was only in their back garden. "And," he went on, forming the shape of a tube with his hands, like a Pringles can, and promptly placing it against his eye, "I even came across the old telescope in the garage, so we can look for the man on the moon like we used to."

Ruby's shoulders dropped. "Tonight?" she asked with a grimace. "Dad, remember, I'm going to that sleepover for Cheryl's sixteenth birthday party," she reminded him, glancing at her watch. "In fact, on that point, I'd better go and get myself looking party-ready."

Ben paused for a moment, performing a scan search through the ol' memory banks. "Oh, bugger. That's right," he said, snapping his fingers in frustration as the specific recollection was retrieved. "Of course, yes. Sorry, Ruby, I'd completely forgotten about that, and there's me waffling on."

"You don't mind me going?"

"No, of course I don't mind. We'll have other nights to spend in the Big Top," he assured her, placing the fresh log he'd procured into the flames. "You have fun!"

Ruby sniffed herself, wrinkling her nose. "Well, I'm going to get out of these clothes and jump into the shower, I suppose," she said. "I'm sure I smell like a barbequed chicken wing right about now, sitting next to the fire like this."

Ben smiled through the disappointment, prodding the burning embers with his stick. But it wasn't a complete loss. After all, he was rather partial to the flavour of ice cream he'd purchased, there were a handful of beers chilling in the fridge, and the clouds were moving along nicely for his telescope session later that evening.

"Dad," Ruby said a moment later, reappearing in the doorway. "Have you by any chance been using my eyeliner to write stuff down again?"

Ben held up his hands as an admission of guilt. "Yes, but would you rather me use it as a pen, or to enhance the natural beauty of my eyes?" he asked.

"Fair enough. But neither option is particularly ideal, to be quite honest," Ruby answered. "Remind me, and I'll treat you to an *actual* pen the next time I'm at the shop," she said.

Soon, with the house now to himself, Ben cracked open a cold beer, stoked his fire, and asked Alexa to play his favourite Beautiful South album. As the frame of his new camping chair was digging into him something awful, he switched to lying on his back on the grass, appreciating the setting sun slowly disappearing for another day. "Cheers," he said to himself, enjoying a swig of his malty hops, reflecting on how one satisfying day could positively impact his outlook on life. He was also pleased with himself for having managed to erect the tent earlier without a single expletive uttered (though whether the air would remain equally clean when he tried to repack the canvas beast into its holdall remained to be seen).

Relaxed, Ben's mind wandered back to the dark days he was now hopefully emerging from. For the first few weeks after the breakup, he'd attempted to suppress all thoughts of his wandering-yet-now-healthy-eating ex. But this had proved impossible and, for Ben, unhealthy. Sleepless nights became the norm as the weight dropped off him. Unmotivated and unhappy, the Bread Pitt had remained closed for days on end as Ben became unable to sort himself out. Customers were forced elsewhere, and the bills soon racked up. Ben had been in a spiral of despair, and, inevitably, something had to give. That something, sadly, being the bakery he'd once nurtured into a thriving business, along with his zest for life as well.

But now, lying there next to the crackling fire, Ben could finally begin to imagine a future without Ruby's mum. Indeed, he could imagine a *future*, full stop.

Giles had asked that afternoon if Ben considered opening another bakery, and that notion had bounced around Ben's head for most of the day. But on reflection, being honest with himself, the bakery was arduous work with too little financial reward. Up at four a.m. most mornings, working non-stop for twelve hours, it wasn't for the faint-hearted. And it certainly wasn't something he could see himself still doing when he was old and grey. So rather than feeling bitter and twisted, Ben considered if this was an opportunity to strike out and try something different. What, exactly, he didn't know just yet. But the prospect was invigorating. Ruby was keen to point out as well that another priority on his road to recovery was to get some meat back on his bones, as he was gaunt, and doing so would likely have the effect of raising his overall energy levels. He knew he needed to start eating sensibly, so if only he knew a *friendly* dietician who could help him out? he pondered. A thought which raised an ironic smile.

Ben dozed off, which was an impressive feat. Not just because he was lying mere inches away from naked flames, but because he had a half-drunk bottle of beer resting precariously on his chest.

Eventually, a burning log crackled, rousing him from slumberland. Peeling one eye open, Ben got the fright of his life. "Bloody hell!" he yelled at the figure looming over him. But fortunately it was only Ruby. "Ruby, is that you? It's not morning already, is it?" he asked in his confused sleepy state, noting there was still a bit of daylight left and wondering if it was still evening or if they'd somehow gone all the way round into the next day.

"Aww, you look just like a little cowboy lying there next to your little fire," Ruby suggested. "Anyway, no, it's not tomorrow. In fact, I only ended up being gone for less than an hour."

Ben retrieved the beer from atop his chest, pushing himself upright with his other hand. "I must have nodded off," he explained, stating the obvious. "Wait, hang on," he said, catching up with what Ruby had just said. "What happened to your sleepover? You haven't fallen out with your mates, have you?"

Ruby parked herself down on one of the less-than-comfortable camping chairs. "I'm fine," she assured him.

"It must have been a pretty rubbish party if you're back here so soon?" Ben remarked, enjoying a nice stretch. "Were there no boys there?" he joked.

"There were plenty. But I decided there's only one fella I really wanted to spend my time with today, and that's you," Ruby told him, reaching for the bag of half-eaten marshmallows. "So, how about I fetch the ice cream from the freezer, and you get that fire roaring again, yeah?"

"You're wanting to camp out with your old man?" Ben asked, delighted, if slightly surprised.

"Sure. Besides, I was worried about you sleeping out here on your own, as there could be bears out there and whatnot," Ruby offered with a playful wink, from over at the doorway now.

"Bears? More like wild wallabies," Ben said with a laugh.

"Either way, I couldn't have you discovering the man on the moon without me, now could I?"

An overwhelmed Ben jumped up, aware of a lump forming in his throat. "In that case, I'll get the telescope set up, Ruby," he said, pleased as Punch. "Oh, do me a favour while you're in there? Grab me another beer, if you don't mind, this one's flippin' roasting."

Chapter Four

Cynthia marched across the open-plan office, the hard, heavy footfalls of her heels against the cold laminate flooring disturbing her colleagues as she passed, leaving a series of raised, inquisitive heads in her wake. Then, upon arrival outside the large corner office, she attempted to compose herself with several deep breaths, in through the nose and out through the mouth. "Knock-knock," she said, giving the door a firm rap of the knuckles as she made her way through, not waiting for an invite. "That email you sent earlier..." she said once inside, trying her best to remain calm. "I'm guessing it's included a typo or two? Because, if I'm reading it correctly, even *you*, Austin, surely cannot be that much of a heartless shit?"

"Why, do come in, Cynthia," Austin suggested, along with an unoffended laugh, almost as if such a greeting from her was to be considered something of a compliment. Austin continued with his biceps curls, admiring his technique in the floor-to-ceiling mirror he'd recently had installed. "You can see the gains, yeah?" he asked. "Yes, I'm sure you can," he said, grunting in satisfaction and not bothering to wait for her answer.

Cynthia wasn't going to answer him anyway, as Austin seemed to be talking more to his own reflection than anything else. Plus, while she couldn't deny he did look well-toned, there was no way in hell she'd be telling him that as it would only serve to increase his already over-inflated ego. "Are you nearly finished?" she asked eventually. "Only, as you pay my wages, you're giving me money to stand here like a flippin' spare part."

"Nearly done," Austin said, his left arm quivering like a bowl of jelly. "There," he added a moment later, placing his weights down on the floor. For a moment, he gave the impression he was about to place a kiss on one of his bulging biceps. Fortunately for Cynthia, however, he instead reached for his towel. "So, how can I help my most exemplary of employees? My most splendid of salespersons, my agent extraordinaire, my—"

"For starters, you can put your bloody shirt back on," Cynthia instructed, reaching for and throwing over his shirt. "Then, you can tell me why you want to evict a hardworking nurse and her ten-year-old son?"

Austin set his shirt aside for the moment, continuing to wipe himself down with his towel, eyes still fixed on the image in the mirror. "Ah, so that's what's got you all worked up into a lather this time of the morning? The nurse? Tell me, Cynthia. This nurse. Is she now all up to date on her arrears?"

Cynthia rolled her eyes. "Austin, that nurse is *Helen*. And her son is *Arthur*. They have names. They're *people*. And Helen is slightly behind schedule because she took unpaid leave from work to care for her father, who'd broken his hip. Austin, she even told us in advance that things would be tight for a few weeks."

"Are we running a charity, Cynthia?" Austin asked, unmoved. "You know that if we don't collect on behalf of our clients, then we don't get paid." Austin then walked over to his window. "Let me show you this, Cynthia," he said, waving her over.

"Put your shirt on first," Cynthia shot back, ambling over in his direction.

"You see that thing of beauty?" Austin asked.

"You're not talking about yourself, are you? One can never be certain where you're concerned," Cynthia said dryly.

"No, not this time," Austin advised, tapping a finger gently on the glass. "I'm talking about the thing of beauty down there, in the carpark."

"Your new car?"

Austin released a contented sigh, gazing lovingly at his fancy new set of wheels. "You don't get yourself a new eighty-grand motor by listening to sob stories, Cynthia. Surely you know this by now?"

"Oh, that's complete bollocks, Austin," Cynthia replied. "We've got dozens of clients whose arrears are *significantly* larger than Helen's, so it doesn't make sense for you to..." she said, trailing off as a thought occurred to her. "Wait. That's it!" she said, suddenly slapping her palm against her forehead as the realisation hit. "You asked me a little while back to look out for a nice flat for your niece, didn't you?"

"One that was spacious," Austin was quick to remind her.

"Right," Cynthia replied, struggling to hide the contempt in her voice. "And it just so happens that Helen's apartment is unusually spacious."

"And with enviable views across Castletown Harbour, no less," Austin was happy to report, now wiggling his hips as he lined up a golf shot out through the window. "So, if you'd be so kind as to get her broke ass out of that apartment..." he said, emphasising the word *broke* as he released an imaginary drive up his pretend fairway.

"I've a good mind to take that putter of yours and place it right where the sun doesn't—"

"It's a *driver*," Austin corrected her, despite the driver being imaginary, and thus completely invisible, meaning there was no way for her to identify it. "And remind me as to why I put up with your impudence, Cynthia?"

"Because I make you more money than the rest of the sales team combined!" Cynthia snapped back, slamming the door on her way out.

Ordinarily, Austin wouldn't stand for such insolence, especially from somebody whose wages he paid. But Cynthia was absolutely spot on in the assessment of her worth to the company. And so long as she continued to deliver the goods, he was willing to forgive the occasional strop. She was, after all, arguably the most talented estate agent on the Isle of Man, and although he was loath to admit it, he probably needed her much more than she needed him. However, her rather more principled approach was a regular source of frustration to Austin. She was already bringing in so much new business playing things entirely by the book, but he knew the sky might be the limit if she could only manage to be a little less rigid with her scruples, like him.

Austin flashed his pearly whites to the other staff members glancing through his office window, likely wondering what the kerfuffle was about. Ever the showman and unable to resist any form of attention, Austin, still shirtless, raised an arm, flexing his right biceps to demonstrate his magnificent physique to his loyal minions. However, before he had the opportunity to give his swollen muscle a tender kiss, the mobile phone buzzing on his desk stole his attention. He glanced casually at the caller ID displayed, but then lurched forward, anxious to take this call judging by the speed in which he moved.

"Yes, Cecil. Talk to me," Austin said, phone now in hand as he walked behind his desk and parked himself onto his chair. He listened intently, nodding his head as he took in what Cecil was telling him. "The old boy's started selling his inventory, has he?" a delighted-sounding Austin asked, the corners of his mouth turning up into a smile. Austin leaned forward, placing both elbows on his desk. "Cecil, your services might be costing me a small fortune, but if that stubborn old bugger is calling it a day and packing things up, you're worth every penny, my friend."

Austin took to his feet, pacing around his office, enjoying what he was hearing. Well, most of what he was hearing, at least...

"He's bloody *what?*" Austin asked, his smile evaporating in an instant. He came to a halt, standing with one hand on his hip. "So, the old boy's *not* packing up and leaving, Cecil, that's what you're actually telling me?" he barked down the phone. "No? Well, that's what it sounds like to me, Cecil." He sat on the corner of his desk, unable to resist a furtive glance at his upper arm, flexing the muscle for his own benefit as doing so often served to calm his nerves to some degree. "Okay," he said after a few moments. "So, if I understand what you're saying, the old boy's calling it a day on that portion of his business, yeah? But instead of washing his hands of the affair entirely, he's first attempting to see if anybody will be stupid enough to take it over for him?"

Once confirmed, Austin's demeanour lifted slightly on hearing this information, the news not being quite as bad as he first imagined. "Well, at least he's accepted the business is on its knees, Cecil. Which is a positive result. Although if he does manage to find some poor muppet to keep things running for him, you need to double down your efforts, my friend. Think outside the box and get creative. Give the old farmer such a headache that he realises his preferred outcome is to simply sell off that section of his land. Do you know what I'm saying?"

Austin listened long enough to receive the assurances he desired. "Excellent, Cecil. I do appreciate a man who's so committed to his work. But I don't need to remind you that the developer needs a signature on that contract in the next three months, or the whole deal is off. And if that happens, I lose my finder's fee and the commission on selling all of those new houses they're building. And you know what that would mean for the whopping great bonus I promised you, don't you?"

Austin's smile returned. "Marvellous. I knew you'd be on precisely the same wavelength as me, Cecil. You're very astute when it comes to such matters. Anyway, I'll let you get back to your normal duties, but keep me up to speed."

With that pressing business addressed, Austin fell back into his chair again, feeling cautiously optimistic. It wasn't the outcome he'd wanted, necessarily, but he at least took some degree of comfort from knowing that his wily comrade Cecil was on the case. And what Cecil lacked in personal hygiene or general charisma, he more than made up for by his unrivalled ability to do whatever was needed to get the job done. Indeed, Austin often wondered how Cecil managed to continually accomplish the seemingly impossible, though for fear of being implicated himself, Austin chose to simply enjoy the fruits of Cecil's accomplishments with minimal questions.

Later that morning, after a post-workout shower and an early protein-rich quinoa power lunch, Austin felt the need for a motivational pick-me-up. The whole business with Cecil was playing on his mind, draining his often-unflappable nature. He needed a distraction.

Austin unlocked his desk, dipping his hand into the drawer at the very bottom. "Who loves ya, baby?" he asked, skimming through a stack of glossy magazines until he located the exact one he'd been looking for. Then, with a cautious glance towards the office door, Austin ran his tongue over his top lip, a shiver of anticipation running down his spine. "Fantastic," he whispered, flicking slowly through the well-thumbed magazine, his eyes lingering over each of the large, magnificent photos to be found therein.

"You can bloody do it yourself!" Cynthia declared, suddenly bursting into Austin's office, nearly taking the door off its hinges. "Honestly, if you think I'm evicting a nurse and her son for a month's worth of arrears, then you've got another thing coming."

"Don't you know how to knock?" a flustered Austin demanded, quickly tossing his magazine back into the drawer and out of view. "I could have been on an important call!" he protested.

"Oh, relax," Cynthia said. "I know precisely what you were doing in here behind closed doors and drawn blinds," she told him. "Staring at those filthy little magazines of yours, weren't you? Same as always."

"Filthy?" Austin replied. "I wouldn't exactly say they were—"

"The ones with the fancy boats in them," Cynthia clarified. "The ones that make the rest of us feel inadequate. Those magazines."

"Ah. *Those.* Yes, guilty as charged, then," Austin replied. "Well, you could buy a boat *yourself*, you know. If you really wanted," he pointed out.

"Not one of those massive jobs you've always got your eye on, Austin. Never for me. A dinghy would probably suit my needs just fine," she answered. "Anyway, what's the current nautical flavour of the month?" she asked, even though she clearly wasn't that interested.

"It's a Sunseeker," Austin said, grabbing the magazine he'd just chucked away and yanking it back out. "Do you want to see her?" he asked, laying the magazine out on his desk and opening it right up to the spot where he'd left off. "She's a beauty."

Cynthia glared across the office. "Do you not see the irony here, Austin? You're looking for a new boat, and that poor nurse and her young son are—"

"*Fine!*" Austin said, cutting her off mid-sermon, throwing his hands above his head. "Fine. She can have a stay of execution," he told her.

"You're serious?" Cynthia asked, scanning his face, waiting to see if there was a punchline a little further on, but seeing no evidence of it. "I can tell her that she's got more time?"

"Sure, yes. But make it very clear to the nurse that she's got one month to get back on her feet, otherwise..."

Cynthia relaxed her shoulders, unclenching her jaw as well. And with the matter she'd come in for settled, "Very good, boss," she said, turning to leave.

"Ah, before you go, Cynthia?" Austin said, calling her back. "The housing scheme in Castletown looks like it might have legs again. You see, I think I've found a way of securing a deal on the land that the developer has failed to do. And, for that, we'll be handsomely rewarded for accomplishing what they couldn't."

"Oh? That's tremendous news, Austin," Cynthia answered. "And we'd be the sole agent for the new properties being built," she noted.

"Every... single... one," Austin said. "That's why I was checking out the new Sunseeker," he confessed, rubbing his thumb and forefinger together as if counting a wad of imaginary cash. "Anyway, I want you to start making calls to prospective buyers. The paperwork isn't signed, but tease them, yeah? Sell them on a new life in lovely Castletown. That way, if I can tell the developer we've already got dozens of prospective buyers, he'll be crawling over bloody broken glass to appoint us as the sole agent."

Cynthia bobbed her head, liking what she was hearing. She was, after all, a salesperson, and this was a challenge right up her street. "Consider it done, Austin," she was happy to advise. "Oh, and by the way, thank you so much for the leeway with Helen's situation," she added.

"Helen...?" Austin responded, confused as to who this Helen person was.

"The nurse? Remember?" Cynthia answered.

"Oh, her. And?"

"And it's nice to see you have some compassion buried somewhere beneath those ribs," Cynthia told him. "Somewhere deep. Somewhere very deep and hidden."

Austin swatted away her kind words. "Yep, that's me. I'm all heart, full of consideration for others," he insisted. "Oh, and one more thing before you go."

"Name it."

"You need to phone my sister, yeah? Tell her the new flat is on hold and that she should cancel my niece's removal van."

Later, Austin drove through the financial district of the island's capital, Douglas, on the way to his next valuation of the day. He didn't attend too many appointments himself these days, and certainly not for anything in the sub-750k bracket, which were, in his words, cesspits and hovels. So yes, Austin was more selective about the clientele worthy of a personal visit from the (self-appointed) pre-eminent property guru on the Isle of Man. As his colleagues were well aware, the usual qualifying criteria for his valuable time was a potential listing with a pool or tennis court and/or an attractive seller. The way Austin figured it, a good proportion of house sales were driven by the breakup of a relationship. And if he, as a caring estate agent, was able to offer a supportive shoulder to the soon-to-be-single — and likely wealthy — wife/girlfriend, then that was just another string to his considerable bow. "All about the personal *touch*," he often liked to remind his staff.

Meanwhile, back on the road...

"Alright, sweetheart?" Austin called out from the driver's seat of his new car, slowing for the traffic lights. He was speaking to a young lady waiting to cross, although she didn't appear to be the least little bit interested in him. Not one to ever let such indifference stop him, he carried right on harassing the poor girl. "V-eight engine," he said, applying the throttle to establish his magnificence to both her and anybody else within earshot. But of course, all he received in response were looks of disdain from those startled by the savage growl of his engine. And if they didn't already think he was something of a pillock, they probably did when he floored it the moment the light turned green, tyres screeching. Although even if they did think he was a pillock, it was all water off a duck's back to Austin. In his mind, *he* was the one looking fabulous driving an eighty-grand V-8 motor, after all.

And next up for Austin was a three-million-pound country pile sitting in seven acres of landscaped gardens and boasting, crucially, an impressive indoor heated pool. Unfortunately, he was unsure if the motive for the sale was a relocation, downsizing, or relationship breakdown. He was hopeful of the last, but if that wasn't to be the case, the sales commission on a property of that stature would certainly help to cushion the blow.

With thoughts drifting to warm evenings spent sipping chilled Bollinger on his new Sunseeker, Austin burst into song, murdering Rod Stewart's classic sailing-themed number as he drove along. However, his ocean-going reveries were rudely interrupted by the office mobile.

"Twice in one day, Cecil?" Austin said, once he'd pressed the hands-free function on his steering wheel. "People will start thinking I like you at this rate," he joked.

Cecil sounded breathless, as if he had just finished the London Marathon wearing a deep-sea diving suit. "Is that you, boss?" he asked, evidently struggling for air.

"Jesus, Cecil," Austin replied, uncharacteristically full of sympathy, or at least making a good show of it in this one particular instance. "You sound like a knackered vacuum cleaner."

"You wanted me to keep you up to speed, boss. So, I ran to the nearest public phone three hundred metres away," Cecil explained.

"Impressive," Austin suggested, pressing out his lower lip, appreciative of Cecil's effort. "Hang on, why didn't you just use your mobile?"

"Not when I'm on active operations," Cecil advised. "You never know who's listening."

Austin couldn't fault the logic. "I suppose now you..." he began to say, but then didn't finish. "Hang on, Cecil, you phoned me from your mobile this morning," Austin pointed out. "Your name was displayed on my screen."

Cecil didn't answer straight away, perhaps reflecting on this apparent lapse in security. "Ehm, well, *usually* I make sure I use a payphone," he said. "When I spoke to you earlier, I was—"

"Never mind. Just get to the bleeding point, Cecil. I'm driving a beautiful car, and some drop-dead gorgeous women around here are suffering from a distinct lack of my attention."

"Right-ho, boss," Cecil answered. It sounded like he was about to say something else as well, but then the line went quiet.

"Cecil...?" Austin asked, a moment or two later.

"Go on, piss off, you nosey old trout!" Cecil snapped, sounding quite agitated from where Austin was sitting.

"What did you say?"

"Oh, sorry, boss. Not you. Some old dear was just outside the phone box with her dog, hanging about. So, I've sent her on her way with a flea in her ear. You never can be too careful in this game."

"Fair enough. Anyway...?"

"Anyway, the old farmer has apparently found someone daft enough to step in and assume responsibility for the business, while also paying the farmer a lease for the privilege."

Austin slapped his hand down on the steering wheel. "Tell me you're joking, Cecil? Over the last several months, you've systematically driven that campsite into the ground. So why would some halfwit come along at this stage to stoke the embers of a dying fire?"

"Dunno, boss," Cecil answered. "The old boy only just broke the news to me. And get this, he was thrilled he'd managed to secure my employment with this new fella, carrying on in my role at the campsite and pledging my services for so many hours a week, as it turns out. Blimey, I actually feel a bit guilty now. You know, him thinking about my career like that, what with everything I've done to him and all."

"Ah, *now* you feel guilty?" Austin scoffed. "But you didn't feel guilty when you left his taps running through the night that one time, flooding the toilet block?"

"Not so much, no."

Austin ran through the various options in his mind. He reasoned that this wasn't ideal, but it needn't be catastrophic. After all, they still had several weeks before the deal with the developer was due to be signed, so, time enough to convince the new leaseholder they'd made a monumental error in judgement by deciding to pick up the reins. "You're just going to have to continue your mission, Cecil. Get yourself in with the new guy, make them feel like you're the employee of the month and, well... you know what you need to do. Cecil, that business cannot be left viable by the time contracts are exchanged, yeah? You understand that?"

"Understood, boss," Cecil said. "But there's one little complication you should know about."

"Which is?"

"Well, the old boy showed me the signed lease, so I know who this new fellow is and where he lives."

"You mean you're going around their house?" Austin asked, unsure if he was entirely on board with such aggressive tactics, but deciding it best to leave matters to Cecil, permitting Cecil to do whatever needed doing no matter how unpleasant. "Well, I reckon you know best what works. So, I'll just leave you to it," Austin allowed, finger poised to end the call. There were, after all, attractive ladies who demanded his attention.

"It's not that, boss, no. See, when I saw this new guy's address, I thought it sounded familiar. It took me a minute or two to realise why, but then I did. Boss, the new person, he lives in your neighbourhood."

"And?" Austin asked, pulling a face. "I don't see as how that changes anything, Cecil," he advised. "You still know what needs to be done."

Cecil likely sensed he was losing his audience at this point. "Boss, when I say this guy lives in your neighbourhood," he went on, "I think it's the smaller houses across the road from you."

"They're *all* a lot smaller than mine," Austin was quick to point out. "And I don't see how that's relevant anyway. Why, what's this new fellow's name?"

"Oh, bollocks. That old dear is back, and she's not alone this time. It might be her son with her, and he's feckin' built like the side of a barn."

"The name of the new leaseholder?" Austin pressed, less concerned about the possibility of Cecil being beaten up.

"Oh, it's Ben Parker, boss. But given that he is a neighbour of yours, right, I'm wondering if you might want to rethink your seek-and-destroy strategy?"

"What? No, of *course* I don't want to rethink my strategy. In fact, this news may even give me some sort of tactical advantage. It's possible. I just need to figure out who the hell *Ben Parker* is."

Just then, the phone line started to crackle, followed by an audible thud and a desperate whimper. "Get your fat, scruffy arse out of that phone box before I drag you out!" were the last words an amused Austin could hear before the call suddenly ended.

"Ah, Cecil," Austin said, chuckling to himself. "What would I do without you?"

Chapter Five

Two magpies were perched atop the wooden fence, one on each side of the open gate between them, both of them surveying the scene before them like watchmen. Either that, or they were simply having a nice rest.

It was impossible not to be impressed by this charming little isle in the middle of the Irish Sea. It was a place where you could enjoy a stroll along a deserted beach one minute and then be surrounded by spectacular mountain landscapes only a short drive away. It was an island of contrasts, enjoyed by tourists for generations, eager to breathe in the bracing sea air and be mesmerised by the open, rolling hillside.

Unfortunately, for the magpies at least, their leisurely afternoon was disturbed by an approaching car, causing them both to take flight in response. Car tyres crunched into the gravel farm track, coming to a halt in front of the gate the birds had just vacated.

"Okay, so you can't see, can you?" Ben asked, applying the handbrake.

Ruby shook her head, the blindfold presently tied around her noggin doing its intended job, it would seem. "Not a thing, Dad," she said. "Although if someone walks past and notices you with a blindfolded schoolgirl in your car, it might raise a question or two," she cautioned.

"Fair point," Ben conceded, promptly checking his side and rear-view mirrors for anybody out walking. "The coast's clear," he was happy to report, jumping out of the car and hurrying to the passenger side door. Ben took his daughter's hand, helping her safely climb out of the vehicle.

"Dad, what's all this about?" Ruby asked. "Have you bought me a puppy or something?"

"Wait and see," Ben suggested, guiding her through the opened gate and slowly up the farm track, taking care to dodge any stray mounds of cow poop in their path. "Nearly there..."

The narrow farm track opened up into a cobbled courtyard, surrounded on three sides by stone outbuildings, which Ben couldn't help but admire.

"I've just stepped in something squidgy," Ruby said. "Dad, what have I just stepped in?"

Ben broke his attention away from the stone structures, worried his mission to avoid cow droppings perhaps wasn't going so well after all. "It's nothing, Ruby," he lied, scanning the ground, hoping there weren't any meadow muffins to be had in their immediate vicinity, though fearful of the worst. "Just waterlogged turf, maybe?" he offered, but it was a weak suggestion at best, and he more wished it to be true than anything else. "Anyway, we're here," he quickly added, hoping to distract Ruby away from what may or may not be soiling her newish school shoes.

Ben placed his hands on Ruby's shoulders, edging her into the correct position so she'd be able to see what he shortly wanted her to see. "Right, you can remove your blindfold," he said.

Ruby did as instructed and, vision restored, glanced immediately down to her sullied shoe. "That... doesn't look like waterlogged turf, Dad?" she suggested, scraping her foot against the cobblestones in a desperate bid to remove the excess muck.

"Never mind that," said Ben, stepping away from her, attempting to focus her attention on the sturdy wooden pole he'd now positioned himself in front of. It was a pole that was supporting a large sign, from the looks of things, though it was difficult to tell for sure on account of the white bedsheet currently draped over it, effectively obscuring it from Ruby's view. "Ta-da!" an enthusiastic Ben announced, offering up his most vigorous jazz hands.

Ruby stared back at him with a wry smile, unsure what was happening but amused by how excited her dad was. "What's going on, Pop?" she asked, looking around to see if there were any clues that might explain the situation. Any clues, that is, beyond an apparent sign that she could not yet read.

Ben gripped the bedsheet, exaggeratedly flapping his eyebrows. "This, my darling daughter, is my future. Or, in actual fact, *our* future," he said, building the tension and now tugging gently on the white bedsheet. Slowly, he revealed more and more of the newly repainted sign beneath, until finally gravity finished the job for him, sending the fabric sinking down to the cobbles. "Whaddya think?" Ben asked, extending his arm like a car salesman trying to seal the deal.

Ruby chewed the inside of her cheek, glancing up at the recently unveiled object. After the drive from school and the cloak-and-dagger blindfolding situation leading up to the big reveal, she was starting to get the impression that this sign was something of a big deal to her dad. She was perceptive like that. "It's, ehm..." she started to say. "Really nice?"

And to be fair to Ruby, it was difficult for her to know just what to make of the thing. Resplendent in British Racing Green against a honey-coloured background, it'd been freshly done, judging by the few errant splashes of paint to be found on the ground, along with a faint chemical smell still hanging in the air. Written on it in sizeable italic lettering were the words *Life's a Pitch*, accompanied by the image of a tent underneath. It was okay, sure, but...

"Really nice?" Ben asked. "Why, she's a thing of *beauty*," he insisted, with a look of wonderment similar to that of a father taking his newborn home from the maternity ward. "Three applications of paint before the signwriter could come and apply the final, finishing touches for me. But it was worth all the effort."

Ruby smiled politely. "It's the nicest sign I've seen in ages," she said, nodding her head and trying to seem more delighted than she actually was.

Sensing he was perhaps losing his audience, Ben came over and placed an arm around Ruby's shoulders, guiding her past the sign towards the side of the courtyard that opened up, permitting access to the surrounding fields. "It's not just the sign, Ruby," Ben was pleased to reveal.

"It's not?"

Ben released the sigh of a contented man. "No, it's not." Once again, Ben extended his arm, this time introducing the expansive field to the right of where they stood. "That, my dear daughter, is the home of Life's a Pitch. Our new campsite."

Ruby started chuckling to herself. Her dad could be a bit batty at times, and she just took this to be another of those occasions. "If you've painted that sign three times..." Ruby began, looking at her dad. "Is there any chance you might've been overcome by fumes?" she asked, wondering if that might explain his current behaviour.

"Very possibly, Ruby. Very possibly. But this is our new business. Signed, sealed, and delivered."

"You've purchased a campsite?"

"Well, technically, I've signed a lease on a campsite rather than purchased it," Ben explained, escorting her onto the grassy field, allowing Ruby to wipe what remained of the cow pie off of her shoe. "Which essentially means that I've agreed to rent the land for three years to operate the campsite. And this change of career direction is all thanks to you."

Ruby was happy to accept the praise, though not entirely sure what she'd done to warrant it. "Erm... how, exactly?" she asked with a nervous laugh.

Ben continued his tour, taking a generous lungful of the fresh country air. "Well, if you hadn't made that appointment for me with Giles, I'd have no idea how absolutely and completely unemployable I was. It also made me realise I had no desire to open another bakery, so the only option was a complete change of direction and a new venture. Or, I could continue to waste away on the sofa, of course."

"I don't even know where to begin with this one, Dad. I mean, how on earth did you decide you wanted to run a campsite, of all things?"

Ben turned, drawing Ruby's attention to the farm buildings in the distance. "The farmer, a lovely chap named Gerry, owns most of the land you can see," he said, running his hand over the vista. "The problem with farming is that it's often arduous work for little financial reward. The reason, then, that Gerry segregated some of his land to set up a campsite, hoping to supplement his income. Only it's turned into something of a disaster, distracting him from the business of farming and costing him a fortune in the process. Not at all what he expected. So that's when he decided to call it a day on this little enterprise and began selling off some of his camping-related inventory."

"Ah, hence, the canvas beast currently pitched in our garden?" Ruby said, before bursting into a fit of giggles.

"What are you laughing at? The tent?" Ben asked, smiling because his daughter was smiling.

"No, not that. *Ben and Gerry*," Ruby told him. "You love ice cream, yeah? So I was just thinking it's a match made in heaven, you and him."

"Hmm. I do like ice cream. But I believe this fellow is a Gerry with a G, rather than Jerry with a J as with the ice cream," Ben offered. "Hopefully still a match made in heaven, though," he added, while thinking about how some lovely cookie dough ice cream would certainly go down a treat. "Anyway," Ben said, forcing himself to get back on track. "According to Gerry, the property developers have circled like vultures for years, desperate to buy that large swath of land the campsite currently sits on and build a massive new estate. Something he was seriously considering until I came along."

"Who'd want to do something like that? Who'd spoil views like this for a building site?"

"Precisely! Although I'd imagine a whole boatload of cash coming Gerry's way might soften the blow. Anyway, after me and you had such a great night under the stars, I popped back to buy one of his firepits and some camping furniture for our next outing. That's when we started talking about the reason for him selling the business. And as fate would have it, I mentioned my newfound appreciation of camping, plus how I was exploring new career opportunities, and the next thing you know, I've signed the lease on a campsite. As a result, he gets some welcome cash each month without listening to the constant racket of diggers all day and his view being destroyed."

"And you can afford it?" Ruby asked with a grimace, wanting to remain positive but also having some knowledge of her dad's precarious finances at present.

Ben looked over his shoulder, making sure he couldn't be overheard. But now, standing in the middle of an empty field, it was unlikely there would be too many eavesdroppers in the vicinity. "Three thousand pounds a month," he explained, grinning like he'd secured the deal of the century. "Included in that price is the use of the land, all of his existing equipment, the shower/toilet block, and several glamping huts he's had built."

Now Ruby, being of school age, wasn't too sure if three thousand pounds a month represented fair value or not. "Do you have three thousand a month spare?"

"Well, no," Ben replied, like this was but a minor inconvenience. "Though it's not like I need to come up with any money in advance. And what we will have is a stream of happy campers generating income, see? All willing to hand over their hard-earned cash for a few nights at Life's a Pitch. And in the meantime, Gerry was happy for me to sign a personal guarantee."

"Right. Which is?"

"A promise on my part to pay him that amount of money each month."

"That's very trusting of him, isn't it?" Ruby pressed.

"Well, I must have a very trustworthy mug," Ben answered, tilting his head, smiling like he was at a photoshoot and offering his face for consideration. "Also," he mumbled, speaking from out of the corner of his mouth, and at a considerably reduced volume, "the personal guarantee is effectively secured by our house."

"What, now?" Ruby asked, picking up on everything he'd said. "So, if you don't pay, the farmer can take our house?"

"It's fine," Ben assured her, turning slowly like the seconds hand on a watch, ticking out each degree of the scenery as he pivoted round, admiring their new kingdom. "I've done the sums, Ruby, and even with the rent payment factored in, we should still be quids in. And I know I don't know that much about running a camping business, but there's where Cecil's experience comes into play."

"Cecil?"

"Cecil is Gerry's farm manager who helped him run the camping business. Gerry has offered us Cecil's assistance for a bit, with Cecil's services being kindly included with what I'm already paying into the lease, not costing me any extra. Meaning we can make use of Cecil's considerable expertise in order to get things up and running at full speed."

"So this Cecil and Gerry couldn't make a go of the business, but you can after one night of camping in the garden?"

"Precisely," Ben was pleased to agree, skipping over the gentle sarcasm in Ruby's voice. "You and me, kiddo," he said, pulling her in close. "We'll soon have the island's finest campsite, with tourists and locals alike arriving in their droves. Life's a Pitch, Ruby. *Life's a Pitch.*"

"You're absolutely bonkers, Dad," Ruby replied. "But if anybody can do this, you can."

Ben kissed the hair on top of her head. "That means a lot, Ruby. Thank you."

"Oh, and the new business name...?" Ruby began, pulling a face.

"Yeah?"

"Absolutely brilliant!"

Chapter Six

It was stupid and a little bit irrational, maybe, but since receiving the call earlier that morning, Ben had been like a giddy child on Christmas morning. Each time he'd heard a vehicle driving up the street, he'd been straight over to the window like an excitable dog hearing the postman walking up the garden path.

Ben had only been without his lawnmower for a few days, but the wait was driving him mad. He just liked everything to be in order, everything working as it should. He took great comfort from things being just so. Life was tidier that way. Hence his elation at getting his mower back from the repair shop today, which would serve to set things right once again. The chap at the garden centre had suggested that, with the projected cost of repair being what it was, it might've made more sense to spend just a bit more, purchasing a new model instead. But Ben, despite having considered that very notion previously, had ignored the sales patter and politely declined the proposal, opting to save that little bit of money and get his tried and tested workhorse back up and running instead. With hindsight, however, and a repair bill of nearly three hundred quid, perhaps a new machine might have been a better idea after all, he pondered.

No matter, the decision had been made, and he was happy to stand by it. And five minutes after the company dropped his refurbished machine at the front of his house, Ben was in his garage digging out his gardening attire.

"Oi!" Ben called out, dropping his right Wellington boot, sprinting from his recently tidied garage as fast as one could wearing only his left wellie. "Don't you flippin' dare!" he yelled, directing his ire towards Atticus, the neighbour's ginger feline, who was currently squatting over Ben's grass without a care in the world. "Go on, sling your hook!" Ben said, removing and throwing a glove in Atticus's general direction, disturbing the cat before it could unleash a motherlode, as Atticus's bowel movements were always unusually, horrifyingly large, the poor chap having some sort of dreadful intestinal troubles.

Rattled but unscathed, Atticus made himself a sharp exit. But before he got too far, he took a moment to look back at his assailant, glaring with a defiant sort of expression that may have translated as *you-may-have-won-the-battle-but-you-haven't-won-the-war*. With that, Atticus was on his way, newspaper under his arm, so to speak, searching out another luscious lawn where he could go about his business undisturbed.

"The bloody cheek of it," Ben remarked, his shoulders back and hands pressed on hips, maintaining his observation post until the area was clear.

Then, with his glove retrieved and both his feet correctly inside a Wellington boot, Ben turned his attention to his lawnmower. He dropped to one knee, topping up the petrol levels, and then couldn't resist running his hand over the smooth metal casing. "Welcome back, old friend," he said, offering his motorised, bladed companion the warmest of smiles before she'd be set loose on his unkempt grass. But before he could tug on the pullcord, a raised voice from across the way attracted his attention. "Bill!" the voice shouted.

Still, Ben didn't pay it too much mind, on account of his name being, well, Ben, as opposed to Bill.

"Bill!" it called out again, only louder and closer this time.

Ben looked up, glancing about, at which point he caught sight of Austin, waving vigorously and headed straight towards him. "Bill!" Austin called out, picking up his pace to a gentle jog. "Lovely day for a spot of gardening?"

Soon, Austin loomed over Ben, looking down on both him and the lawnmower. "So, you got the old girl back then, Bill?"

he asked, retrieving his wallet from his trouser pocket.

"Oh, it's actually Ben," Ben said with a gentle laugh, figuring it best to correct the error before it spiralled into an uncomfortable situation.

Austin started to chuckle to himself. "Oh, Bill, that's priceless," he said. "You're the only person I know who'd give their lawnmower a name."

Ben took a moment to work out what Austin was saying, wondering what his neighbour could possibly be on about. "Ah," he said a moment later, once the penny had dropped. "No, no, Austin. *My* name is Ben. Not the lawnmower's," Ben explained, gently patting the lawnmower.

"You're sure?"

"What, about my name being Ben? Yes, quite sure."

"Ah. Well, I suppose Ben does sound like Bill," Austin suggested. "I knew you were named after one of the Flower Pot Men," he said, setting himself off laughing. "I just went for the wrong one."

Ben, polite as he ever was, added his own laughter. "It's an easy mistake to make, Austin," he offered.

Austin shifted his attention towards the bulging wallet in his hand. "Well, I couldn't help feeling a spot of guilt over the broken lawnmower situation," he said, which was generous considering it was likely his fault it needed to be repaired in the first place, Ben reckoned. "And I just wanted to contribute to the repairs," Austin told him, counting out several notes and handing them over.

By now, Ben's folded-up leg was starting to get a bit numb. "Ah," he said, pushing himself up to a standing position. "You didn't need to, Austin. But it's gratefully received."

The two men stood staring at each other, both sporting an awkward smile. Then, finally, when neither of them spoke after what seemed like an interminable and uncomfortable silence, Ben felt the need to fill it. "Oh. Well. You know you can borrow the mower any time you'd like," he said, saying the precise opposite of what he was thinking. In fact, as the words exited his mouth, he could see Ruby in his mind's eye, gently shaking her head in disapproval.

"No need, Ben, but thank you," Austin said. "I've just treated myself to one of those fancy ride-on jobs," he advised, operating an imaginary steering wheel. "It cost a lot more than yours, of course, but it'll make life easier, what with my lawn being so very much larger. No more breaking a sweat for me."

"I'll look forward to seeing it in action," Ben replied. "Anyway, ehm... this grass isn't going to cut itself," he added.

Austin didn't react to what was clearly a polite request for him to please bugger off.

"So. What sort of work are you in, Ben?" Austin asked instead, although it was delivered in a tone suggesting Austin probably already knew the answer.

"Me?" Ben said, slightly caught off guard by this sudden line of questioning. "Well, I've just left a lengthy career in the catering industry, and I'm diversifying into the outdoor accommodation sector," he explained, somewhat vaguely, immediately wondering why he didn't just come straight out with it.

"Outdoor accommodation?" Austin said, doing an impressive job of pretending this was all news to him. "That sounds a bit like camping, no?"

Ben nodded in confirmation. "Yeah, the very same thing," he admitted. "I've recently assumed a lease on a campsite just outside of town," he added, a proud sparkle in his eye.

"Gerry's place?" Austin ventured, even though he already knew the answer. "I'd heard he was thinking of calling it a day."

"You know Gerry?"

"Not so much, but I'm familiar with the campsite. You don't become the island's most successful estate agent without knowing these things," Austin said, tapping the side of his head. "After all, that's how I can afford the largest house in the neighbourhood," he added, pointing a haughty thumb over his shoulder. "Anyway, we should go for a coffee, Ben, yes?" Austin offered. "One of my many specialities is the hospitality sector, so I might be able to add some value? Give you some advice?

Steer you towards the right people?" Then, in a complete change of direction, Austin ran his eyes over the exterior of Ben's house. "It's just the two of you now?" he asked. "You and your daughter, I mean? Since your wife, well..."

"Just the pair of us. Yes," Ben said through a forced smile. "Like two peas in a pod."

"It's a big house for two," Austin remarked. "If you ever need to downsize, let me know. I could sell this place in twenty-four hours, you know." Austin snapped his fingers as he said this, as if that, in some way, emphasised his brilliance. Then, jabbing his fingers into his own chest, he added, "Number one estate agent in the Isle of Man! And remember, if you ever need any help with anything, you know where I am."

"Oh, I didn't doubt your credentials for a moment, Austin," Ben replied. "And thanks for the offer of that coffee."

"Did I tell you about the time I sold twelve houses in one day?" Austin continued.

Ben groaned, silently, in his head. "No, you didn't," Ben said in answer, though realising this response would, sadly, most likely result in a lengthy property-based anecdote demonstrating just how brilliant indeed Austin was. Just then, however, Ben's unlikely saviour came into view, visible from a distance. "Austin, I think Atticus is about to get himself comfortable on your lawn," he advised, cutting off Austin's anecdote before he had a chance to begin it.

Austin spun round to see where Ben's extended finger was pointing. "Who?" he asked, confused at first, not seeing anybody there, but then immediately putting two and two together. And then, to Atticus, he said, "Don't even think about it, you furry little rodent, or I'll turn you into a hat!"

Even though Austin wouldn't be top of Ben's list of potential coffee companions, Ben couldn't deny the offer of assistance was a generous one. Of course, with his brash ways, Austin may not have been everybody's cup of tea, necessarily. But as Ben reasoned, Austin was a man with his finger on the hospitality pulse, and probably knew the key movers and shakers in that sector better than he knew himself. A powerful ally, then, and someone he'd be crazy not to want to have there in his corner, helping him to fight the good fight, he thought, as he attended to his grass.

Ben's newly refurbished mower hadn't missed a beat, and in no time at all, his lawn, now pristine, resembled the playing surface at Lord's Cricket Ground. And with that task sorted, it was now off to lovely Life's a Pitch.

It was only a short drive to his new enterprise, and Ben couldn't contain his excitement, beaming all the way, ideas for the business whirring through his mind. The new lease took effect at three p.m. that afternoon, and he'd been counting down the minutes for most of the day. He'd hoped Ruby could duck out of school early and join him on his first 'official' visit, but sadly an essential English exam took precedent, so he was flying solo. Regardless, previous visits to the site had been helpful, and now, as the man at the helm, Ben could really get his teeth in and put his own unique stamp on things. It was also his first opportunity to meet Cecil, Gerry's farm manager, whose assistance was negotiated as part of the lease agreement. Well, at least for the next three months.

Ben drove up the gravel farm track, taking in the new surroundings once more, rubbernecking. Again, there was just something about being out in the country that raised his spirits, removing any remaining weight from his shoulders — although part of that, as well, could be due to him having an extremely overdue haircut, his long, curly locks now consigned to the barbershop's bin.

Rather than heading towards the farm courtyard, Ben took a slight detour towards the campsite's allocated parking area. At first, he wondered if he'd taken a wrong turn owing to the distinct lack of any other vehicles parked there. Then, climbing out of his car, the next thing that struck him was the eerie quiet. On his previous visit, he'd been charmed by the sound of children squealing with delight over in the playground, as well as the raucous laughter from parents chatting around a BBQ whilst enjoying a beer or two. It'd been splendid and sunny so far today, though, so perhaps his happy campers were out enjoying themselves someplace else this afternoon, exploring the various charms of this fair isle?

Curious, Ben wandered along the raised wooden walkway leading from the parking area to the campsite, with birdsong being the only sounds he could hear at present. The official visitors entrance was an impressive privet hedge archway flanked by dense hedgerows, the hedgerows forming a natural wall around the front of the site. Walking through the archway, first into view was the smallest of his three fields and home to a row of glamping pods, installed for the convenience of those who wanted to camp but didn't relish the prospect of getting cold or wet. So, much like staying at home, purists in the camping fraternity might argue.

Not wanting to come across as a nosey parker, Ben cast a discreet sideways glance through the window of each of the pods he passed by, hoping to find some movement inside. But from his limited view, they were all vacant with no sign of life.

"What's going on here?" a despondent Ben said to himself, continuing through into the adjacent field, rigged out with electric hook-up points for the motorhome community. But again, there was nothing, only empty space here, and the only indication this field was once crammed with vehicles was the collection of vacant, faded areas of grass they'd once occupied, along with numerous ruts carved into the turf.

This was all starting to get a little freaky, like something from an episode of *The Twilight Zone*, Ben reckoned. Because the last time he'd visited, a little over a week ago, the place was packed with giddy holidaymakers. And now this. The grand total of nothing.

The final destination on Ben's reconnaissance mission was the largest of the three fields, home to the shower/toilet block, communal area, and where most campers with free-standing tents were ordinarily welcomed. But not today. In fact, a few discarded beer cans scattered about, along with one abandoned, disposable BBQ surrounded by a scorched patch of earth, were the only clues Ben could find suggesting a campsite existed.

"The communal area," Ben thought aloud, hoping a visit there might offer him some sort of explanation as to why he was walking through a ghost town.

It was one of the areas previously earmarked by Ben for immediate attention. Long overdue any cosmetic care of note, the wood-constructed shed housed a kitchen area for the campers to use and a generous-sized lounge for when they wanted to mingle with their fellow residents. As Ruby had excellently suggested, with a bit of a spruce up here and there, the communal area could also be fitted with a camp grocery shop as a way of generating additional income, as well as, of course, providing a useful service to the campers. And as long as they were selling food items, the idea of utilising Ben's baking skills was bandied about also. After all, running a campsite meant you had a steady stream of customers who were, in essence, a captive audience.

There was, at present, unfortunately, a flaw in their enthusiastic master plan to turn around the business. And that was the fact that there were currently no customers to speak of.

Unfortunately, the exterior of the communal area was in a worse state than he remembered, Ben noted on approach. Perhaps due to him wearing his rose-tinted spectacles on his previous visits. And as he now realised, it wasn't just cosmetic. A quick inspection — minus the rose-coloured glasses this time — around the structure revealed misplaced roof tiles, strips of rotting wood, and drainpipes which looked as if they might give way from their moorings at any given moment. And while he consoled himself that the condition may not have been terminal, the communal area would undoubtedly need some financial investment before implementing his plans for it.

Just then, Ben's ears pricked up, detecting as they did a faint grumbling sound, something he initially took to be a motorbike approaching from a distance. But when no motorbike or other motor-propelled vehicle appeared in view and the low rumbling noise continued, Ben tilted his head, struggling to work out where the sound originated. "If not a bike, then what *is* that?" he said to himself, walking around to the front of the building, climbing a short set of steps to the balcony area. There, he repeated the process, tilting his head like an inquisitive puppy, attempting to tune his ears into the source. Finally, Ben reached for the door handle, now convinced the sound was originating from within the structure itself, and, sure enough, the moment the door was ajar, the grumbling sound immediately intensified.

And then the audible mystery was solved. Because there, lying on a tatty couch, was a somewhat corpulent human form stretched out like a sunbathing seal, snoring its head off. Ordinarily, for Ben, the sight of an unshaven man with drool pooling around his mouth wasn't something that'd raise a smile. But as this was the first person he'd found enjoying the facilities at his new campsite, for that reason alone, Ben was delighted to see him.

Opting to leave Sleeping Beauty to enjoy his afternoon nap in peace, Ben reckoned his only remaining option was to call Gerry the farmer and ask if he had insight he could share as to why, aside from this one fellow, there wasn't anybody about. Irrational thoughts rattled through Ben's mind: Had there been a local bomb threat resulting in a mass evacuation? Or perhaps an outbreak of the Ebola virus, or some new variant? There must have been some logical reason for the exodus, although he hadn't a clue what.

Ben glanced into the adjoining kitchen, noting the worktops were clear and the sink empty. Again, an area which didn't appear to have received any recent visitors.

Entering the kitchen, and not looking where he was going, Ben stumbled into a metal trash bin, sending the bin crashing to the floor. "Damn!" he said, concerned the resulting racket would surely wake his snoozing guest enjoying forty winks.

And if the noise of the bin didn't do it, then he supposed his sudden shouting probably would. And sure enough...

"What is it, Lassie? Is someone trapped down the mine again...?" the chap from the other room could be heard to say, his voice groggy and confused as he transitioned from dreaming to an awake state. As Ben stepped out of the kitchen and back into the lounge area, he could see the fellow sitting upright, rubbing the sleepybugs from his eyes and the excess saliva from around his chin.

"That'll be me that's woken you up," Ben offered, holding out his hands by way of apology. "I just clattered into the bin," he explained, releasing a *what-am-I-like* sigh.

"It's fine," the chap replied, adjusting his shirt, which had risen up over his protruding midriff. "I'm actually meant to be working, truth be told," he explained, glancing about, trying to get his bearings now that he was becoming more or less wide awake. "I suppose I must have nodded off," he remarked.

Ben laughed along in solidarity until the fellow's words completely registered. "Wait, so you're not a guest here?" he asked.

"A guest? Oh, no," came the reply, his arms now stretched out above his head. "No, I work here."

At this point, Ben didn't really need the investigative prowess of Hercule Poirot to figure out the identity of the slovenly fellow before him. After all, there was only one employee that he was aware of. "In that case, you must be Cecil?" he deduced.

"At your service," Cecil replied, pushing himself to his feet, leaving behind a deep imprint on the worn sofa.

Ben considered extending a hand to introduce himself, but the thought of the drool likely still coating Cecil's hand convinced him otherwise. "I'm Ben," Ben said instead, along with a generous smile.

Cecil narrowed one eye, like the name was familiar to him but he couldn't quite place it. "Ben...?" he said, as if the answer was on the tip of his tongue.

"Ben, as in I've just taken the business over, Ben."

Cecil's eye remained half shut. Perhaps he was still a little sleepy. "Oh. *Ben*," he said eventually, his powers of recall taking a moment to catch up. "Ah. It's a pleasure to finally meet you, Ben," Cecil offered, throwing out a hand Ben couldn't politely refuse this time. "I was just catching up on some overdue sleep," Cecil told him, explaining why he'd had a nap on the sofa. "I was down the Dog and Crown last night for our darts match, you see," he elaborated, throwing an imaginary dart with precision. "Sadly, we didn't win. But then, afterwards, the landlord announced a lock-in. So not a *complete* disaster, mind you."

"Ah, I see. A late evening, then," Ben remarked, catching a whiff of stale ale in the air. "Well, I am very sorry to hear you lost your darts match," he offered sympathetically. "But, anyway..." Ben said, moving the conversation to more pressing matters, namely his new business. "Gerry's kindly offered us your services for the next few months?" he asked, hoping this information had been relayed accordingly.

"At your service," Cecil said again, offering a smart salute. "Two or more hours a day until further notice," he added. "Whatever I can do to assist, you just have to name it. I'm here to help."

"There was one quick thing I wanted to discuss, actually. At least for starters," Ben said, turning and walking towards the front window, his expression grave.

Cecil followed, taking up a position standing next to Ben. "It's not about me bathing in the hot tub, is it?" he asked, head slightly bowed. "Because I promise that's only a temporary measure while I sort a few things out with the ol' trouble and strife."

Ben slowly turned his head, unsure where to go with that little packet of information. "No, it wasn't that, Cecil," Ben assured him, taking a mental note to give the glamping pod hot tubs a thorough bleaching. "No, what I wanted to talk to you about was *that*," Ben said, extending a finger towards the empty field in front.

"Yeah, it's a magnificent view, isn't it?" Cecil was quick to agree, though appearing not entirely sure what it was that he was meant to be looking at.

Ben nodded. "Yes, but the problem is that it's only the *two* of us enjoying it," he pointed out. "So where on earth *is* everyone?"

"You mean the campers?" Cecil asked, receiving a further nod. "Ah. Well they're all gone, aren't they?" Cecil noted, looking decidedly pleased with himself. "It took me all day to cancel the reservations after the current guests left, but it's all done. Once Cecil puts his mind to something, Cecil gets it done," he insisted.

Ben ran his eyes over Cecil's jowly face, hoping to see some sort of smile emerge. "Cancel the reservations?" Ben asked eventually, when no such smile appeared. "What do you mean you've cancelled all of the reservations?" Ben said with a nervous laugh. "Gerry did tell you I was taking over the business, didn't he?"

"Of course!" Cecil was happy to confirm. "But I just assumed you'd want to start things all afresh, you know? New business, new beginnings, right?"

Ben placed a hand to his forehead. "So, you didn't think the new owner would be delighted to welcome those campers who'd already booked?" he asked, hardly believing what he was hearing.

"Hmm. Interesting," Cecil replied, appearing to entertain this notion for the very first time. "Yeah, now you mention it, I suppose that approach might have made more sense, mightn't it?" he offered. "Yeah. Yeah, I definitely feel a little bit silly now, actually."

"You feel a bit *silly*...?" Ben said, now chewing on his knuckle. "What about all of the money from those guests who were due to arrive?" he asked with his mouth half-full, almost afraid to hear the answer.

"Oh, don't you worry about that, it's all been sorted," Cecil said, perfectly happy to have been of service. "I've refunded everyone, so you needn't concern yourself with it. I knew you'd be busy with other matters, yeah?"

Ben was on the verge of tears at this stage. "So, you're saying that our reservations book is emptier than the three fields out-side, and you've now given back any money we once had nestled in the bank account?"

Cecil shifted uneasily, rubbing the stubble on the upper-most of his various chins. "Ehm... yeah. Pretty much. But, you know, Ben... onwards and upwards?"

"Right, then. Let's phone them all back?" Ben suggested, hav-ing something of a eureka moment.

"How do you mean?" Cecil asked. "Phone who back?"

Ben paused for a moment, wondering if Cecil's brain was perhaps still soaked with alcohol from the night before.

"The guests who you've just cancelled, yes? We phone them all back, tell them there's been a huge mistake, and look for-ward to seeing them soon."

"Oh, right. Sorry," Cecil replied with a chuckle. "But, no. Sadly not."

"Sadly not?" Ben answered, repeating Cecil's words back to him in hopes that it might prompt some sort of further expla-nation.

"I've deleted all of their details, Ben. I didn't want you to get in trouble with the data protection police. So, I thought it better safe than sorry."

Ben cradled his face in his hands, moaning quietly.

Cecil, for his part, took a step closer, appearing as if he might want to give Ben a cuddle but unsure if they were at that stage in their relationship yet. "Keep yer pecker up, Ben!" Cecil of-fered instead. "You're at the start of an exciting journey. No, scrap that, we're at the start of an exciting journey," he said, smiling broadly.

Ben peeled his hands from his face, glancing down at his watch. "Exciting journey?" he answered through gritted teeth. "Cecil, I don't think I've got any money in the business bank ac-count, and thanks to your considerable efforts, I've now got the grand total of naff-all customers," he said with a weary shake of his head. "Cecil, I've been in charge for a mere forty-two minutes, and I think the business is bankrupt already."

Chapter Seven

Ben didn't enjoy lying. It doesn't come to him naturally. And even when he attempted a small fib, his cheeks flushed to such an extent that they glowed like a Belisha beacon. For that reason, it was often fairly easy to spot when he was stretching the truth.

Indeed, when his ex-wife Olivia had asked on one fateful occasion if her bum "looked big" in some particular article of clothing, Ben had ably provided the necessary assurances, doing a convincing enough job of allaying her fears. That is, until his cheeks changed colour quicker than a frightened chameleon. And it was after this little incident, in fact, that Olivia had sought out the services of a dietician. And the rest, as they say, is history.

But despite his best efforts, Ben, by his own admission, was still rather useless at telling the occasional untruth, his unwelcome affliction returning whenever Ruby asked about the campsite. Only this time, his reddening cheeks brought a friend along with them in the form of a rather irritating twitch in his left eyelid, the gravity of the situation and the dire state of his new business only heightening his symptoms. And thus, it didn't take Ruby too long to figure out that all wasn't sunshine and rainbows.

But a problem shared is a problem halved, or so the saying goes. And far from being judgemental, Ruby sat with her dad for hours on end, brainstorming ideas, throwing out suggestions that could drum up some much-needed trade to fill their empty grass with tents. Luckily, being a teenage girl, Ruby was somewhat *au fait* with social media, what with having her nose constantly pressed to her phone screen. As such, she was willing and able to assume responsibility for updating and maintaining the campsite's online presence. Meanwhile, Ben, for his part, wasn't necessarily sitting on his hands either. He'd spent hours that week promoting the business on the phone, speaking with travel agents, the local tourist board, coach excursion companies, and anybody who'd listen to him. The two of them had even tossed around the benefits of advertising in magazines catering to a camping audience. Unfortunately, where that was concerned at least, any spare cash in the coffers was already earmarked for long-overdue renovations, particularly in the communal areas.

Fortunately, there was still a trickle of new business, primarily from returning customers or from those that hadn't opened or received Cecil's cancellation notice and turned up for their holiday none the wiser. But while it was an immense relief to see a few names in the reservations book, the modest income generated from these new arrivals being most welcome, it certainly wasn't enough to keep the wolf from the door in the long term. If the business was going to flourish, Ben and Ruby needed a serious influx of campers and fast.

Currently, Ben was fielding the occasional phone call, including those querying the impersonal cancellation email they'd received and checking to see if there'd been some kind of mistake somehow. Sadly, many who received the notice had simply made alternative arrangements without further communication. But for those who did make the effort to phone, Ben was desperate to make amends. And one of those who bothered enough to ring Ben up and query the cancellation message he'd received, as it should happen, was Louis from Wolverhampton.

Ben eased back in his chair, feet resting on the desk he'd set up in his makeshift campsite office. Ordinarily, this area next to the kitchen served as the laundry room, but without too many visitors to worry about just yet, Ben was presently putting it to another use.

"Yes, that's right, Louis," Ben said brightly, directing his voice towards the speakerphone, a smile emerging for his own benefit. "Yes, I've renamed the business *Life's a Pitch*," he confirmed. "And, as you'll know if you've stayed here before, we're ideally located near Castletown. So, a short walk to the local shops and plenty of opportunity for a beer or two if the mood takes."

"I dunno, Ben," a sceptical-sounding Louis replied from his end. "We've stayed at your site for, what, six, maybe seven years? Regular as clockwork. So when we got this recent email saying our reservation had been cancelled without notice, it left something of a sour taste in our mouths."

Ben briefly curled his fingers into a fist, shaking his head as well, frustrated by Cecil's inexplicable actions. "It's all been a genuine mistake, Louis, and one we're eager to rectify," he replied earnestly. "And if you and the other mountain bikers in your group agree to come back to Life's a Pitch, I'll give you..." Ben added, looking to the ceiling for inspiration. "A twenty percent discount?"

"Make it twenty-five," Louis immediately countered. "And if it sweetens things for you, we've over thirty club members making the trip to the island this year."

Ben unfurled his fingers, figuring seventy-five percent of something was better than a hundred percent of nothing. "Louis, you've got a deal. And I look forward to welcoming you in person."

Louis went silent for a long moment, with it seeming like he was mulling things over for a bit. "There was one thing, Ben..."

"Please, anything. All feedback is gratefully received," Ben responded.

"Well, ever since our reservation was cancelled, I've been looking at other campsites on the island, you see, and—"

"But I've already got you booked in," Ben protested, fearing he hadn't sealed the deal after all.

"No, it's not that, Ben. That's sorted," Louis told him. "It's just, well, looking at the other campsites made me realise the one you've taken over is a little tired, is all."

"Tired?"

"Yeah. In a desperate state. A bit run down. Sorry, no offence meant."

"Don't worry, none taken," Ben quickly assured him, as it's not as if it was an assessment he could really disagree with. In fact, right now, he was staring forlornly at a giant mould patch that'd formed above one of the washing machines. And if that wasn't bad enough in itself, paint was peeling from the walls like skin from sunburnt shoulders. "As it should happen, Louis, I've committed to a series of extensive renovations, which should be completed in the next couple of weeks. You won't recognise the place."

"In that case, get the beer on ice, and we'll all definitely see you in a few weeks, Ben. Also, dust off your bike, if you've got one, and you can come out with us on a few trails, yeah? We'll go easy on you, I promise!"

"Only if you promise," Ben joked, sharing the laugh and imagining himself riding his daughter's undersized girl's bicycle in the company of seasoned mountain bikers.

Of course, it was only a small victory, but securing the booking for the mountain bikers offered Ben a welcome boost, giving him a glimmer of hope. And, as Ben had mentioned on the phone, Operation Camp Refurb was already well underway. Ordinarily, any refurbishment works would have been scheduled for the closed season over the long winter months when customer inconvenience would be minimised. But there was the current state of things. And with only a handful of campers on site for the next couple of weeks, it was safe enough to get things underway right now, Ben figured.

So, following several productive, if expensive, visits to B & Q for DIY supplies, Ben had effectively obtained the required materials to get the renovations started. He wasn't exactly known for his handyman abilities, of course. A point Ruby had to remind him of, while back at home, by gently pointing out the door he'd hung in the spare room of the house that would never close properly without a firm application of the shoulder. And even if you *did* manage to get it shut, getting it back open again was another matter in itself.

But what Ben may have lacked in experience, he more than made up for in enthusiasm, burning the midnight oil for days on end, hoping to make a dent at the campsite in what was, after all, a daunting schedule of work.

Fortunately, though, like an angel from above, an unexpected godsend proving themselves to be invaluable was Cecil. After Ben's first meeting with his new part-time employee, his early expectations hadn't been exceptionally high. But for someone so listless in appearance, Cecil was proving himself to be something of a DIY superhero. Surprising, then, that the campsite was in such a sorry state in the first place, when Ben had taken things over. But that was a discussion for another day, Ben reckoned.

Cecil could turn his hand to anything, or so it appeared to Ben. And before too long, rotting floorboards were replaced on the communal patio area, drainpipes were hanging the way they were meant to, and tired, cracked tiles in the shower block were restored to their former glory. Indeed, it was proving to be quite the productive partnership, with Cecil focussing his efforts on the more skilled tasks like carpentry and such, and Ben spending his time on the strictly cosmetic side of things, the stuff he was genuinely good at. After all, he was a dab hand with a paintbrush and a roll of masking tape. The difficulty, however, was the sheer time investment required. For his part alone, the interior of all the glamping pods were requiring a good lick of paint, sometimes two full applications, and the entire communal area was still in need of some serious attention as well. And progress was painfully slow, to the extent it felt to Ben like he was using a toothbrush to apply his choice of magnolia paint, an unimaginative yet safe option, as it was a nice neutral cream colour.

So far, Ben had successfully refreshed the paint in six of the seven glamping pods. Although to call them merely 'pods' was, perhaps, doing them something of a disservice. Rather than the modest typical curved shingle roof design that he'd seen on other campsites, these were more akin to mini houses, each with two bedrooms, a small but functional kitchen, and a modern bathroom arguably nicer than the one in his own home. However, contributing to the overall protracted nature of his progress was the fact that each of the pods had required a thoroughly good scrubbing before he could even *think* about proceeding with any of the painting. He wasn't entirely sure who'd previously assumed cleaning responsibilities, but whoever it was, they clearly didn't have their heart in that particular task judging by the dust and grime he'd encountered. In addition to the general dinge, he'd discovered rotten fruit fermenting in one pod, congealed milk in the fridge of another, and the interior of one particular oven would likely require an acid bath to remove what had exploded within.

And so, other than a brief interlude to say hello to Louis the mountain biker, it was back to work, no rest for the wicked, as Ben had a full day with the paintbrush ahead of him.

A little later on in the morning, with the steady, assured hand of a brain surgeon, Ben was carefully cutting in around an interior window frame, leaving a perfectly neat application of paint as he went along. "Smashing job," Ben said, complimenting himself as he surveyed his work, and then shuffling over to the opposite side of the window to continue on his ministrations over there. Unfortunately, the two-seater sofa was sitting a little too close for comfort, and having so far avoided covering any of the soft furnishings in magnolia, he had no wish to start now. "You just wait there a moment," Ben instructed to his tin of paint, laying it on the windowsill and carefully resting the brush across the opening so any spillage would fall safely back inside.

"Right," he said, first checking that his hands were clean, and then giving one end of the sofa a shove until it was clear of where he wanted to stand. "Oh, for the love of..." he moaned, clapping his eyes on the thick layer of dust suddenly revealed, that portion of the sofa no longer hiding it. "Why didn't I think to look under there earlier, when I was cleaning?" he said, chastising himself.

He wondered if he should go fetch Henry the Hoover to immediately tidy things up, or if it might make more sense to simply wait until later, after he was done painting. But just then, his attention was drawn to what looked at first blush like a pink ball, caught there on the wooden foot of the couch. For a moment, he thought it might be one of those squeaky toys that dogs liked to torture their owners with. Whatever it was, it was just one more indication he'd have to have some profound words with the current cleaning team (if there even *was* one).

Ben dropped to one knee, lifting the corner of the couch to free up the item in question. And now that he was a little closer to it, it became evident it wasn't a pooch's squeaky toy at all, as it was made of fabric, not rubber. He now thought it could very well be a rolled-up sock, but that proved not to be the case either, once the item was dislodged and finally unravelled. Because there, dangling between his thumb and forefinger like a spaniel's ear, was a pair of women's lacy pink knickers. And there wasn't too much to them, curiously enough, as they were the sort of design where the more money you paid out for them, the less material you actually got in return.

Judging by his vacant expression, what Ben was holding wasn't fully registering, even though he was staring straight at it. It could have been because he'd not been in the company of such intimate apparel for quite some time, or it could simply have been bewilderment as to why it was there, under the couch, in the first place. And then the precise realisation of what he was holding finally clicked into place.

"Eww!" Ben said, tossing the knickers away like a hand grenade — a dirty, *filthy* hand grenade — before wiping the palm of his hand on his paint-splattered overalls.

He eased himself down, coming to rest lying flat on his stomach, looking to see what else might possibly be found beneath the couch, hidden from view. And sure enough, the knickers hadn't been the only thing keeping the dust bunnies company. Stretching out an arm, Ben hooked a finger around a pink strap, pulling out a bra like a lingerie fisherman, and then hurriedly chucked this article to the side as well. He suspected both of these items as having been removed with a great deal of haste and little care. A further inspection thankfully revealed no companion garments, only more dust that Ben would soon have to attend to by unleashing Henry the Hoover.

Ben pushed himself upright, grumbling away, heading to the bathroom to urgently wash his hands, even though there was very little physical dirt on them to speak of. While scrubbing furiously, he reasoned that the only saving grace was that he'd come across the discarded underwear himself and not the next guest. After all, that sort of discovery didn't often make for a favourable review on TripAdvisor.

With his hands sterilised and smelling of vanilla and lily blossom, Ben returned to his brush, conscious the walls weren't going to paint themselves. However, he couldn't resist a wry smile, imagining the former owner of the unmentionables wondering where on earth she'd left them. A quick glance at his watch told Ben it was a little under an hour until lunchtime. Plenty of time, he reasoned, to finish the first coat on the interior walls if he didn't get distracted again. However...

"Dad!" Ruby's familiar voice called out, just as paint bristles were about to make contact with the wall. "Dad, are you down here?" she asked, sounding reasonably close, but somewhere outside.

Ben pressed his nose up against the pod window, spotting Ruby wandering through the campsite with several of her mates. Once again, Ben carefully laid his brush across his paint tin, resigned that this particular job might take a little longer than he'd initially anticipated. Still, as far as interruptions went, seeing his lovely daughter was one that Ben didn't mind so much at all.

"I'm in here!" Ben called out, rattling a knuckle against the windowpane. But his greeting went unheard, the girls continuing along their way.

With the group in danger of disappearing from view behind another of the glamping pods, Ben moved over to the patio entrance a short distance away. But as he reached to open the sliding glass door, he noticed the undergarments he'd previously cast aside, now sitting there at his feet, just before the glass, basking in the sun.

Diving in like an osprey snatching a fish from the water, he swiftly scooped the offending articles from the floor and promptly stuffed them inside his painting overalls, all in one magnificent fluid motion. Then, and only then, did he open the sliding glass door. "Ruby! Ruby, I'm over here!" he called out, waving them over as he caught their attention.

"Hiya, girls," Ben said a moment later, giving them a friendly wave as they strolled over, meeting him at his location. But he was acting a little funny, from Ruby's point of view, behaving as if he'd just been caught scrumping apples.

"I thought you had hockey practice this afternoon?" Ben asked of Ruby, followed by a nervous laugh.

"It was netball," Ruby replied, eying him suspiciously, as he was, at present, acting suspiciously. "Everything okay, Dad?" Ruby asked, noting the peculiar way he was standing, a protective arm draped across his chest. "We've not caught you at an awkward time?"

"Oh no, Ruby. Not at all," Ben suggested. "This is the final pod that—"

But Ruby cut him off mid-explanation, stepping forward now that she was closer and tugging on the end of a pink strap she could see dangling out the side of his overalls. Then, like a magician pulling hankies from their sleeve, she liberated the entirety of the bra that'd formerly been concealed, sending the accompanying knickers, as well, tumbling to the wooden decking in the process.

"Have you got someone in there with you?" Ruby asked, with the bra still secured in her fingertips, swinging it slowly like a lacy pink pendulum while trying to look around her father for a view inside.

Ben started to laugh. "What, me?" he asked, jabbing a thumb into his chest. Instinct taking over, he placed a foot over the knickers as he said this, attempting to conceal them, even though Ruby and her mates had surely already spotted them by now. "No, no, of course I've not got anybody in there with me," he said nervously, letting out a playful sigh as well, which could have been interpreted as an additional, *That would be nice. But no. Sadly, I don't.*"

"I'm all on my own," Ben insisted, his eyes falling down to the bra pinched between Ruby's fingers. "Just me," he continued, before suddenly realising that being on his own, with these types of objects in his sweaty possession, may, on reflection, have looked even *worse* for him than the alternative. "Ah. There's a funny story about the bra and knickers..." he began to explain, but then trailed away, deciding the less said about it the better, actually. "Anyway. Enough about me, girls. How was hockey practice?" he said, swiftly changing tack.

"*Netball*, Dad. And it was fine."

"Six cups of tea," Cecil announced, proceeding with caution, taking care not to spill the contents. "And..." he teased, placing the tray down on the lounge table, "I've found a packet of unopened HobNobs in the biscuit barrel."

One by one, the eager painters stopped what they were doing, congregating around the table like buffalo around a watering hole. "Thanks, Cecil," Ben said with a wink, procuring one of the chocolate-covered biscuit beauties and dunking it squarely into his tea. "Ah. Lovely, this," Ben said to the others.

Ben couldn't help but smile. There was the nice cup of tea in hand, but also there'd been the unexpected arrival of Ruby and her netball teammates. Unbeknownst to him, Ruby had spoken to her friends about the campsite and how she was intending to head there after practice to surprise her old dad, chipping in with some DIY while she was at it. And Ben was held in high regard by her circle of friends, not just because he was a thoroughly decent bloke, but because he'd kept most of them supplied with delicious glazed goods during his time as a baker. For both these reasons, when they heard he needed assistance, they were quick to volunteer their services. Even their netball coach, Abigail, had put in an appearance at one point, happy to get stuck in, and proving herself quite the dab hand with the roller, as it should happen.

Fortunately for Ben, the new arrivals had been so engrossed in what they were doing that they'd soon stopped ribbing him about what he'd been up to with the undergarments. However, he suspected it wasn't the last he'd ever hear on that particular subject, as it was ripe for poking fun. By this time, as they sat around for tea, Ben had finished the first coat on the remaining glamping pod, his efforts then shifting to helping the gang in the communal area. In a relatively short amount of time, serious progress had been made, much to his immense delight.

"Is that you heading off, Cecil?" Ben asked, noting his wingman patting his trouser pockets, presumably looking for his keys. "Thanks again for your fine efforts today, mate," Ben told him. "Much appreciated."

"No, I'm just looking for my phone, Ben. I'm going to ring the better half and tell her I'm here to stay for a bit longer. I thought I'd lend a hand with the painting and help you finish up, if you don't mind?"

"Mind? No, of course I don't mind, Cecil!" Ben responded, pleased at having an extra body thrown into the mix, helping to speed things along. "Hang on a minute, Cecil," he added, a thought presenting itself to him. "Today's Saturday, yeah? Is Saturday not supposed to be your day off?"

Cecil offered a casual shrug. "It's fine," he answered, pressing a few buttons on his phone. "To be honest with you, I enjoy seeing the campsite with a new burst of life," he said, placing the phone against his ear. "Plus," he said bravely, directly before the call connected, "it means I'm not getting under the wife's feet, now doesn't it?" And then, shortly thereafter, "Oh, hello, luv. It's just me..."

Ben felt a wave of guilt wash over him, feeling a bit of shame for having thought poorly of Cecil for his previous mistakes. Yet here he was willing to put in a further shift, without being asked, all on his day off. It was a noble gesture that left Ben with a lump in his throat. The netball girls also putting in an appearance made Ben realise that there really were good people in the world, selfless folk willing to help others in their time of need just because it was a nice thing to do.

"Here, Ruby," Ben said a short time later, standing at the foot of the stepladder she was working up now that they were all back at it.

"Yeah?" Ruby asked, still focussed on what she was doing, inheriting her father's eye for detail as she had. "Do you need this ladder or something?"

"No, no, it's not that," he said, placing his foot on the bottom step. "No, I was just admiring your steady hand," he told her. "And I was *also* just thinking about how I painted your bedroom last year. As I recall, having to work around you while you lay on the bed?"

"And an excellent job you did of it, too," Ruby put forth.

Ben laughed to show he wasn't too serious about his subtle dig at her expense. "Well, looking at the standard of your work, Ruby, I think I can find another painting job for you to do back at home. Maybe *my* room will need painting next?"

"I'll see what I can do, Dad. It'll be a few weeks until I can get you in the diary, though," she advised. "You see, I'm tied up working for this complete crackpot right at the moment, someone who thought he'd buy a campsite on a wing and a prayer."

"Sounds like my kind of guy," Ben said with a chuckle.

But before Ruby could offer up any kind of response, the lounge area was suddenly filled with the unmistakable sound of "Dancing Queen," ABBA's classic hit. And the netball girls didn't need asking twice to join in, even those up a ladder, all happily belting out the catchy lyrics.

"Apologies!" Cecil called out, holding up his mobile to clarify where the music originated — namely, his phone's ringtone.

"Don't answer it!" Ruby joked. "We're only just getting to the good bit!"

"He'd better, as that might be his wife!" Ben chipped in. "And I imagine he's already in enough trouble as it is for working on his day off!"

Cecil wiggled his bum to the beat, enjoying the tune also, along with the playful banter as well. "We'll continue the karaoke session in a minute," he said after a moment, looking down to the phone screen to see who was calling, thinking he really ought to answer it by now. And immediately, his playful expression evaporated.

"I'll, ehm… I'll just take this outside," Cecil advised, shuffling towards the front door, the wind suddenly taken from his sails. And once outside, Cecil glanced over his shoulder, even, before answering the call…

"Yeah. Hello, Austin," Cecil whispered, only now noticing that he was still holding his paintbrush in his other hand. Cecil listened intently, putting a small bit of distance between himself and the area where he'd just been working. "Oh, you've been around my house, have you?" he asked, in response to what he was hearing. "My wife said I was working extra hours to help the new owners out, did she?" Cecil said, glancing at his paintbrush.

"Ehm… yeah, I'm here, boss," Cecil said, after a few moments of remaining quiet. He listened on as the rather animated voice blared through his phone's speaker, moving the phone a few inches away from his face so as to protect his poor eardrums from damage. "What's that?" Cecil asked with a forced laugh, and then, "Helping him out, boss? Of course not, no. No, I was just, you know… well, trying to take him down from the inside, as it were."

That explanation appeared to placate Austin, at least for the time being, judging by the decreased overall volume coming through Cecil's phone. Then, after listening to Austin prattle on for a bit longer, Cecil worked up the courage to speak up, revealing something that was on his mind. "There was actually one thing I wanted to mention, boss, if I may," he offered, while giving his paintbrush a little shake, the excess paint now coating the nearby hedgerow in a small spattering of droplets. "It's this Ben chap, you see... Yes. Ben. No, not Bill. Yes, I'm sure... What about him, then? Well, he's actually a pretty stand-up guy, once you get to know him. And I was just wondering, see, if we really needed to turn the screw? Because, as I said—"

But it was time for Cecil to once again move the phone a safe distance away from his ear while Austin had his say.

"Yes, Austin, I do know how much you're paying me," Cecil conceded, once he could eventually get a word in. "Yes, you're absolutely correct, my gambling debts will not pay themselves off," he reluctantly admitted.

Cecil sat down on a bench he'd only just fixed that morning. From there, he had a clear view of the short distance across the field, spying Ben and his merry band of helpers through windows he'd recently cleaned for the first time in ages. And even though he'd taken the ABBA soundtrack with him, they were still leaping about, dancing to the beat of their own drum, Cecil couldn't help but observe. Finally, he had to look away, unwilling to watch them enjoying themselves like that, knowing their efforts to make the place nicer were ultimately, and most likely, going to be all for nought. Especially if he had anything to do with it. Which, sadly, he did.

"What?" Cecil answered. "No, I'm still here, boss," he said into his phone. "No, you're right, I don't suppose there is another way," he replied with a sigh, responding to what he was being told. "Yes, you can count on me, boss," he said, although without too terribly much conviction, and also unable to block out the sound of giddy laughter filtering across the field. "No, I won't let you down, I promise," he insisted. "When Cecil Crumpet accepts a mission, he never lets personal feelings get in the way, much less anything else."

Chapter Eight

T his can't be it, Billy," Tommo insisted, jabbing his finger onto the delivery note resting on his knee. "We can't possibly be going the right way."

Billy slowed the van to a crawl, clicking his tongue against the roof of his mouth, something he did when thinking. "Hmm..." he said, casting an uncertain eye over the expansive countryside. "So why'd you send us up this country lane, then?" he offered abruptly, glaring over to his mate in the passenger seat, the contemplation portion of Billy's thinking process apparently concluded and now moving straight on to the accusation stage.

Tommo extended a finger towards the windscreen. "What are you blaming *me* for? It's *'er* bloody fault, not mine," he protested, pointing at the sat-nav secured to the glass by its sucker. *"She's* the one that sent us up a country lane in the arse end of nowhere, not me," he said, sulking, crossing his arms over his chest like a petulant child who'd just dropped their lolly. And then, just as he appeared ready to deploy his bottom lip as well... "There!" he said, unfolding his arms as he clapped his eyes on the sign ahead, a most welcome sight. *"Life's a Pitch,"* he declared, cross-referencing the name on the sign with the one detailed on his delivery note, just to be sure. "Yep. We're right where we should be," he confirmed. And then, "Sorry, Gloria," he said to the sat-nav, apologetic for ever having doubted her sense of direction.

Parked up on the cobbles, the two of them climbed out of their trusty white Ford Transit van, sucking in a deep lungful of the fresh, clean country air. Or at least one of them did.

"I could get used to this," Tommo suggested, adjusting his hat as he took a good gander, admiring the scenery. "Imagine waking up with that view every day," he said dreamily. "The smell of—"

"Cow shit?" Billy answered, paying more attention to his phone than the captivating views on offer.

Tommo shook his head. "Nature," he replied. "I was going to say *nature*. But I wouldn't expect you to appreciate the great outdoors, Billy, what with you being something of a philistine."

"Philistine? Dunno what you're talking about. I don't collect stamps," Billy answered, without bothering to look up. "But there can be good money in stamps. So you shouldn't knock it."

"Uncultured," Tommo said with a sigh. "Although I'm not sure I'd have expected anything else from a man who eats Pot Noodle for breakfast."

"It's a glorious breakfast. Sets you up for the day, dunnit? Bloody breakfast of champions, Tommo," Billy offered, popping his phone into his pocket and walking round to the rear of the van. "Right. Come on, then. This oven's not going to unload itself."

Tommo followed close behind, scrutinising the delivery note in one hand while caressing his chin with the other. "Hmm, I'm not sure about this, Billy."

"About what, exactly?"

"That we're in the right place," Tommo suggested, briefly taking in the agricultural surroundings once more.

"You're the one who just insisted we were at the right spot," Billy had to remind him.

"Yeah, but I mean, what would a farmer want with an industrial catering oven?" replied Tommo.

Billy gave a shrug of his shoulders before pulling open the rear door of the van. "Delivery note ties up with the name on that signpost we just saw," he said. "So that's good enough for me."

"I dunno, I think I'm going to find someone before we start unloading," Tommo decided, and then started heading towards the farm building to do precisely that. But before he'd advanced too far, a spirited voice called out from the opposite direction.

"Yes, hello!" a breathless Ben shouted over, jogging towards their location while offering a cheery way. "Are you fine gentlemen here to deliver my new oven?" he asked upon arrival.

Billy couldn't resist glancing at their van. Their van, that is, with the giant image of an oven plastered across the side along with the words INDUSTRIAL CATERING EQUIPMENT in large, prominent lettering above it. "Eh, yeah, that's us, mate," Billy offered. "How did you know?" he asked with a wry smile.

"I saw you coming up the lane," Ben answered, allowing the gentle sarcasm to wash over him. "I was hoping to direct you to the other entrance, but you'd already driven past."

"Wait, this isn't where the oven's being delivered?" Billy asked, gesturing towards the nearby farmhouse situated only a very close distance away.

Ben turned, gesturing himself, towards an area in the distance. "No, it's going over to my official Guest Entertainment Centre," he said, releasing a contented sigh, pleased with the name he'd chosen for his refurbished communal area. "It's just a short walk through those fields," he added, delighted, it would appear, by the arrival of his new oven.

"*Short walk?*" a returning Tommo exclaimed, squinting his eyes at the building on the horizon. "You mean that one over there?" he asked.

Ben followed the direction of Tommo's extended finger. "Yes, that's the one. Just a short walk."

Billy and Tommo's shoulders both dropped. "If you're carrying a bloody half-ton oven, that's not exactly a short walk," Tommo observed. "Ah, well. It'll keep us fit, I suppose," he added with a laugh.

"I'll get the trolley ready," Billy suggested, receiving a nod from his colleague.

"Anything I can do to help?" Ben asked, sensing this might be a more challenging task than he'd initially assumed. He told the lads they could drive back to a different access point, which would bring them a bit closer to their target. But by this time they had already loaded the huge beast of an oven onto a trolley, and decided they may as well simply carry on as is, readying themselves to hoof it across the fields.

"You've got a kettle at this Guest Entertainment Centre of yours?" Tommo asked.

"Absolutely. And some chocolate brownies as well, if that'll help things at all," Ben answered.

"We'll see you there," Tommo advised, before then shifting his attention to his partner. "Right. Well, Billy, I suppose you best hope the surgeon did a proper job sewing up that hernia of yours, yeah?"

And a bit later...

"Oh, *yes*, baby," Ben cooed, pressing his cheek flat against the polished stainless steel while caressing the worktop with the palm of his right hand, as if he'd just been reunited with a long-lost lover.

"So you like?" an amused Tommo enquired, whilst enjoying his well-deserved cuppa.

"Mm-hmm," Ben offered in response, arms draped over his new oven and worktop like he was afraid someone might suddenly take it away from him. "Yes, it's *wonderful*."

The installation of Ben's new object of desire had taken a little under two hours. And a large portion of that time was spent hauling the massive weight over the grass, the trolley wheels sinking into the soil at every turn. Fortunately, a helpful group of newly arrived orienteers had delayed erecting their tents in order to render some last-minute aid, kindly assisting the boys in completing their task.

In the kitchen area of the newly christened Guest Entertainment Centre, Ben's master plan was now coming to fruition. The area had benefited from a complete overhaul, with the walls given a long-overdue thick coating of paint, threadbare sections of carpet replaced, et cetera, with any tired fixtures and fittings now thankfully gone. And the other thing *gone*, unfortunately, was the contents of Ben's bank account. His financial contingency, buffer, safety blanket, or whatever you should like to call it, was now exhausted, a distant memory. And not only that, but Ben was also now spending money he didn't have, courtesy of an attractive buy-now-pay-later deal offered by the friendly branch of his local industrial equipment centre. But tents were popping up all over the campsite, with a steady trickle of new reservations coming in as well, so, as far as Ben was concerned, this expenditure was a safe investment in the future of his new business.

"So, all of this isn't a bit overkill?" Billy asked, mid-chomp, working on stuffing the brownie Ben had given him into his face. "I mean, that's the type of oven we ordinarily deliver to the big, fancy restaurants. And here you've got one in a *campsite*," he pondered aloud. "No offence meant, of course," he added, shoving the remainder of the brownie into his greedy gob.

"Oh, I've big plans," Ben advised, finally peeling his cheek from the cool, shiny surface and offering his new oven an adoring glance. "I'm a baker by trade," he explained, unable to contain his gratified smile. "Not only will I sell my lovely campers freshly baked goods, but I'm also going to offer baking workshops. So, you can come for a lovely camping experience and also learn to make bread, cake, croissants, and other goodies."

"I'm in!" Tommo declared without hesitation.

Ben smiled politely. "In?" he asked, wishing to make sure he understood correctly.

"Yeah, I'm in. The missus is always saying I never take her anywhere. And we both like bread, cake, and croissants. So you can put our names on the list."

"Now you mention it," Billy entered in, after running the idea around his noggin. "Yeah, go on. If he's signing up, then put me down as well."

"You're being serious?" Ben asked, thoroughly delighted. "Oh, lads, that's really made my day. Thank you."

"You're welcome," said Billy, before draining the contents of his cup. "C'mon, Tommo. We've got that fridge in the van that still has to be delivered today."

Ben removed a pen from the breast pocket of his shirt, ready to take some details. "The first paying customers for my Baking Break Vacation," he announced, bursting with pride. "Hmm, I just need a few more bookings, and I might actually be able to pay for that oven you've just delivered," he added, though talking more to himself now than to the others.

"What's that?" Billy asked.

"Nothing. I was just thinking out loud, lads. Don't mind me," Ben answered with a wave of the hand. "So anyway, you'd better go home and dig your apron and oven gloves out, yeah?" Ben suggested, escorting the two of them out into the fresh air. "You know, gentlemen, again, you've really made my day," Ben reiterated. "And I've got this sneaking suspicion things are starting to take a turn for the better around here," he said with a confident sniff. "Yep, I've got a feeling in my water that things are on the up for Life's a Pitch."

Three overly enthusiastic fellows with nary a tooth between them squealed with delight, briefly hugging each other before leaping about like crazed Morris dancers. "Go on, ya beauty!" one of them screamed, shaking a triumphant fist towards the widescreen TV secured on the wall. "I told you, didn't I!" the same man yelled, looking around to his mates, happy to receive a few hearty slaps between the shoulder blades in response. *"Twelve to one,"* he said, singing the words which left his lips, just before puckering up to kiss the slip of paper he was gripping for dear life.

Then, watching as the jubilant jockey climbed down from his sweat-covered mount, waving to the cameras, a joyous cheer arose from the group of gummy punters. In contrast, another high roller offered them a look of disdain, after which he crumpled his betting slip into a tight ball and launched it in their general direction.

"Like I told you earlier, you should have listened to me!" came the gloating response, followed by a forty-fag-a-day sort of cackle. "Didn't I say he should've listened to me, lads?" the fellow from the luckier group added, waving his winning betting slip at Doubting Thomas on his way to the cashier's desk, a spring in his step.

Sitting in the corner of the betting shop on a grubby padded swivel stool, Austin Fletcher couldn't have looked more like a fish out of water if he tried. It's fair to say that his snappy designer grey suit wasn't the usual attire seen in this establishment, judging by the number of sideways glances he attracted.

Presently, an elderly chap wearing a lovely ensemble of dingy sleeveless white top, old tracksuit bottoms, and comfortable-looking night-time footwear was hovering directly in front of Austin. Uncomfortably close.

"Can I help?" said Austin, in a tone suggesting he had absolutely no desire to help, actually. But there was no answer.

"I said, can I *help*?" Austin repeated, leaning back on his stool to put as much distance between them as possible. But every time Austin moved in any direction, the man in front of him countered it. It might have looked, to the casual observer, as if the two of them were engaged in some sort of choreographed dance routine. And, still, no response was offered by the man, the fellow staring intently towards Austin, a half-smoked Woodbine stuck to his lower lip.

"I *said*—"

"Will you shut up?" the old boy barked. "I'm researching the next race," he advised, pointing out the *Racing Post* form guide pinned to the wall behind Austin.

"It's just that you're nearly sat on my knee," Austin indicated, although his warning was promptly ignored. "I said that..." he continued, about to repeat himself yet again, but then suspecting it might be pointless to try and reason with a man wearing a pair of furry slippers in the daytime. "How about I just move," Austin suggested, before doing precisely that, giving his new acquaintance an unobstructed view of the form guide.

Austin glanced at the wall-mounted digital clock, making no attempt to disguise his frustration. Then, appearing to have had quite enough of his present location, he rose to his feet and began making his way past the heavily tattooed lady currently shovelling coins down the throat of a gambling machine. However, before he could make good his exit, a familiar face appeared through the doorway ahead.

"Good afternoon, Austin!" Cecil announced brightly, newspaper tucked under his arm.

"*Is it?*" came Austin's indignant reply, spoken through a set of gritted teeth. "I shouldn't think so. Sitting in this dilapidated hovel is making my skin crawl," he said, giving a little shudder. "Why on earth you wanted to meet up in a place like this is beyond me."

"It's nice and quiet, Austin," Cecil answered. "No prying eyes, if you take my meaning."

"Cecil, I've just been talking to some halfwit wearing a vest and a pair of fluffy slippers, for god's sake. And they were *bunny* slippers, at that," Austin advised. "Have you seen the state of this place and the sort of Neanderthals they let in?"

"Afternoon, Cecil!" the tattooed, sturdily built lass playing the fruit machine said, greeting the current arrival. Then, turning to Austin, she looked him up and down like he was something filthy she'd just stepped in. "And did you just call me a bloody troglodyte?" she added, glaring.

Austin gulped hard, his bravado evaporating as the large woman reared up, too fearful to even correct her. "I– that is... well, not that I– I mean, ehm..."

"It's fine, Bella," said Cecil, playing the role of peacekeeper, resting a calming hand on her stout shoulder. "He's not from around these parts, yeah? More used to the fancy-schmancy wine bars than a real man's bookies," he offered. Cecil then realised what he'd just said. "And a real *lady's* bookies as well, of course," he quickly added, not wishing to offend. "Here. Let's get you out of harm's way," Cecil said to Austin, pulling him aside and leading him towards the rear of the shop.

"I take it you're a regular in this place?" Austin surmised, throwing a cautious glance over his shoulder.

"It's fair to say it's not my first visit," Cecil answered, offering the cashier a cordial wave. "Looking good, Karen," he said, following it up with a friendly wink as they passed. Cecil then took a seat at an empty table, inviting Austin to join him there. "We shouldn't be disturbed here, Austin," he said, using his hand to brush away a pile of cigarette ash from the table's surface. "So," he continued, once Austin had sat down. "You said you wanted to see me?"

Austin screwed up his eyes, drawn to the stubble beneath Cecil's mouth. "You do know you've got egg all over your chin?" he asked, appearing visibly nauseated.

Cecil chuckled, wetting his thumb to remove the dried yolk. "I was at the greasy spoon across the road a bit earlier," he explained, wiping away the remnants of his prior breakfast. "We could have met in there, but, you know, I didn't think it was really you."

"And this place *is*?" Austin scoffed, rolling his eyes before reaching inside his jacket. "You're worrying me, Cecil, I won't lie," he said, removing a white envelope from his suit pocket and placing it down on the table.

Cecil was drawn to the plump-looking package like a drunk to a kebab, daring to guess what was contained within. "Worried?" he asked, without shifting his attention.

Austin eased the envelope across the table, leaving one protective finger when it came to a rest. "Yes, worried, Cecil. We have an agreement, and it very much sounded like you were losing your nerve?"

Cecil considered his response for a moment or two. "No, I'm not losing my nerve, boss," he replied, leaning back in his seat. "I was just saying before that this Ben fellow is actually a nice chap once you get to know him."

"So, after all the various unscrupulous tasks you've undertaken, you're finally developing a conscience?" Austin asked with the sarcasm dripping from his words, withdrawing the envelope just a touch.

"Oh, I'm as unscrupulous as they come," Cecil suggested, as

if this were, in some way, a badge of honour.

Satisfied, Austin pressed down on the envelope, sliding it all the way across the table like a croupier dealing cards. "For you, then," he said with a nod.

Cecil lurched forward in his chair before Austin had a chance to change his mind. "For me?" Cecil asked, reaching out with greedy sausage-shaped fingers. "Ah, you shouldn't have," he added, peering inside the envelope and thumbing through the banknotes with a contented smile on his face. "Very generous, boss. Thank you."

Austin pushed his chair back like he'd finally had enough of this particular establishment. "I thought this little bonus might serve to focus your attention, Cecil," Austin told him. "Help you see where your loyalties lie, and help encourage you to set certain wheels in motion. If you take my meaning."

A sufficiently chuffed Cecil placed the envelope in his trouser pocket. "Oh, I do, Austin," Cecil answered. "But you needn't worry on that last point. That particular mission is now well underway, you see."

"It is? So I didn't even need to give you that envelope, or darken the door of this vile cesspit?"

"I suppose not," Cecil said with a shrug. "But no takesy backsies, yeah? Oh, and always a pleasure to see you in person, Austin."

Austin stood, eyeing his companion frostily. "Just so we're clear, your conscience isn't going to cause complications or get in the way of dealing with your new best mate Ben?"

Cecil eased out of his chair. "Ben? Ben who?" he asked, letting out a little snort as he said it.

"I need to get out of here," Austin said, turning towards the exit. "I'm starting to itch. You coming?"

"What? Oh, sorry, no," Cecil replied, advancing towards Karen over at the cashier's desk. "I've got a cast-iron tip on the next race at Kempton," he advised, reaching for the envelope in his pocket, an envelope which was soon to get a bit lighter, it would appear.

Austin began his way towards the exit. "Keep me up to date, Cecil?" he said by way of instruction rather than a question, offering tattooed, broad-shouldered Bella a wide berth. "Oh, and Cecil?" he added as an afterthought, turning again for a moment.

"Yeah?"

"You've still got dried egg all over your chin."

Chapter Nine

The morning sun rose sleepily, almost as if it wanted another five minutes snuggled under the duvet. But a lie-in proved elusive, and the Isle of Man was soon illuminated by the sun's warming golden rays.

As a former baker, Ben wasn't afraid of crawling out of bed at an ungodly hour. And now, as he partook in a leisurely stroll around the campsite, making his morning rounds with only the dawn chorus for company, he was loving life. True, he was putting in more hours these days, but it hardly felt like work. Moreover, it seemed like his efforts were starting to bear fruit, which further spurred him on. The campsite was nowhere near capacity just yet, but because of his persistent marketing efforts — helped in large part by Ruby's social media savvy — more tents were starting to spring up all over the place.

In addition, there were several unexpected benefactors in the form of Ben's fellow island campsite owners, whose generosity he'd never seen coming. Rather than offering Ben, as their competition, something of a cold shoulder as Ben would have expected, the complete opposite turned out to be the case. With it being the peak time of the tourist season, many other sites were completely full, as it should happen. But rather than simply turning guests away, the other site owners were only too happy to provide the contact details for Life's a Pitch, and this was because the island as a whole benefited from a healthy tourist trade. Plus, as it was explained to Ben, those in the hospitality sector generally stuck together, helping each other out whenever they could. This type of kindness, the kindness of strangers, was something that very nearly brought a tear to

Ben's eye. Recently, he'd encountered folk he'd never previously met, willing and able to give him a leg up when he needed it the most. It was the sort of generosity he wouldn't soon forget, and one he hoped, someday soon, to be in a position to reciprocate.

Nearing the conclusion of his morning rounds, Ben continued to tiptoe around the site, not wishing to disturb his sleeping guests. Ordinarily, coming across an overspilling wheelie bin would cause Ben some considerable frustration. But not today. Instead, reaching down to pick up some rogue beer cans was a task he was delighted to attend to. The bins had previously been empty for days, with nary a soul around to fill them. So to see them now, packed to the brim and overflowing, was a positive sign that folks were in attendance and having a good time.

"Ah, there we go," Ben whispered to himself, talking to his vibrating watch. "It's already that time, is it?" he remarked, picking up the pace and heading back to the Guest Entertainment Centre.

Once inside, Ben's nostrils flared, his lungs filling with the glorious scent of today's freshly baked bread. "Come to papa, you magnificent beauties," Ben cooed, kneeling down before his new oven almost as if he was praying, pressing his hands together in perfect delight. It was fine timing, as the bread was just ready to come out.

By his own admission, the oven had been an extravagance, something he couldn't really afford. But, as he often reassured himself, he reckoned it was likely to pay for itself in next to no time at all. Already, for instance, he'd developed a modest yet appetising breakfast menu that had the campers forming an orderly queue each and every morning without fail. And he didn't need to sound an alarm to wake them, either. All that was required was to throw open the patio doors, and the smell of fresh bread and delicious bacon wafting across the grass indicated the kitchen was open for trade.

And it wasn't just the breakfast shift bringing in a new stream of income, as Ben's idea of a baking workshop was being realised as well. In return for a not unreasonable fee, his would-be bakers were offered the opportunity to learn the tricks of the trade from a professional, have a few cheeky glasses of vino, and then spend a night under canvas out amongst the stars. The concept was untested, to him a least, but the initial indicators were positive, with over twenty already booked in (including Tommo and Billy, along with their two better halves). And while Ben did have to shell out a few quid on extra supplies, he was fairly confident it would all turn into a regular feature and provide a much-needed, further stream of income.

Then, with another well-received breakfast service having soon been concluded and a few more pounds in the till, Ben's next task was to welcome a party of visiting wedding guests who'd hired all of the glamping pods for a few days. And once again, this booking resulted from another referral, this time coming from the wedding venue, which couldn't accommodate all of the invited guests for the several days they were staying on the Isle of Man.

"Welcome to Life's a Pitch!" Ben announced, bright and breezy, standing out on the decking area of the Guest Entertainment Centre. "Let me help you with that," he added, reaching for a bag from one of the more elderly of his new arrivals. "Come on inside, and I'll soon have you all checked in."

Ben had laid out tempting plates of freshly baked croissants in advance for them, along with an assortment of various soft drinks and a tray of Buck's Fizz.

"I don't mind if I do," said the giggly lady whose bag Ben had just carried, zeroing right in on the latter of the drinks choices. "It's five o'clock somewhere," she reasoned, taking a generous swig of the mildly alcoholic beverage. "Here's to a happy holiday," she said, once some of the others in her group had armed themselves with a drink as well. "Cheers!"

"You take it easy with that drink, Mum," said her concerned yet smiling son, as he made his way to Ben's reception desk. "We don't want a repeat of Cousin Helen's wedding," he advised, without further explanation, raising his left eyebrow. "Right.

I'll check us all in," he said, shifting his attention to an amused Ben.

"Should I brace myself for trouble from your mum later?" Ben asked with a smile, sliding over the keys for the glamping pods.

The woman's son nodded in the affirmative. "Let's just say that if you hear reports of a conga line in the early hours, you won't need to look too far for the instigator. She has form."

Ben laughed at the thought, accepting the credit card handed his way. "Am I charging for the entire party, sir?"

"Yes, please," the fellow replied, before briefly glancing over his shoulder. "I think she's already on the second glass," he remarked, with a *what-can-you-do* sort of shrug. "And, please, call me Henry."

"A pleasure to welcome you, Henry. I'm your host, Ben."

Ben then extended his arm towards the card reader sat beside his computer keyboard, doing so without looking as he already knew precisely where it was. He did this in full expectation of processing his guest's payment. But when his hand failed to make contact with the card reader as anticipated, he had to look down. "Strange," Ben said, confused at not observing the device in residence at its usual, customary location.

"I won't be a moment, Henry," Ben said by way of a placeholder, crouching down to see if the card reader had perhaps fallen underneath his desk. "Where are you?" he muttered to himself, opening each drawer in turn, hopeful it may have somehow found itself inside one for some reason, though without any success.

Henry, for his part, glanced down on the other side of the desk, spotting an errant wire poking out like a mouse's tail, the end of it not being attached to anything. "There's a cable near my feet. Just there," he said helpfully, although Ben couldn't see where he was looking, crouched under the desk as he was. "Here you go," Henry added, bending down to shove the thing round to Ben's side of the desk so that Ben could take hold of it.

"A-ha, got it," Ben confirmed, emerging a moment later with

the cable held between his fingers. "Yes, that appears to be what I'm looking for," Ben remarked, offering it a quizzical eye. "And yet…"

"No card reader attached to it," a perceptive Henry remarked.

"Yes, it would appear so," Ben agreed, dropping the now-useless cable back under the desk, along with a weary sigh. "Well, rather than delay you further," Ben decided, "how about I just check you in, and we can arrange payment later?"

"Perfect. I'll be staying right nearby," Henry joked, jiggling the keys in his hand.

Ben tapped away on his keyboard. "Just a few details, and we'll have you on your way," he said cheerily. And then, pressing the keys with increased vigour, Ben's smile became somewhat forced. "I won't be a moment," he said, through gritted teeth, feeling a dribble of sweat running down the curve of his back. "It *is* my bloody password, I can *assure* you," Ben insisted, speaking to his computer now, unable to progress beyond the login screen and sensing a vein in his neck beginning to pulse.

"You're not having much luck this morning," Henry observed, just as Ben gripped the keyboard in both hands, appearing for all the world like he was about to launch it across the reception area and out the window.

"How about we just take care of *all* the formalities once you're settled in?" Ben suggested, breathing deeply and walking around to the customer side of the desk. "Allow me to help you with your bags, and I hope you have a very special stay at Life's a Pitch."

It's fair to say that Ben's morning didn't improve any over the next hour. With his wedding party guests safely attended to and Henry's mother likely sleeping off the four or five glasses of Buck's Fizz she'd quaffed on arrival, Ben subsequently managed to completely lock himself out of his computer system. How, he didn't know.

Ben was one of those types who wrote everything down, including passwords and PINs, not really considering the potential hazards. "If a thief can manage to find anything worth taking, they're welcome to it!" Ben once remarked when his daughter challenged him on his data security protocols. But it was for *this very reason*, him writing everything down, that Ben could be absolutely certain the password he'd entered was the correct one. Further, it was also why he continued inputting the same password until he'd eventually locked himself out. And with his card reader seemingly vanished off the face of the earth, and now with no computer access as well, Ben found himself in a situation where he couldn't easily take new reservations. And even if he could, he had no way of accepting payment for them.

"Bloody technology," Ben grumbled to himself, deciding to pull on his wellies and take a wander around the campsite, as there was little else he could do at present. Along his stroll, he encountered a handful of weeds that needed pulling, at least affording him the opportunity to make himself feel moderately useful. Besides, yanking the little blighters up by the roots allowed him some degree of satisfaction, if only fleeting.

Uncertain what to do next, Ben wondered if perhaps, for some unknown reason, Cecil might have changed the password. Ben had seen him lingering around the reception area the previous evening, now he thought about it, so maybe Cecil could shed some light on the situation? Although adding to Ben's elevated stress levels, Cecil's mobile went straight to voicemail every time Ben tried calling him. As such, Ben headed towards the farm, hoping to find Cecil working there so he could speak to him in person directly.

"Flippin' thing," Ben moaned, when his thirteenth call in a row went unanswered. But by this time he'd made his way up to the farm, so he poked his head inside the cattle sheds. "Cecil!" he called out, his voice echoing around the cavernous building. But all Ben received in reply was a round of mooing from the ruminating residents whose lunch he'd temporarily interrupted.

Unfortunately, Cecil was nowhere to be found. He could be

anywhere, and with the farm, as a whole, extending to over one hundred and fifty acres in size, Ben didn't have either the time or the inclination to go on a wild goose chase in search of him.

Hopeful that Cecil would eventually return his call, Ben moseyed across the farm courtyard, considering his options. But his pondering was disturbed by the sudden sound of a door slamming shut. Ben spun around, irrationally wondering if somehow the cows had broken free and were now tailing him. But instead, he caught a flash of vibrant yellow, near to the ground, through the corner of his eye. And knowing of only one person on the farm who owned a distinctive pair of yellow Wellington boots, Ben took off in hot pursuit. "Cecil!" he yelled, now realising it wasn't terribly easy to move at pace wearing wellies, although Cecil seemed to be doing a remarkable job of it somehow. "Cecil!" Ben said again, catching sight of Cecil's considerable form. "Cecil, wait there!"

But Cecil didn't respond, pulling further away from the pursuing Ben. For such a rotund, generously padded individual, he could undoubtedly shift, Ben noted, especially considering he bounded along with the grace of an ogre being chased from his swampy home by pitchfork-wielding villagers.

Ben continued to make haste, watching as Cecil came to a stop, fumbling through his trouser pocket, eventually retrieving his keys and then jumping into his car without looking back. "Cecil!" Ben hollered. "Cecil, hang on!"

But that slight delay in locating his keys had allowed Ben the opportunity to catch up. "Cecil?" he said, drawing alongside Cecil's vehicle, gasping for air. "I've been calling!" Ben explained, rapping his knuckles on the car window, and then spreading his thumb and pinkie apart to resemble the shape of a phone. "I've been calling you!"

Cecil looked up from his position in the driver's seat, offering a forced smile. *"I can't hear you,"* he said, mouthing the words as he spoke through the glass, shaking his head, and then pointing to his ear to reinforce what he was saying.

"I said..." Ben replied, reaching for the handle and pulling open the door. "That I've been trying to call you," he explained, the door now open.

For a moment, Cecil looked like a deer caught in the head-lights. "Oh, sorry, Ben," he offered. "I was just off to... ehm, that is... I was just heading..."

"Everything okay, Cecil?" Ben asked.

"Okay? What? Oh, yes. Yes, of course," Cecil answered, accompanying this with an awkward laugh. "It's just that I've got this, em... this awful toothache. It's just come on, you see. So I'm off to the, erm, doctors."

Ben took a sniff of the air, wondering if Cecil had been on the sauce and whether he should be confiscating Cecil's keys before he could drive away. "Doctors? For a toothache?"

"Ah. *Ha-ha*. Did I say doctors? I meant *dentist*, of course," came Cecil's reply. "Anyway, I should probably..."

Satisfied that he could detect no presence of alcohol on Cecil's breath, Ben released his grip on the door. "In that case, Cecil, just a really quick question. Cecil, by any chance, have you changed the password on the reception computer or know where the credit card machine has gone?"

Cecil narrowed one eye, chewing the inside of his cheek like he was giving this question sincere consideration. "No," he offered a moment later. "No, I can't say I know anything about those things. In fact, I've not even been in the reception area for, I dunno, two, maybe three days?"

This response took Ben by surprise. "Eh?" he said, scratching the side of his head. "But I saw you walking out from there when I was completing my evening rounds, just last night. Didn't I?"

Cecil took a gulp of air, expelling it with such force that his lips vibrated. "Not me, Ben," he suggested, glancing down at a watch he wasn't wearing. "No, that must've been someone else," he said. "Anyway, I need to get to the doc—" he began, before quickly correcting himself. "Sorry, *dentists*, I meant to say. How about I pop round later and help you search?"

And with that, Cecil fired up the car's engine, giving the impression of a man who would rather be anywhere else but there.

"Poor chap. He must be in terrible pain," Ben remarked, offering a sympathetic wave to the departing automobile before returning his thoughts to the matter at hand. Namely, his ongoing technology situation.

Ben massaged his two eyeballs with his thumb and index finger, Ruby's warning about him working too hard rattling around his skull. He absolutely loved what he was doing, but perhaps burning the candle at both ends was beginning to take its toll. Sleep had been something of a luxury these past few days, so maybe he was mistaken about seeing Cecil the previous evening. And could this same lack of downtime have left him befuddled, he wondered, contributing as well to his password issue and confusion about the misplaced card reader?

Ben headed back in the direction of the campsite, stopping only briefly to provide a couple of hikers directions towards the Calf of Man, a small island they could view off the southwest coast, likely from the comfort of The Sound Café, a lovely eatery overlooking Calf Sound. Ben's mind was awash with password combinations. But the more he thought about it, the more confidence he had that'd he input it correctly in the first place. *"How could I forget the name of my first childhood pet and my date of birth?"* he reasoned. Still, considering the lack of sleep, he couldn't be sure of himself, wondering if he wasn't in fact going doolally.

However, his musings were cut short by the sight of two delivery men leaving his Guest Entertainment Centre, both sweating and appearing to have recently put in a solid shift.

"Hello, chaps!" Ben called out, picking up the pace and hurrying across the field. "Hello there!" he repeated a little louder, catching the man's attention on the right, resulting in the both of them turning. "Were you dropping off my baking supplies?" he asked upon arrival, nodding in the direction they'd just travelled from.

"Eh, you could say that," one of the men replied, glancing down at the impressive sweat patch on his polo shirt. "We've placed your order down in the kitchen area, if that's okay? The delivery note is next to the microwave."

"Are you feeding the five thousand?" his mate asked with a smile, plucking the front of his own shirt away from his skin to get the air circulating. "Lugging that lot across your fields," he added, throwing a weary thumb over this shoulder, "is one way to get fit."

"It's the supplies for my baking workshop," Ben proudly announced. "Can I get you gents a glass of water before you go?" he asked. "Or a towel, perhaps?" he added, in reference to the moisture dripping down their faces.

"No, but thanks," one of the men said, nursing his lower back. "We didn't factor in the time for so many trips to the van and back."

"And we need to be in Laxey by eleven," his mate helpfully reminded him.

"And we need to be in Laxey by eleven," the first man agreed.

Ben waved the deliverymen on their way, slightly confused by how knackered they were, if their damp patches were anything to go by. Fair enough, it was a bit of a stomp from the car park. But he thought a couple of sacks of flour and a few bags of baking supplies shouldn't have left them in their present physical state. Especially considering they were two professionals and likely used to such exertions.

Ben rubbed his hands together, the thought of his upcoming baking class offering him a moment of relief on an otherwise frustrating day. "Right. Now let's find this bloomin' card reader," he told himself, determined to make the rest of this day a good one as well.

"In the bin?" he wondered aloud, as he opened the door to the Guest Entertainment Centre. He couldn't be sure if he'd already checked in there, so it was an excellent place to start, he reckoned. Once inside, Ben strolled through his refurbished kitchen, offering an admiring glance in the direction of his new oven. He walked on past, continuing merrily along his way, until what he'd just seen suddenly registered in the depths of his brain.

Ben came to an abrupt halt, looking over his shoulder to verify that what he *thought* he just saw was what he actually *did* see. He'd been a little bit stressed of late, by his own admission, and for a moment, he wondered if hallucinations were a by-product of that particular affliction. He certainly bloody hoped so.

"What the dickens?" he asked, turning to fully take in what was now before him. Blinking so slowly his eyeballs started to dry, he tried to make sense of what he was seeing, but alas, it wasn't a hallucination as he'd hoped. Because there, stacked up in the kitchen area like sandbags in a wartime bunker, were dozens upon dozens of flour sacks. And keeping them company were trays of eggs piled up to chest height, along with numerous boxes labelled as marzipan, chocolate chips, brown sugar, and who knew what else. At that moment, Ben could now understand why the two delivery men had appeared as completely worn out as they did.

Ben wandered slowly around the perimeter of his delivery, not entirely sure what to do next. In advance of its arrival, he'd cleared out a spare cupboard to accommodate it. But this would need an entire spare *kitchen* to house it all. He placed his hand to his forehead. "What the ffff..." he started to say, trailing away, his curse left incomplete, as he suddenly clapped eyes on a white envelope which he was hoping contained the invoice, as well as some potential answers.

"Right," he said, ripping it open and removing the folded page inside. He snapped the paper open, running his finger down the long list of items that ran to the bottom of the page, continuing overleaf. "*Thirty bags of flour?*" he spat out, incredulous, flicking his eyes over to the heap and back again. "But I only ordered *three!*" he protested. Ticking off the items delivered against the mental shopping list held in his head, Ben could see that each of the items he'd ordered had been increased by a factor of ten. How or why this occurred, he couldn't be certain. And then, "Oh, bloody hell! You've *got* to be kidding me!" he yelled, reaching the part of the invoice detailing how much he owed. *"One thousand, two hundred and eighty-six pounds...?"* he said, unsure as to whether he ought to laugh or to cry.

However, before any tears might arrive, a lanky chap wearing cycling attire wandered in. It was a lone cyclist, perhaps one of the on-site mountain bikers, a tyre innertube dangling from his hand. "You don't by any chance have a bicycle pump I could borrow, old bean?" the cheerful fellow asked of Ben, hope written all over his face. "A blasted puncture, it was, which I've managed to repair well enough. But silly fool that I am, I left my pump back at home, sitting in the garage."

Ben looked up from his invoice, happy for any distraction provided at this point. "No problem at all, sir," he replied. "I just so happen to have one on hand, assuming it hasn't disappeared on me like some other things. I won't be a moment."

It was a good thing Ben had thought to keep a bicycle pump handy. With the large group of mountain bikers booked to the campsite, he reckoned it would be a good idea. In a pinch, it could also be used to help fill a camper's air mattress as well, and Ben was all about service, happy to cater to the needs of his guests.

"A busy day ahead?" the cyclist remarked upon Ben's return. He was motioning towards the tower of flour over in Ben's kitchen, visible from where he was standing.

"What, that?" Ben answered, walking over and giving one of the topmost bags on the pile a good slap. The slap caused a small rupture, it would seem, as a fine mist of white flour was thus brought forth, the escaped particles briefly filling the air.

"The ingredients for my inaugural baking workshop," Ben explained, after coughing on the cloud of flour he'd just produced. "You can come if you like?" Ben offered, handing over the retrieved bicycle pump. "I've got a sneaking suspicion we might have enough supplies to squeeze another person or fifty in..."

Chapter Ten

I t's probably that busty divorcée whose house he valued last week," Barry suggested, standing idly beside the office photocopier with his mug millimetres from his lips. "The way he's been skipping about, singing to himself and whatnot."

"Nah," Ricky, his co-conspirator, offered with a shrug. "Nah, Bazza, I've never known a woman to make him that happy," he said, at which point he tilted his head, pondering as to what the alternative explanation might be. "What about money?" he proposed, peering in the direction of Austin's office. "Money always seems to lift his spirits."

"That's true enough," Barry was happy to concede, taking a generous slurp of his morning brew. "But you know what Austin's like, yeah? Every time he lands a whopping deal, he rings that bell on his desk and then does that tawdry little stripper dance he likes to do, letting everyone know what a legend he is. And I don't know about you, but I've not heard any bells dinging."

"Or seen him taking his shirt off recently," Ricky considered. "Except when he's doing his biceps curls. Which might mean..." he said, lowering his voice lest any nosey work colleagues overhear.

"Yeah?"

"Which might mean he's up to no good."

"No good?" Barry said, repeating the words back. "What do you mean, exactly?"

Ricky offered a shrug. He didn't have all the answers. "Dunno, mate," he said. "I mean, not the specifics of it anyway. But whatever's got him all giddy lately, you can bet it'll be at someone else's expense."

"Or illegal," Barry remarked.

"Illegal? Could be, yeah," Ricky agreed, raising an eyebrow as he entertained this possibility. "I wouldn't put it past him. And it might explain why he's keeping his cards so close to his chest as well."

"Have you ladies not got any work to do?" Cynthia asked, bringing their deliberations to an early conclusion. "Honestly, you're like a couple of old women gossiping over a tea cake in the local café," she chided them, while placing a paper into the copy machine and pressing the 'Copy' button. "And who's the subject of your little tittle-tattle?" she asked, mildly curious, as she waited to retrieve her documents from the copier.

"Ricky was just talking about the boss," Barry promptly replied, throwing his mate under the proverbial bus.

"Whaddya mean, *I* was?" Ricky shot back, a little too loudly, before cautiously glancing over his shoulder. "And we *weren't* gossiping," he told Cynthia, carefully lowering his voice again. "Not really. I mean, we were just discussing how happy Austin has been lately."

"So what's the inside track, then?" Barry asked, sidling up to Cynthia. "Ricky reckons he's up to something, you know... *un-eth-i-cal*," he added, mouthing out the final word of his sentence so as not to be heard outside their circle.

"I bloody didn't!" Ricky whispered, cheeks reddening, throwing his officemate a stern glance. "I *didn't*," he stressed, before turning to face Cynthia again. "Although, Cynthia, if you did happen to have any insight...?"

"How would I know?" Cynthia said coldly, clearly unimpressed that they'd think she should have anything to do with such things.

"Because you're the golden girl," Barry was quick to point out, though it didn't sound like much of a compliment in the tone used. "Plus, as a company director, if the boss man *was* up to any sort of mischief, like Ricky said, then you'd end up standing in the dock next to him. So, spill it, yeah?"

Ricky shook his head furiously. "You're an arsehole, Bazza," he told Barry. "That's the last time I speculate with you," he muttered, turning to go, and then walking back to his desk in a huff.

"Ricky's right," Cynthia offered, after Ricky had gone.

"About the boss being up to no good?" Barry asked.

"No, about you being an arsehole, Barry," Cynthia answered, though it was delivered with the flicker of a smile. "Anyway, I can't stand around talking nonsense with you all morning," she added, gathering her papers and leaving Barry to finish his brew, alone.

Cynthia returned to her desk, shaking her head as she observed Ricky launch a succession of paperclips in Barry's general direction via a stretched rubber band. "Children," she remarked, releasing a weary sigh.

Ordinarily, Cynthia didn't pay too much attention to the idle gossip from Tweedledee and Tweedledum, as she'd affectionately named them. But now she came to think of it, Austin had indeed been chirpier than she'd seen him in a while. She'd even heard him singing earlier that week, and nearly tripped over a kerb when she witnessed him dropping money into a charity bucket as they were on their way to a meeting across town. So maybe the office gossips did have a point, she mused.

"Right," Cynthia said, returning to work mode. After all, she did have three property purchases closing that week. Staring at the legal document in hand, however, the words melted without meaning. She shook her head like a dog climbing out of the bath. "Concentrate," she admonished herself, staring intently. "Oh, bugger," she said a few moments later, giving up on concentrating and falling back in her chair instead, Barry's recent words still echoing in her head: *"You'd end up standing in the dock next to him."*

She knew Austin wasn't exactly pure as the driven snow, often sailing close to the wind in his dealings. But he'd never done anything outright illegal. Or at least, not that she knew of. But what if Ricky and Barry's suspicions were correct, she wondered, looking over to Austin's office. She'd never really considered that if Austin were ever to do anything *"un-eth-i-cal"* or illegal, then, as company director, she might actually be found guilty by association.

Seeing her looking in his direction, Austin responded by grinning broadly, and then bringing his fingertips to his lips and sending her a kiss in a rare display of affection. "Why are you so bloody happy?" she said to herself, ignoring the kiss wafting its way across the room. "What the hell are you up to?"

Shortly, Austin emerged from his office with a spring in his step, along with a song in his heart, if his joyous smile was anything to go by. "Who loves you?" he asked of his industrious employees, jabbing both thumbs into his chest as he spoke. "Yes, *Austin Fletcher* loves you, *that's* who," he said, lest there be any doubt as to who it was that loved them. "You're all smashing it out of the park!" he said with encouragement, making his way towards the main door. "And when I come back in a bit, I'm bringing cakes for everyone!"

Cynthia set the kettle on in preparation for the promised cakes they'd soon be receiving. She wasn't sure what time Austin would return, exactly, but it couldn't hurt to be ready in advance. While she waited for the water to come to a boil, she wandered over to Carol, one of her colleagues, and then parked herself down beside her, casting her eyes towards Austin's now-vacant office. "Carol," she said. "Did Austin happen to mention to you where he was going, by any chance?"

"No, he didn't say anything to me," Carol replied. "But he did say he was coming back with cake, right? And that's the important thing, yes?" she added, licking her lips at the prospect of some lovely cake. "Hmm, I wonder what type of cakes he'll bring for us..."

Cynthia sat, stewing in her own juices, as something seemed a bit off to her, though she couldn't quite place a finger on what it was. Then, after a few moments of consideration, "No, wait. That's it! Cake!" she said, incredulous. "Austin has never bought us cake. Not once. Not ever. In fact, it was your fiftieth birthday last week, Carol. And did he buy you a cake for that?"

"No," Carol replied. "No, he didn't."

"My point exactly," Cynthia told her.

"But *you* did," Carol noted. "You bought me cake."

"Precisely, Carol," Cynthia answered. "And that's because I'm a nice person, while Austin *isn't*," she suggested, rising up from her chair, certain now that something was afoot. She stomped across the office towards Barry's desk, eyes fixed on Austin's office.

"Barry, where's Austin disappeared to?"

"How should I know? What am I, his personal assistant or something?" Barry remarked, looking up at Cynthia looming over him.

Cynthia responded by raising one eyebrow. "Ehm, well *yeah*, Barry," she added. "Yeah, that's *exactly* what you are, as a matter of fact. Although why he needs a dedicated PA is still beyond me. Unless it's to impress his mates down at the golf club or something."

"Oh, you love me, really," Barry said, chuckling away to himself, opening his onscreen calendar. "Let's see, he's gone to meet..." he began, manoeuvring his mouse, searching for the relevant entry. "Ah. Here it is. Miles Frampton," Barry confirmed a moment later.

"Miles Frampton? Who's that?"

"Dunno?" Barry replied. "Austin stuck the appointment in the diary himself, it would seem."

"Miles is one of the salesmen at Heritage Homes," Ricky offered helpfully, moseying over and inserting himself into the conversation. "Maybe they're talking about that new housing development on the old campsite?"

"Eh? A salesman? That makes absolutely no sense," Cynthia suggested, furrowing her brow and creating deep lines across her forehead. "Austin doesn't bother speaking with the foot soldiers," she continued, although talking more to herself at this stage. "Austin would *never* leave his office to speak to anybody below the CEO level. He'd send one of us. Me, more than likely."

"He does often say that he won't waste time speaking to plebs," Ricky concurred.

"Exactly right," Cynthia said, starting off towards Austin's office. "Something is most definitely not right."

"Hang on, you're not going sneaking around the boss's office, are you?" Barry asked, wagging a cautionary finger.

"*Moi?*" Cynthia replied over her shoulder, easing open Austin's office door. "*Pfft*, of course I'm not, Barry. I'm just going to..." she began, but trailed off at the crucial portion of her explanation as Barry was no longer within earshot by that point anyway.

"What are you up to, mister?" Cynthia said, now she was inside, casting her eyes over the group of papers strewn over the surface of Austin's desk. But there was nothing untoward that she could spot, only documents about property sales that one would expect to see on an estate agent's desk. She moved around to the business end of Austin's desk, edging closer to his desk drawers. Sensing Barry's eyes presently boring a hole into her skull through the office glass, she paused for a moment, realising that rummaging through Austin's personal belongings wouldn't just be overstepping the mark, it'd be bloody flying over it wearing a jetpack. Still, she'd come this far, she reasoned, so she might as well be hanged for a sheep as a lamb.

The first drawer she teased open was relatively uneventful, containing only general office supplies, along with a giant chocolate cock someone had given him as a joke in the previous year's Secret Santa gift exchange. Then, dipping her hand into one of the other drawers, she came across the glossy magazines showcasing exotic-looking yachts he'd previously been lusting over. And unfortunately, it wasn't just fancy *ships* that floated his boat, as it should happen, if the buxom lady looking up at Cynthia from another one of the magazine covers was anything to go by. "Dirty old sod," she said, screwing up her face, although perfectly able to appreciate the piriform nature of the breasts staring back at her as, well, anyone could admire a good pair of chesticles.

Ultimately, however, she discovered nothing of any genuine interest. She didn't know what she'd expected to come across. Maybe a smoking gun, a cyanide tablet, or even a masterplan for world domination, maybe? But her debut spy mission was an abject failure. Indeed, James Bond wouldn't be impressed at only discovering a chocolatey phallus and a jazz mag, she couldn't help but think, closing over the desk drawers.

"Bugger," she said, still no further forward, and sensing it to be an excellent opportunity to perhaps get out while the getting was still good. But then something out of the corner of her eye caught her attention. Underneath the documents piled atop the desk was a leatherbound desk mat, the sort you'd scribble down telephone notes on. And indeed, half-hidden, she could just make out a fragment of one of these notes. "*Hello there*," she said, first glancing up to check the coast was still clear, and then sliding away the documents obscuring the rest of Austin's scribblings, revealing details previously obscured:

Pay Cecil the Chubster £300

Offer to buy losers in office some cake

Make appt for teeth bleaching

Cash for MF

Of the lines scribbled down, only the final one remained uncrossed, suggesting that this particular agenda item remained open. "Cash for MF," Cynthia said, running a curious finger over the words. "Who is MF...?" she asked, while carefully repositioning the documents to where they once were in hopes of hiding any trace she'd been there. "And who the heck is Cecil the Chubster...?"

"Got what you need?" a sneering Barry asked, as Cynthia passed by his workstation. "I'm sure the boss will be absolutely delighted to learn you've been poking your nose through his drawers the moment he steps out of the office," he added with a grin, though it remained unclear just how serious he was about making good on this implied threat.

Cynthia appeared unconcerned, however. *"Ahem,"* she said, "I suppose Austin will *also* be interested in knowing how you used the company credit card in a strip club?"

"He was with me at the time!" Barry shot back, with an *is-that-all-you've-got* type of expression.

"Yeah," Ricky entered in, leaning over from his nearby desk. "But he doesn't know it was you what drunk drove a golf buggy into his Porsche last year, does he, Bazza?" he asked, still sore, it would appear, at being thrown under the proverbial bus a bit earlier.

"Whose side are you on?" Barry protested to his mate.

"Wait. I thought the parking brake failed on the golf buggy, and it simply rolled down the car park?" Cynthia interjected, a sly smirk emerging. "Because if that *wasn't* the case, then I'm sure the insurance company would be *very* interested, as would Austin. He bloody loved that car."

"I've also got that little incident recorded on my phone," Ricky revealed, enjoying his moment in the limelight, throwing his mate a *how-do-you-like-those-apples* look.

"So, we won't be saying anything about...?" Cynthia asked, nodding her head in the direction of Austin's office.

"Dunno what you mean, Cynthia," Barry replied with a shrug. "I've only just returned from a trip to the loo, haven't I, so I didn't see a blessed thing."

"Splendid. Oh, and Ricky. I owe you a beer," Cynthia said, giving Ricky a grateful wink.

After fetching herself a cuppa, Cynthia returned to her desk, wondering who on earth Cecil the Chubster was, and who or what 'MF' could possibly be. She lifted her tea to her nose, hoping the aroma and rising steam might warm her brain and generate some ideas. "Wait! Miles Frampton!" she proclaimed in a eureka moment, proud of herself for solving at least that one riddle.

Fully immersing herself in her new Miss Marple investigative persona, Cynthia lowered her cup, reaching for her keyboard. "I wonder...?" she said to herself, logging onto the com-

pany's online banking, of which she was a signatory, and leaning in close. "Stone the crows!" she declared a moment later,
once the page had loaded. According to the online statement,
she could see that a cash withdrawal of fifteen thousand
pounds had recently been debited. Of course, as the business
belonged to Austin, Austin could withdraw what he liked from
the bank account. But 15k in cash? That was a lot of dosh, and
just didn't feel right to Cynthia. First, he'd been acting strangely
all week — cheerful and pleasant, which wasn't like him at all
— and now he was off galivanting with the sales manager of a
new prestigious housing development, armed with 15k in cash
to boot.

"It must be a bribe," Cynthia muttered to herself, the gravity
of the situation smacking her square in the face. "And if that
devious shite weasel gets caught, then I'll end up in the next
bloody prison cell over."

"Would you like a biscuit, dear?" a helpful Carol asked, stopping by Cynthia's desk and teasingly jiggling a pack of Jammie
Dodgers.

"What? Oh, no, but thanks, Carol," Cynthia replied, glancing
far off into the distance. "No, I've suddenly lost my appetite, I'm
afraid."

Chapter Eleven

And that should be it," the bespectacled Harry Potter lookalike declared, tapping a few final keys on Ben's keyboard like a concert pianist concluding his virtuoso performance.

"Seriously?" Ben asked, hovering behind, looking over the lad's shoulder. "You mean I can actually get back into my computer system?" he asked with hope-filled eyes, resisting the urge to place a giant smacker on the young fella's cheek.

Simeon, the IT consultant, slid his chair to one side, offering Ben an unobstructed view. "Yes indeed," he was happy to confirm. "You just need to create a new password, and that's you all good to go again."

Ben caressed his keyboard with a tenderness usually reserved for an intimate moment. "I can access my reservations calendar?" he said. "And my emails?"

Simeon nodded, and whilst he might not have actually been the boy wizard, what he'd managed to do was magical in Ben's eyes.

"I shouldn't be this happy over a bloody computer," Ben confessed, offering a relieved sigh. "But these last few days without it have been a complete nightmare, I don't mind telling you."

"It's only when they stop working that we realise how much we need them," Simeon offered sympathetically, as he packed away his gear. "Anyway, I must press on," he advised, rising to his feet, his belongings in hand. "I've got several other people to visit today who are likely ripping their hair out as we speak."

"I nearly ended up with a bald patch myself," Ben suggested, rubbing his bonce. "So do you know what happened here, exactly? Is there anything I need to do differently?"

Ben smiled politely at Simeon's subsequent response, nodding at the required intervals and maintaining eye contact throughout the lengthy explanation as to what had likely happened, how it had been resolved, and what Ben might do in the future to avoid similar troubles. But Ben wasn't exactly computer literate, so, mostly, the words washed over him. Sure, he knew his way around email, Excel, and other programmes, but he didn't have a clue about the nitty-gritty regarding the detailed workings. It was a little bit like with his Wi-Fi, in that, yes, Ben could use the internet, but he had absolutely no idea how the little box next to his phone offered him a portal to the world. So, he just went with it.

"... and call me if you have any further problems," Simeon said in closing, likely fearing he was losing his audience by this point.

"You wouldn't happen to have a spare card reader, would you?" Ben asked, half-joking, half in hope. "Mine's gone missing, you see. And the bank's informed me that it's a minimum of two weeks to get a replacement."

"A card reader?" Simeon responded. "No, sorry, I'm afraid I can't help you there."

"Ah, don't worry about it, it was just a shot in the dark," Ben answered, offering Simeon a grateful pat on the back. "Anyway, as for what you've done, hopefully, in the nicest possible way, I won't be seeing you again for quite a while. But truly, thank you. You've saved me from throwing my computer straight out the window."

With the reception area soon to himself, Ben rested his head in his hands, relieved that computer access was finally restored. It was a positive outcome in what was otherwise a rather lousy week, not to mention a rather *expensive* week. Unfortunately, as wonderful a result as Simeon had accomplished, his yet-to-be-received invoice would only add to Ben's pile of expenses (not to mention worry levels), likely running into the hundreds following four hours of intensive investigation work. And of course there was still the matter of the unresolved issue regarding the gargantuan baking supplies delivery, the primary source of Ben's stress and anxiety.

Despite speaking at length with the catering wholesalers, they remained insistent that the delivery had been valid, having received a phone call, according to them, to increase the quantities from the original amount. And as they'd had to order in additional stock just to facilitate the revised order, they'd remained insistent, also, that they would be unable to accept any returns. Fortunately, Ben shifted some flour sacks and other items onto a few of his former baking contacts. Still, he remained considerably out of pocket, with his modest stockroom presently bursting at the seams with an overabundance of supplies he could not fully make use of.

But it wasn't all doom and gloom, Ben had to regularly remind himself. Tents were popping up all over the site, for instance, phone bookings remained lively, and he had a fully subscribed inaugural baking workshop to look forward to that evening as well.

With his students due to soon arrive for the baking masterclass, Ben was beavering away in the Guest Entertainment Centre with the recently arrived Ruby helping him with the final preparations.

"Here you go, Dad," Ruby said, armed with a stack of papers, coming fresh from the printer behind the reception desk. "That's the recipes all printed for you," she advised, placing them in a neat pile on the large oak table in the centre of the room. "And I've taken the liberty of running off a few extra in case they get messed up, or if you get a few latecomers signing up."

"You're the absolute best, Ruby," Ben said in answer, laying out a rolling pin next to each designated workspace, along with a few other select implements. "And now you mention it, I've had a few further enquiries about availability, so we might hopefully have a few extra people to accommodate."

"Which might serve to relieve some pressure on the overcrowded storeroom," Ruby said with a wry smile, unsure if it was acceptable to pick at this particular scab or if the wound was perhaps a bit too fresh, still. However, she needn't have worried, receiving a friendly growl in response. "Anyway," she said, moving the conversation in a slightly different direction. "What happens if we get any latecomers who want to pay by card? Oh, and what about payment for the pop-up bar later on?"

"I've stuck a sign on the door advising we have an issue with the card reader and can only accept cash at the moment," Ben replied. "It's a bloody pain, Ruby. When the wedding party checked out earlier, I had to drive them down the cash point in Castletown, which was far from ideal. Luckily, they were good sports about it all."

"Ah, I wondered what that enormous stash of cash in the till was all about," Ruby said, lowering her voice as she did so, just in case anyone should happen to be about. "So..."

"So?" asked Ben.

"So what's next, Chef?" Ruby replied. "Whaddya need me to do?"

Chef Ben placed his hands on his hips, surveying his kingdom and working through the to-do list in his head. "Well..." he began, turning slowly, pivoting round, until he spied, there in the kitchen area, a small stack of boxes left in front of the fridge. "Ah, fudge," he said.

"You bought fudge?" asked Ruby, unaware of any such fudge on the premises but very pleased to hear about it nonetheless.

"What? Oh, sorry, no. Cecil's just taken out a load of the excess stock I managed to sell on," Ben explained. "But he must've forgotten those few boxes of marzipan, or didn't have room for them in the wheelbarrow. He's ferrying everything up to the car park in a wheelbarrow, you see, so if you're quick enough, you might—"

"On it!" Ruby said, promptly fetching the stray boxes her father had mentioned. "Won't be too long, Chef," she added, darting towards the exit, boxes in hand.

Once outside in the warm Manx sunshine, Ruby weaved her

way between the assembled tents, delighted to see more canvas on display than lonely grass. "That smells delicious!" she remarked to one group of campers she'd spoken to earlier, all seated now around a gas stove cooking up what smelled very much like bacon, if her nose didn't deceive her, the wonderful aroma carrying through the air.

"There's plenty to spare," someone from the group kindly called out over the sizzle. "Pop by on your way back!"

Ruby turned for a moment, chin resting on the pile of boxes in her arms. "I just may have to take you up on that offer," she promised, taking in the glorious scent that was wafting her way.

It was remarkable how the allure of a bacon sarnie could spur you on, bacon being perfectly lovely any time of the day, and mere moments later, Ruby approached the busy car park, her cargo hopefully still intact. "Now where are you...?" she wondered aloud, slowing her pace, uncertain as to which car belonged to Cecil. She had seen it once or twice before, and had an inkling it was dull beige in colour, if memory served. Although beyond that, any further details remained elusive. Also, boring beige appeared to be a fairly popular colour choice amidst the camping fraternity, for reasons unknown, making Ruby's search even more challenging.

Then, scrutinising the car park, Ruby narrowed down her list of target vehicles to just one — a shabby-looking hatchback with its rear suspension presently buckling under considerable strain. Indeed, the rear bumper hovered mere inches away from the ground, giving the impression the car was transporting a large shipment of perhaps iron or lead. "A-ha," Ruby said as she got closer, the catering supplies piled high obscuring her view into the front of the car, but confirming that she was in fact approaching the correct vehicle. "Cecil!" she called out, struggling with one of the boxes in her arms, making one final dash for freedom. "Cecil, help!" she yelled with a laugh, as the unruly box of marzipan on top of her pile tumbled to the earth.

But, approaching the passenger side window, she could now

see that the driver's seat was empty. "Ah, crap," she moaned, contemplating her options and wondering what she should do.

Shifting the load in her arms and grabbing the door handle, she prayed to the boring-beige car gods. "Please be unlocked?" she implored, just as the door majestically opened. "Yes!" she said, and decided she'd just place her boxes down onto the empty passenger seat. After all, they were headed to the same destination as the load in back that was currently battling with the car's rear suspension. "Hang on, what if Cecil's already headed back to fetch what I've just brought up?" she considered, while collecting the stray box that had fallen behind the front wheel. But she was certain she could still smell bacon in the air, off in the distance, and was anxious to follow the scent back to its source. "Ah, well," she said, placing the final box with its fellows there on the front seat, certain that Cecil would figure it all out, perceptive chap that he was.

She was just getting ready to close the passenger door, her tum offering a well-timed grumble for good measure, when something odd caught Ruby's attention. She tilted her head, narrowing her eyes, trying to work out if what she was seeing was actually what she thought she was seeing. "Hold on. What's this?" she said, keeping the door held open.

She glanced over her shoulder, first taking care that she wasn't being observed, and then plunged her hand into the narrow door compartment. With a cautious finger, she shifted a stale, half-eaten sandwich to one side, her face wrinkling at both the sight and the feel of it. Then, she took hold of the thing that'd caught her attention in the first place, wondering how the devil it'd ended up there, stuffed down the bloody side pocket of Cecil's car. "What are *you* doing here?" she said, perplexed. She stared at it for a long moment, wracking her brains for a reasonable explanation, but coming up with nothing.

"Dad's going to go mad. He'll be *furious*," she said, deciding to take the device with her. She headed back, making a beeline to HQ and completely forgetting about the earlier promise of a bacon sarnie. "Why was the missing card reader in Cecil's car??"

"I'm going to wring his neck!" Ruby insisted, extending her arms to demonstrate how, precisely, she would be doing the wringing.

Ben set down the mixing bowls he was carrying and gently waved his hands, like a hypnotist, hoping to reduce his daughter's elevated blood pressure. "Now just calm down, Ruby," he told her. "It's more than likely a simple mistake, yeah?"

"A simple mistake?" Ruby shot back, incredulous. "Dad, it was stuffed in the passenger compartment of that horrid little car of his!" she said, letting loose a shudder at the memory of the disgusting, half-eaten sandwich she'd had to move out of the way with her fingers, and praying she hadn't picked up any germs in the process. "Do you think the card reader simply got a bit bored, wandering up to Cecil's car all by itself in hopes of a lovely afternoon drive?"

"Well, no," Ben conceded, searching for any other reasonable explanation though failing miserably. So instead, he walked towards Ruby, who was, by this stage, pacing in circles with clenched teeth. "I've already left a message on his mobile, so he'll hopefully phone me back before you know it," he suggested brightly.

But Ruby wasn't for convincing. "Dad, I've seen how stressed you've been all week because of that stupid plastic box, and Cecil had it *all along*," she reminded him, giving her foot a little stamp for emphasis. She took several deep breaths, attempting to compose herself, and then, "He was even pretending to help you look for it the other day!" she pointed out, the recollection of this one particular detail setting her teeth to grinding all over again.

"At least we have it back," Ben offered, attempting to put a positive spin on things. "And with any luck, it'll be getting plenty of use a bit later, when all of our baking apprentices turn up. Now, come on, Rubster, chin up, and let's go and get all of their tents set up, all right?"

Two hours later, Life's a Pitch was fully prepared for its first baking workshop experience, and Ben couldn't wait. He'd invested a lot of time, effort, and energy into what would, with any luck, become a regular feature, bringing along with it some much-needed cash. And he knew it might be a touch mushy, but watching on as Ruby straightened out the cheery tablecloth he'd set down, he couldn't help but feel like the luckiest man alive. Here he was, at the start of a new and hopefully prosperous business journey, and he had the pleasure of sharing the adventure with his beautiful daughter. It was times like this that he would never forget.

"Allow me," Ben offered, grabbing one end of the tablecloth so they could get it just right. "Are you still thinking about Cecil?" he asked, noting his daughter's distant expression. "Cecil's a bit..." he started to say, trying to think of the right words. "Well, a little unorthodox," he finally settled on. "But his heart is in the right place, I think, and he's been an absolute godsend helping me with all the renovations."

Ruby used the palm of her hand to straighten out a few remaining creases in the tablecloth, and then adjusted a rolling pin that had gone slightly askew. "But the card reader in his car?" she said.

But before Ben could respond one way or the other, he was distracted by the sound of bottles chinking together. "A-ha," he said, spotting the source of the familiar-sounding noise.

"I hope you're thirsty!" said Brian, of Wine Cellar Wholesalers, cheerfully announcing his arrival as he lugged in three boxes, followed closely behind by a colleague loaded with several more.

"The liquid refreshment for tonight has arrived," Ben told Ruby, rubbing his hands together in delight. "And the bar is now open," he remarked with a chuckle. "Let's get the party started!"

"Right, there we are," said Brian, he and his associate placing down the boxes where directed. "Wow," Brian offered once upright, having a good look around. "I camped down here last year, Ben, and I have to say, what you've done with the place is extraordinary."

"A team effort," Ben suggested. "There's still a good way to go, but we're getting there," he said, pleased that Brian was impressed. "Time for a cuppa before you go?"

Brian glanced down at his watch. "No time. Though it's kind of you to offer," he replied. "We've a van full of Prosecco to drop off at some fancy shindig in Douglas," Brian explained, and yet, despite having said this, made no immediate attempt to move.

"Ah. Best not to keep them waiting, then," Ben agreed, smiling awkwardly when Brian, strangely, remained rooted to the spot several long moments later.

Brian returned the smile, shifting his attention to the boxes, and then back over to Ben. "So. We'll just settle up and be on our way?"

"Sounds like a plan," Ben replied, before eventually catching up. "Oh! You need to be paid!" he realised, slapping a palm against his forehead.

"That always helps," Brian said with a laugh. "But don't worry, it's only cash-on-delivery until your third order," he advised. "Then we can get you set up on account."

Ben marched over to his reception desk with a *what-am-I-like* sort of chuckle. "Perfectly reasonable," Ben responded, reaching for the cash register. "And, hopefully, that'll not be too long following tonight's roaring success," he declared, tapping down on one of the buttons to release the till.

Ben went silent, head down, staring intently into the black abyss that was his cash drawer. "Ehm..." he said a moment later, uncomfortably shifting his weight from one foot to the other. "Ruby...?" he said, forcing a smile. "Ruby, I don't suppose you've taken the wedding party's cash from the till, have you?"

Ruby looked up from what she was doing. "No, why would I?" she asked, from across the room.

"Oh, right. Erm, okay, then."

Sensing the fraught tone in her dad's voice, Ruby headed over and joined him behind the reception desk. Once there, she peered over his shoulder, greeted by the unfortunate sight of a cash drawer completely lacking in any currency beyond a small handful of coins. "There's... only coins?" Ruby remarked, though this was a fact her father was obviously already acutely aware of.

"Everything okay?" Brian asked, appearing like he was ready to leave, save for the small matter of receiving payment.

"Oh, yes! Perfect!" Ben offered with a spirited thumbs-up. "Yes, couldn't be better!"

"Dad..." Ruby whispered. "Dad, there was cash in there earlier, and now it's gone."

"I can see that," Ben answered, talking through the corner of his mouth. "What the hell am I supposed to do now, Ruby? I've got seven boxes of wine and assorted spirits to pay for, and the grand sum of..." he said, stirring a finger through the coins tray. "Roughly sixty-two pence."

Ruby clenched her hand into a fist, looking as if she was searching for something to punch with it. "It must be that low-life, Cecil," she said, grinding her teeth.

"Cecil?"

"Yes. *Cecil*," Ruby replied. "Dad, open your eyes. First, I find the card reader stashed in the door of his car. And now, not long after that, several hundred pounds have mysteriously vanished from the till. It *can't* be a coincidence," Ruby told him. "I'm telling you, there was always something funny about that man, but I couldn't quite place my finger on what it was."

"But why would Cecil do that, Ruby?" Ben asked, entirely perplexed. "It doesn't make sense. He's always been so good to us."

Ruby shrugged her shoulders, searching for something logical. "I dunno," she said, just as two suited gentlemen entered the building. "Perhaps he's out to get us."

Ben gently laughed off the suggestion. "Nobody is out to get us, Ruby, don't be silly," he said, trying to alleviate her fears. "I mean, who would want to ever *get* us in the first place?" he added, before shifting his attention to the men now standing before him.

"Hello! You're a bit early for the baking workshop," Ben said by way of salutation. "And a little overdressed?" he added, flicking his eyes down to their formal suits.

"Ben Parker?" one of the men asked, unamused, his voice utterly devoid of levity.

"Ehm, yes. Can I help?" Ben asked, his Spidey senses telling him that this wasn't going to be good news.

"James Hobson," the man on the left introduced himself. "We're inspectors from building control," he added, producing a business card and handing it over. "We've received a report of dangerous and substandard building protocols on the premises."

"What, now?" Ben asked in disbelief, glancing over to Ruby, and then looking back to the men.

"What does that mean, exactly?" Ruby entered in.

"What it means," the first of the inspectors answered. "Is that we need to conduct an urgent review of the buildings here in order to ensure compliance."

"Compliance?" Ruby pressed.

"Yes. To make sure they're safe," came the succinct reply.

"Safe from what?" Ruby asked, confused and slightly annoyed.

Ben held his hands aloft, hoping to de-escalate the situation. "Gentlemen," he interjected, friendly as you like. "Gentlemen, I'm sure we can work this out in no time at all," he said. "But the thing is, I've people due to arrive for a baking workshop in the next half hour. So, if we could just reschedule, and—"

"Reschedule?" one of the inspectors replied with a sharp laugh.

"Yes, please," Ben said. "That would be greatly appreciated."

"Em... no," the man answered, looking at his colleague with an *is-this-guy-serious* sort of expression. "What it means, Mr Parker, is that this building, along with the shower block, are now closed to public access until such time as we've concluded a complete and thorough investigation."

"B-b-but..." Ben sputtered. "But my baking workshop!" he finally managed to spit out.

Ruby rubbed her hand along her father's back, hoping to calm him down before he possibly ruptured something. "Dad, I'm sorry to say this," she whispered. "But I think somebody is *definitely* out to get us..."

Chapter Twelve

An excitable child of about five years of age sprinted away from his mother's grasp, giggling as he made his daring break for freedom. His floppy blond fringe virtually covered his eyes, and for a moment, it appeared that he might run directly into a marble-effect column towering to the gilded ceiling up high. Fortunately, he spotted the obstacle just in time to avoid a nasty collision, taking evasive action, but, unfortunately, dropping what he'd been gripping tightly in his left palm. "Oh, poop," he moaned, watching as the gold-coloured coins rolled across the tiled floor in different directions. Unable to chase them all, he settled on one, following its trajectory, and then abruptly lurching forward before it got lost amongst the threatening cluster of feet and legs that loomed ahead.

"Harry!" the lad's flustered mum called out, just as Harry's head made contact with a sour-faced woman's shin.

"I got it, Mum!" Harry replied, holding up the gold coin like a proud Olympian parading on the top step.

"I can see that, Harry, but where's the rest?" Mum asked like a seasoned debt collector. "Don't tell me you've lost them already?" she said, in her finest 'Mum' tone.

Young Harry brushed his fringe to one side, desperately looking this way and that. "No, I've not," he insisted, falling down onto his knees, hoping an ant's-eye view would improve his rescue mission. "I think they went... no, wait, that's not it... now where did they..."

Witnessing the unfolding events, Ben pushed himself up from the elegant sofa in the corner of the banking hall, as he'd watched as two of the coins had rolled in his direction, one to the left of the sofa he'd been sitting on and one to the right. He picked both of them up, happy to be of service, and then raised a finger, hoping to attract the mum's attention before Harry received too much of a tongue lashing. "I think this is the rest of what he's looking for," Ben said, walking over and presenting himself before them.

Harry scurried in and snatched up the two remaining coins, suspicious as to how they'd come into this man's possession. But now that the money was firmly ensconced in his paw, back in its rightful owner's custody, the boy's steely expression changed. "Thanks, mister," young Harry offered, his demeanour quickly softening.

Mum offered Ben a grateful smile. "Thanks for that. He's only just received his pocket money from his gran, and there he is throwing it away moments later," she said with a laugh, giving her son a playful hair ruffling. "Most kids with a few coins jingling in their pocket want to head straight to the sweet shop," she explained to Ben. "But not Harry. He's happier bringing it along to the bank to place into his Junior Savers account."

"Impressive," Ben remarked.

"He's just like his dad in that respect," Harry's mum whispered. "Doesn't like spending money," she confided. "Either that, or he's smitten with the pretty girl behind the counter, and that's why he likes coming here."

"That could also be the reason your husband is so frugal," Ben joked, chuckling away at his impeccable comedic timing.

"Oh, dear. I'd never thought of that," Mum responded, filling her cheeks with air and then expelling her breath, looking somewhat dejected. "Ah, well!" she added, immediately brightening up. "If it stops him spending it down the pub or at the bookies, then who am I to grumble, yeah?"

"Are we talking about Harry or his dad?" Ben asked, now on an impressive roll.

"Come on, Mum!" Harry cut in, fidgeting like he was desperate for a wee. "Zoe's free," he advised, pointing in the direction of his favourite bank cashier.

"Okay, mister," Mum said. And then, turning her attention to Ben, "Thanks again for finding his money."

"Very happy to help," Ben answered. "And I hope Zoe's just as pleased to see him as he appears to be about seeing her."

Ben watched Harry skipping his way happily across the banking hall, which raised a welcome smile. "Mr Parker?" a voice enquired, approaching from behind.

"Yes, hello there," Ben said, spinning round, receiving the hand thrust in his direction. "Dave?"

"Dave Griffiths, Small Business Manager, yes. A pleasure to meet you," Dave cordially replied. "Please," he said, inviting Ben towards a door of solid chestnut.

"This is an impressive building," Ben said by way of small talk, admiring the elegant décor as they walked forward. "It's like something from a bygone age," he noted.

"We're privileged to call this place our business home," Dave answered, escorting Ben inside his office. "Sadly, most old buildings like this have been converted to trendy wine bars. But not this one, fortunately. Please, take a seat."

Ben did as instructed, placing the folder he'd been carrying into his lap. "I appreciate you seeing me at such short notice, Dave."

"Not at all, Mr Parker, it's—"

"Please, call me Ben," Ben insisted.

"Sorry, a force of habit. Now, I've spotted a few of your adverts on social media, Ben, so I was quite excited to meet up and hear all about what you've been doing."

Ben unzipped his folder, placing down a formal business plan he'd compiled the previous evening, utilising Ruby's helpful skills with PowerPoint. Then, like an advertising executive delivering a killer pitch, he walked Dave through the progress they'd made to date — including several before and after shots — along with his optimistic plans for the future. And, for Dave, it would've been difficult not to be impressed. After all, Ben & co had transformed the campsite from a tired destination to a modern facility in a relatively short amount of time. Further, as

Ben's colourful graphs and bar charts illustrated, there was a healthy pipeline of new bookings in the diary and several exciting initiatives in the offing, all of which would bolster the crucial bottom line of the business accounts. Indeed, on paper, the business appeared to be in rude health, with an enthusiastic crew onboard to steer the ship and a steady influx of passengers eager to climb aboard.

"What can I say? You've done a remarkable job," Dave offered, duly impressed. "And in fact the next thing I'm going to do, once you leave, is to book the family in for a weekend stay, weather permitting."

"In that case, I'll put an order in for some sunshine," Ben suggested, accompanied by a nervous laugh.

Dave eased back in his chair, twirling his engraved pen like a cheerleader's baton between his fingers. "So, your email mentioned that you'd like to discuss some sort of finance? An overdraft or loan for the business?" he said, moving to the salient agenda item for the meeting.

Ben nodded, offering his warmest of smiles. "Yes, please. That would be wonderful," he said, without further explanation, hopeful of any assistance, it would appear.

Dave offered a half-laugh in return. "I might need a little more detail than that," he said, though not in an unkind way. "Ben, the business appears brisk on the face of it, so why...?"

"Ah," Ben said, raising a finger like a pupil asking a question in class. "It does. But..." he said, pausing for a moment to choose his words. "But we're having a few technical difficulties at present," he continued. "Difficulties that are having an immediate impact on cash flow."

"I see. Yes. *Mmm-hmm*," Dave replied, offering noises of encouragement as he twisted his pen, releasing the nib to take notes. "And what appears to be impacting your cash flow?"

Ben sucked in air like he was building up to a big reveal. "Well, the fact that our communal areas have been closed and our kitchen has been condemned. Is that the right word? Condemned?"

Dave glanced up, putting his pen on standby. "Your communal areas have been closed down and your kitchen's been condemned...?" he said, making sure he understood correctly. "By whom?" he asked, unsure what else he could say.

"By building control," Ben answered. "Oh, and Environmental Health and Safety. Both, in fact. They were quite insistent."

Dave removed his glasses, massaging the bridge of his nose. "I'm not in the camping business, Ben, but that doesn't sound good?"

Ben nodded in agreement. "No, it's not ideal," he said, smiling away the inner pain. "We can't be sure, but we think we've been the victims of some type of campaign."

"Campaign? What sort of campaign?

"We're not too sure at this stage," Ben confided. "Sabotage, hate, or possibly smear? Maybe all three."

Dave smiled politely, perhaps wondering who he'd invited into his office, retracting the nib on his pen, indicating the meeting was drawing to a close.

"Allow me to explain," Ben offered in response to the confused expression radiating from across the desk.

Ben proceeded to fill Dave in on the unfortunate situation the business had found itself in. As Ruby had suspected, Cecil wasn't quite the model employee he'd made himself out to be, as it turned out. Indeed, since the cash disappeared from the till, there wasn't a trace to be found of old Cecil, who had, by this point, disconnected his phone. And in addition to his 'sticky fingers,' the quality and workmanship of his recent renovations was now being questioned as well. Not by Ben, necessarily, but the chaps from building control weren't exactly effusive in appraising Cecil's efforts. *"Substandard," "dangerous,"* and *"shoddy"* were some of the more generous of the descriptors used. *"Negligent"* and *"cowboy"* were some of the other highlights from the written report provided to Ben.

Compounding Ben's issues was the gang's arrival from Environmental Health, alerted to the supposed vermin infestation and storage of hazardous chemicals in the food preparation areas. Neither of which Ben believed to be true, of course, but with Ben's business shut down in the meantime while thoroughly investigated, as such accusations were taken very seriously by the relevant authorities.

And, as it should happen, both agencies had been alerted to the various issues by a mystery whistle-blower, supposedly 'concerned' about potential dangers. No small coincidence, either, Ruby had been quick to point out, that all of this transpired soon after Cecil had smartly buggered off with the contents of the till.

And with the benefit of hindsight, Cecil was now in the frame for the IT sabotage as well. So the only questions that remained were where Cecil was at present, and why the devil he appeared so intent on destroying Ben's business.

"Blimey, that's awful news, Ben," Dave said once he'd uploaded Ben's tale of woe.

"You're not wrong there, Dave," Ben agreed. "Unfortunately, I've had to refund all of the money from the baking workshop, and the only reason I've still got campers on site is that the local swimming pool nearby is allowing kind access to their shower and toilet facilities on a short-term basis."

"And you're sure it's this Cecil fellow?"

Ben shrugged his shoulders. "It has to be," he said. "My daughter Ruby found the missing card reader stashed away in Cecil's car, and his work was so bad that building control concluded his shoddy efforts had to be *deliberate rather than simply ham-fisted,*' as they so eloquently put it."

"And the environmental health situation?"

"No furry little critters were found, so I suspect the mouse droppings that were discovered had been strategically placed," Ben wearily advised. "Still, they were none too impressed. And even more so when they recovered the chemical bottles from the food storage cupboards. Chemical bottles I most certainly did *not* put there, I might add. So, sorry to go on, Dave, but I wanted to bring you up to speed with the current situation."

"So, I take it you need finance to remedy the substandard

building works before you can re-open the public areas of the business?" Dave smartly surmised.

"Exactly! We can continue operating the campsite, but we're not likely to be on the recommended list at The Caravan Club without available toilets and a shower."

"May I?" Dave asked, taking possession of the printed slide deck, scrutinising the figures that Ben had prepared ahead of the meeting.

Ben nervously fidgeted in his seat, watching the top of Dave's head as he pored over the data. "If you need any clarity...?" Ben whispered, not wanting to break his hopeful saviour's attention too much.

Then, after what felt to Ben like hours, Dave raised his head. "I'll just need to have a quick look over the activity in your company bank account, Ben," Dave told him, turning his attention to the computer positioned on the far side of his desk.

Ben leaned forward a smidge, hoping to gain some insight into whatever information was contained on Dave's computer. But the screen's angle left it frustratingly out of view, and Ben was in danger of falling off his seat if he stretched forward any further.

Eventually, after much tapping of the keyboard, Dave rotated in his chair, now staring directly at Ben. "Ben," he said, in the sombre tone a doctor might adopt before discussing an unwanted diagnosis. "Ben, there's probably no easy way to say this..."

"Ah, bugger," Ben said, kneading his forehead.

"Ben, I could prepare a case for our credit team to consider, but I know time is against you, and I doubt the response would be favourable. It's no reflection on you, Ben, but without any assets to secure the facility and the fact your business account has only been open a few weeks..."

"I understand," Ben said. "But thank you for looking anyway."

It was clear that Dave took no pleasure in delivering such disappointing news, and Ben appreciated the quick 'no' rather than a drawn-out affair.

"I am sorry," Dave added, pushing the slide deck back across his desk. "And for what it's worth, I'm genuinely impressed with what you've accomplished at the campsite. Hopefully, we'll come for a stay once you get back up and running."

Back out in the banking hall, seeing Ben off, Dave extended his hand. "I genuinely hope it all works out for you, Ben."

"We look forward to seeing you at Life's a Pitch," Ben offered. "Although, just remember to bring a portaloo with you," he joked, attempting to lighten the mood.

"Just before you go," Dave said, as Ben turned to leave.

Delighted to hear any possible solution to the pickle he was in, Ben stopped in his tracks. "Yes?" he said, ready to hang on Dave's every word.

"Have you considered a private investor?" Dave suggested.

"Private investor?" Ben responded.

"Yes, a shareholder to come on board with you. Once you resolve your current issues, you potentially have an exciting, thriving business that could be an attractive proposition to the right person," Dave explained. "Plus, a private investor wouldn't have the same administrative hoops to jump through as a traditional lender, so might be able to move quickly."

"I hadn't thought of that option," Ben advised, giving it some thought. "You know, that might be a promising idea," he added a moment later. "You don't happen to know anybody, do you?" Ben asked, though receiving a shake of the head in response.

Once outside in the warm Manx sunshine, Ben wandered along Athol Street, the island's financial district, which was bustling with office workers enjoying their lunch break. And even though confidence hadn't been high ahead of his meeting with the bank, he couldn't shake the feeling he'd now exhausted his final option. The idea of an outside investor had sounded like a good one. But with no specific suggestions in that regard, Ben felt he was now more or less back to square one. *Is this the end of the line?* he wondered, unable to escape the gut-wrenching feeling that'd been consuming him for days. Perhaps it was irrational, but he wasn't concerned so much for himself, either. Rather, it was more that he didn't want to disappoint his daughter, who had remained a rock by his side.

Ben had by now invested every penny he had into the business as things stood and then some. There was no contingency, no buffer zone or wealthy parents to phone for a bailout. Nothing. If Life's a Pitch had any chance of surviving, the business had to be operational. And that wasn't possible until he'd satisfied the requirements of building control. And if that wasn't enough, he also had to convince Environmental Health & Safety that he didn't have a rodent-infested bloody chemical weapons facility. All of this required a cash injection that he simply didn't have.

Ben strolled vacantly, unsure where he was going, in something of a daze, the faces of those walking towards him melting like something from a surreal dream. Understandable, then, that the cracked paving slab crept up on Ben, all unseen and stealth-like.

"Ahh!" Ben exclaimed, snapped from troubled thoughts by the fragment of fractured concrete his toe had suddenly made contact with. With his hands tucked firmly in his pockets, Ben didn't even have the luxury of cushioning his subsequent fall, that thankless task landing firmly on his startled face.

An indeterminate amount of time later — he wasn't sure how long, exactly — Ben moaned, the ringing bells in his ears rousing him from the unscheduled afternoon nap he'd apparently just taken. He'd never been a fighter, which wouldn't have come as a surprise to many, but at that moment he felt like he'd just been knocked to the canvas by Mike Tyson, or perhaps a revolving door. Ben unsheathed a hand, placing it against his throbbing jaw.

"Are you all right?" a concerned voice could be heard to say, from somewhere above. "Do you want me to phone an ambulance? Yes, we'll phone an ambulance."

Ben turned slowly over like a sizzling rotisserie chicken, using a finger as he did so to check that all of his teeth remained where nature intended. Then, finally, he looked up, greeted by the strange vision of silhouetted figures forming a circle above him, a halo of light shining around their heads. "What's going on? Am I... am I in heaven...?" Ben asked, still dazed from his fall, and wiping away a trickle of blood from his squashed beak.

"No, you're still very much alive," the same female voice from a moment ago assured him. "You've taken a tumble, and we're just about to call an ambulance to come and check you over."

"It's... it's not heaven," said Ben, sounding almost disappointed at this, and still very much confused.

"Give the man some room," the woman told the others, waving her arm to shoo them away a bit. "You're all crowding him."

The tangle of figures parted, allowing Ben a proper glimpse of his surroundings, bright sunlight flooding back in. "I've just been to the bank," he said, putting together the pieces of his recent experience. "And then I fell," he added, a fact the group were probably already aware of. "The man at the bank said no," he went on, resulting in confused expressions from above. "Oh. He said no," Ben muttered, the reality of his dire business situation dawning on him like he'd just woken from a deep sleep, which in essence he had.

Then, through a gap in his concerned onlookers' legs, Ben's eyes were drawn to a building on the opposite side of the road. His eyes widened, a moment of elation washing away the pain. Ben pushed himself up on his elbows, forcing a smile through his bruised jaw. "It's a sign!" he declared triumphantly.

"Yes, it's a sign," the woman said, having no idea what sort of epiphany Ben might be having, but appeasing him until such time as the ambulance arrived.

"No, I mean, it's *really* a sign," Ben said, extending a finger towards the thing that had captured his attention. "It's a sign hanging over that shop."

The woman looked over her shoulder, following the direction of her patient's finger. "Over there?" she asked, uncertain as to which one in particular she should be looking at. "You mean the sign advertising Austin Fletcher's Estate Agency?"

"Yes!" Ben said enthusiastically, the pain in his face forgotten. "Austin Fletcher, he's the man who can help me!" he insisted, as the sound of an ambulance siren carried through the air.

Chapter Thirteen

H ave some of that!" Austin yelled, hoping his words would encourage his golf ball on a few extra yards. "You know, Miles," he said with a smug sense of satisfaction, "there are days when all is well in the world, do you know what I mean?"

"I hear that," Miles replied, stepping forward and jamming his tee into the dirt. "Three birdies on the bounce, Austin. You're on fire."

Austin simply nodded, happy to accept the praise.

With his ball in position, Miles lifted his club over his head with both hands, twisting his torso from side to side, stretching out his spine as he surveyed the next fairway. "I have to tell you, Austin, when you first suggested golf, I had this image that you'd be one of those all-the-gear, no-idea sorts," he said. "The kind of bloke with a five-grand set of golf clubs but couldn't hit a cow's arse with a banjo, if you know what I mean. That sort of bloke."

"Ah, well now you know, Miles. I discovered many years ago that the most lucrative deals often take place on the golf course," Austin advised.

"And the nineteenth hole as well," Miles suggested, focussing once again on his ball. With a satisfying *thwack*, he sent the ball hurtling skyward, where it soared gracefully before coming to rest several yards behind Austin's effort. "I can hear you smiling from here," Miles said, without turning around to confirm.

"*Moi?*" Austin replied, placing a hand against his heart. "Oh, I would never kick a man while he's down, Miles. Especially someone who's having such a stinker of a round."

Miles threw his club into his bag like a dart, the club landing perfectly into place. He only wished his shot down the fairway had been just as precise. "Bloody stupid game anyway," he said with a laugh.

"So," Austin said, once the two of them were aboard the hired buggy and on their way. "Talk to me about the old man."

"Seven holes completed before you finally start talking business, Austin?" Miles answered, one eyebrow raised. "I'm surprised it's taken you this long."

"I was planning on letting you get into your golfing stride, Miles. But that strategy appears to have fallen out the window," Austin joked.

"Well, as for business, Sebastian told me he'll make a final decision at the end of the week," Miles informed Austin. "Then, he'll formally announce which estate agent has exclusivity for the new development."

"Marvellous. And I'm hoping the list of potential candidates is short?"

"Short? I suppose you could say that," Miles replied with a chuckle. "Most formal tenders didn't even arrive on Sebastian's desk, Austin. I did allow a couple through, so that it wasn't completely obvious what was going on. But those agencies that did make the cut, to use a golfing term, had their quotes inflated more than Pamela Anderson's whatsits. So in other words, I've done my bit, Austin. You just need to do yours now."

Austin parked up the golf buggy, taking care not to plough over their balls. "Oh, don't you worry about that, my old friend," he replied, looking to his passenger once again. "My insider assures me that all is going to plan in that regard. Apparently, business is not too brisk at that rubbish little campsite. *Only a matter of time now* to use my associate's words."

Miles rubbed his hands together, appreciating what he was hearing. "Splendid news, Austin. And my final payment?"

"Now *you're* the one keen to discuss business," Austin observed with a smirk, climbing out of their buggy. "And don't you worry about the rest of your money. The minute the old boy signs the contract appointing my agency, you'll be receiving a rather large, fat envelope, yes?" he assured Miles. "Now. Let me show you just how this little game should be played," he added, reaching for his nine iron.

Later that same day, Austin paced around his well-appointed office back at estate agency HQ, listening to the woman talking on his speakerphone. And while he *was* paying attention to a certain extent, he was also able to floss his teeth simultaneously. "Uh-huh," he offered, indicating to the caller that he was still there and listening, whilst then checking out the results of his handiwork in the wall-mounted mirror. "Looking good," he suggested, with an approving wink.

"Looking good...?" the caller asked, knocked off her stride, and confused as to what Austin could possibly mean by that.

"What? Oh, sorry, Dorothy, not you. I was talking about me," Austin advised, returning to his chair. Austin rolled his eyes as he listened on, the frustrations apparent in his face, though of course Dorothy couldn't see it. "Dorothy, I completely understand what you're saying," he told her. "That you need time to think about the sale, and—"

"My late husband built that house with his own hands," Dorothy cut in. "I just don't know if I'm ready to proceed with the sale."

Austin placed his head in his hands, groaning quietly. "Dorothy, like I said in person, it's a seller's market, yeah? But I don't know how long I can keep my buyer on the hook, my love. And the other thing you need to think about is the heating."

"The heating?"

"Yes, the heating, Dorothy. Have you watched the news lately? Heating bills are soaring, and don't forget it's just you rattling around in there, paying to heat rooms you'll never use, Dorothy. And don't forget about the roof."

"My roof?"

"Yes, Dorothy, your roof. It's showing serious signs of wear and tear," Austin stressed. "And to replace a roof that size..." he added, sucking in air to emphasise the gravity of the situation. "Well, you could be looking close to a hundred grand to sort it all out."

Dorothy went quiet for a moment, likely digesting this grave piece of news she was hearing. "But– but the roof was replaced only four years ago," she said, sounding worried and confused. "And it already needs to be replaced...?"

Then, sensing he had her exactly where he wanted her, he feigned frustration on her behalf. "Oh, I *know*, Dorothy. I witness this sort of thing all the *time*," Austin told her. "And it really does make my blood boil to see good people, such as yourself, subjected to poor workmanship like that. It's a shame, really. A crying shame. But if you're not interested in selling at the peak of the market, maximising your profit and avoiding those unwanted bills, then I completely—"

"No, no!" Dorothy cut in, sounding much more certain now as to what she ought to do. "After what you've told me, I think I'd be a fool not to sell at this time."

Austin punched the air in triumph. "Marvellous news, Dorothy. Leave it with me, and I'll set the wheels in motion. Oh, but before you go..."

"Yes?"

"As it should happen, I've just had the details for a charming little cottage arrive on my desk. If you like, I can pull a few strings and make sure you're at the head of the queue for what's certain to be a property in great demand?"

"Oh, Austin. I'd be exceptionally grateful if you could do that for me? I really don't know what I'd do without you."

"Not all heroes wear capes, Dorothy. It's just what I do. Austin Fletcher goes the extra mile for his clients."

With that call ended and another deal, possibly two, thrashing around his fishing net, ready to be landed, Austin decided he'd done enough for one day. "Ah, the old roof repair story. It works every time," he said, closing over Dorothy's file and patting it gently.

"Knock-knock," Barry announced, letting himself into Austin's office. "I'm guessing by the smile that you've secured Dorothy's sale?"

"Was it ever in doubt?" Austin asked, rising to his feet and getting his things together. "It's like shooting fish in a barrel, Barry."

"Good work, boss," Barry said. "Though I couldn't help noticing you're on your way out the door?"

Austin slipped an arm inside his jacket. "That's why I pay your salary, Bazza. You're perceptive like that."

"I appreciate that, boss," Barry said, completely missing the sarcastic tone. "But the thing is, someone is waiting for you in reception."

"What? I'm off to the tanning salon, Bazza. Unless they're trying to sell a multi-million-pound house that I can steal for a tiny fraction of its real value, you can deal with it? Just tell them I'm not here."

Barry scratched his head, uncertain how to proceed. "Yeah, but from the reception area, they can see you through the glass, boss," he pointed out. "So, they already know you're here."

"Gawdssake, Bazza. Remind me why I pay your wages?" Austin responded, stamping all over his earlier compliment. "Well, who is it?" he asked, not bothering to look for himself.

Barry glanced down at the yellow post-it note held in his palm. "Ben Parker," he revealed, reading his own scribbled handwriting.

"I've no idea who that is, Bazza. So sling him out, and I'll slope out the back door, yeah?"

"But he says he knows you and needs to talk to you urgently."

Austin glanced up, finally catching a glimpse of the man stood patiently waiting for him. "Oh, shit!" he said, taking an immediate step to his right, hoping to conceal himself, even though they were presently surrounded by glass. "That's my neighbour."

"Oh," Barry said, unsure what to do with that information or how he was meant to proceed. "So, you still want me to sling him out...?"

Austin's mind started to race, anxiously wondering if Ben knew about Cecil, as why else would his neighbour be darkening his door?

"Did he seem very angry?" Austin asked Barry.

Barry offered a casual shrug. "No, not at all," he said. "He doesn't appear the sort, if I'm being honest. In fact he looks like the type you'd administer a wedgie to at school." With this critical assessment delivered, Barry glanced over his shoulder for a moment. "I reckon you could take him in a fight, Austin, if that's what you're worried about?" he advised, cosying up to his boss with a well-timed compliment.

"I'm not going to get into any kind of physical altercation, Bazza, not with *these* teeth to protect," Austin said, flashing him a smile. "That's why I pay you what I do."

"Very generous, too, Austin, which I appreciate. Anyway...?"

Austin darted his eyes, trying to work out if there was some way to possibly slip out the back as he'd suggested. But there didn't seem to be. "Oh, show him in, then," Austin eventually decided, returning to the business end of his desk. "But I want you to remain vigilant, yeah? Nothing happens to these teeth, Bazza."

"I'm never off duty," Barry commented, tapping the side of his nose like he had all the answers. "And if anything kicks off, I'll be in here before you can say, ehm..." he offered, searching for just the right thing to say. "Erm, before you can say..." he repeated, still in search of something clever.

"Bazza, just show him in, yeah?" Austin snapped, rapping a set of impatient knuckles on his desk.

"Straight away, Austin."

A moment or two later, Ben, escorted by Bazza, appeared in Austin's doorway. "Ben Parker to see you," Barry announced, tapping the side of his nose once again.

"Neighbourino!" Austin cheerily replied, rising from his chair. "Please, come into my humble office," he offered, scanning Ben's face for any threat.

Ben took a seat as directed, smiling nervously like a pupil being invited into the headmaster's office. "You're very kind to see me without an appointment, Austin," Ben answered, glancing around and admiring Austin's workspace. "You're buying a boat?" he added by way of small talk.

"What? *What* boat?" Austin said, going on the defensive and wondering how on earth Ben had got wind about the first purchase with his ill-gotten gains. "Who said I was buying a boat?"

"Uhm, I just saw the yacht magazine on your desk, and, you know..." Ben said, lowering his head, concerned he'd destroyed the meeting before it had a chance to even properly begin.

"What, *this* magazine?" Austin asked. "Ah. I wish," he said with a nervous laugh. "No, I stole this when I was at the dentist the other day, that's all," he fibbed. "Anyway, what can I do for my favourite neighbour?"

Ben relaxed into his seat, holding up a copy of his business plan. "Well," Ben said, clearing his throat. "You might recall me telling you about my new business venture?"

Austin screwed up his face, as if this was the last thing he could remember, though of course the very opposite was true. "Business venture...?" he said, tilting his head, playing like he was struggling to recall what Ben might be referring to. "Oh. It was a campsite, wasn't it?" he asked, with impressive acting skills.

"Life's a Pitch," Ben was pleased to confirm, pointing to the title on his business plan. "Anyway, Austin," he went on, offering his most cordial of smiles. "When I mentioned it to you previously, you kindly offered to help me should the need arise. And, well, unfortunately, that particular need has now arisen, Austin."

"I see," Austin said with a flourish of the hand, eager to hear more. "Do continue."

Encouraged by the warm reception, Ben slid a copy of his business plan across the desk. "Well, I won't lie, Austin. My new business venture has encountered some severe headwinds, I guess you could say, and I'm wondering if you might be able to help me get back on course?" he asked, eyes filled with hope.

Ben proceeded to fill Austin in on some of the finer detail, speaking faster than he usually would, unsure how much time was allotted to him. But Austin, for his part, listened intently, nodding his head and offering noises of encouragement throughout the unscheduled presentation. And, before too long, Ben's nerves settled, and his passion for the business shone through.

"... So," Ben said, drawing towards a conclusion, "I think you can see from the financial figures that there's a genuine opportunity for the right investor to come on board, I hope. And that's when your kind offer of assistance came to mind, as you mentioned to me that you know everyone in this business that's worth knowing."

Austin relaxed back in his chair, gently caressing his chin. "And you're just looking for a cash injection to assist with the repairs and aid cash flow?" he asked, in summation of what he'd heard.

"Exactly, Austin. It won't take too much to get the business on track, and I'm confident it would be a solid investment for the right person," Ben said, sounding like he was pitching an invention on *Dragons' Den*. "So, as a man in the know, Austin, I suppose I was hopeful you might be aware of a particular investor who might like to become part of the Life's a Pitch journey? Or even someone to provide a loan in return for a healthy interest rate?"

"Be aware of anybody?" Austin replied, replaying Ben's words back to him. "Of *course* I do," he said, leaning forward.

Ben's face lit up in response. "You do?" he asked. "Who?"

"Why, *me*, of course," Austin declared, as if the answer should have been obvious. "How could I resist the opportunity of working with my favourite neighbour?" he added. Austin extended a hand across his desk, flashing his precious pearly whites. "Put it there, buddy," he said, shaking Ben's hand. "I'll be happy to lend you the money you need."

Chapter Fourteen

W hat?" Cecil asked with a scowl, nursing the dregs in the bottom of his pint glass. "But that makes absolutely no sense," he said, swirling the murky liquid before tossing it down his grateful gullet. Shaking his head in dismay, he licked the surplus foam from his top lip, and then looked down forlornly at his empty glass. "Another?" he asked Austin.

"First off, Cecil, you don't need to understand," Austin replied. "And second, yes, I'll have another Diet Coke," he added, with a dismissive flick of the hand.

Cecil traipsed to the counter where the bartender was already poised and ready to dispense more liquid refreshment. "Same again, Cecil?" the barkeep asked accommodatingly, receiving the required confirmation.

"Quiet in here tonight," Cecil commented, running his eyes over the array of empty seats.

The bartender handed over the first drink in the order. "Yeah, there's not been many in since that little fracas at the weekend," he explained.

"Fracas?" Cecil said with a laugh. "It was a full-on mass brawl from what I heard."

"It wasn't pretty, Cecil, I can tell you that much," the bartender gravely advised. "It was like something from a Wild West saloon. Bottles chucked in every direction, fists flying, and I think I even saw a few knuckle dusters, if I'm not mistaken. And that was just the *women*."

"The regulars in here can certainly look after themselves," Cecil readily agreed, enjoying a generous slurp of his beer, not bothering to wait until he was back at the table with Austin. "Still, it doesn't look too bad?" he offered optimistically.

"The broken windows are being replaced later today, and the carpet cleaner arrives tomorrow. He thinks he'll be able to get most of the blood out. So, that's something to look forward to."

"We won't be able to recognise the place," Cecil said with a smirk, taking hold of the second drink. "Stick it on my tab, yeah?" he said, turning his back before the barkeep could decline the request.

"There you are," Cecil said a moment later, placing Austin's fizzy pop in front of him. "You *do* know you're in a pub, right? And that you can order a proper drink?"

Austin turned up his nose. "I have to watch my figure, Cecil. A body like this doesn't just happen, you know."

"I suppose not," Cecil answered with a shrug. "Still, I'll stick to my Guinness."

"And speaking of this place," Austin continued, "I really don't know why I let you drag me into such establishments for our little meetings, Cecil, I really don't."

"It's not too bad once you get used to it," Cecil suggested, inspecting the rim of his glass and plucking away a few suspicious curly hairs that'd somehow found their way there. "It's characterful, as they say."

"Oh? And who says that, precisely?" Austin asked sceptically, remaining unconvinced that anyone would say such a thing.

"Well, I just did," Cecil said with another shrug, after which he took another large swig of his beer, all hairs having been successfully removed. "Besides, it's not like I could venture into the town centre, is it?" he added with a scowl, lowering his voice even though the pub was virtually empty. "If Ben catches up with me, he'll skin me alive for what I've done to him at your urging."

"You weren't exactly flavour of the month when your name came up during our recent meeting," Austin revealed with a grin. "Anyway, you should count your blessings that he's not phoned the Old Bill over that cash you nicked out of his till."

"Dunno what you mean," Cecil said with a sniff, as if he were offended by Austin's insinuation, even though he very clearly wasn't. "People were coming and going all throughout the day at that campsite. Could've been any one of them."

"And that's the only reason Ben's not shopped you to the police," Austin suggested. "So, it's fortunate that he's found a friendly face in the form of yours truly."

"As you mentioned a few minutes ago," Cecil said with a further scowl. "And I'm looking forward to hearing the explanation for this. First, you pay me to force the wheels off his business, and then, just as everything is going to plan, you open your wallet to bail him out? It makes absolutely no sense."

"It was the only option given the circumstances," Austin insisted.

"Eh...?"

"Well, Ben's banker unhelpfully suggested he try and attract an investor to come on board with him, yeah? After all, on paper, the business is quite attractive. So, if by some chance he'd succeeded in doing that, there was a slim possibility the business would remain viable beyond the time I need him packed up and gone so the farmer will sign on the dotted line. And to avoid that unpalatable situation, I've stepped in, so that Ben won't look any further."

The stubbly corner of Cecil's lip turned up. "You're a devious bugger, Austin," he said, before pausing to completely register what he'd just been told. "Wait, hang on. But if you don't hand over any money to pay to correct what I sabotaged, then he'll know something's not right, surely? I mean, the guy's not stupid, Austin."

"Yes, and that's why I've ventured out to this dump to see you now, Cecil, as I'll need your kind assistance for the next phase of Operation Sabotage."

"What, it's not because you wanted to share a pint with your old pal?" Cecil joked, taking another sip of his brown nectar. "Wait," he said, as realisation struck him again. "Don't think you're getting me involved in anything *else* shifty, Austin. After

I finished that last mission, I told you I'd be out," he said, waving a firm hand through the air. *"Finito,"* he added. "Me and the missus are swapping cold winters for the glorious sunshine in sunny Spain. The flight tickets are getting booked this week."

"I know that, Cecil," Austin replied, sounding like this was only a minor inconvenience to his master plan. "But do you know how many cocktails on the beach five grand will buy you? Because that's what I'm offering."

"Five grand?" Cecil answered, eyes widening. "Well, why didn't you say so before now?" he remarked.

"So, I can count on you, Cecil?" Austin asked, raising his glass of Diet Coke to seal the deal.

"I'll phone the missus and ask her to put the passports back in the kitchen drawer, just for the time being, Austin."

"Marvellous."

"So, you can do everything?" Ben asked, escorting the building contractors from the shower block over at Life's a Pitch.

"Sure, absolutely," one of the men in a high-viz jacket replied. "And you know, you're incredibly lucky to call this your office," he commented, by way of nothing, extending a hand towards the rolling hillside as he took in his countryside surroundings.

"If you couldn't fix what needed fixing, it wouldn't be my office for too much longer," Ben suggested nervously. "And you can start straight away?"

"Uh-huh," the other chap offered, following the direction of his colleague's hand and appearing equally captivated by the tranquil view. "We'll get on with the more urgent jobs first, yeah? That way, you'll keep the guys from building control happy so you can continue operating."

"And then we'll move onto the other mainly cosmetic jobs," the first chap suggested as they approached the Guest Entertainment Centre. "If all goes to plan, you'll be operational again in no time at all. So, if you'd like us to get cracking..."

"Yes, that would be amazing," Ben answered, raising a grateful thumb in the air. Which appeared to be appreciated, though not quite the response the fellow had been after, as evidenced by the *is-there-something-you've-forgotten* sort of look which Ben received in polite response. "Oh!" Ben exclaimed, when he eventually caught up. "Yes, you'll be needing some cash, then," he added, inviting the guys inside. "Two thousand up front, with the remainder to be paid on completion?" Ben asked, confirming the agreement as per their previous conversation over the phone.

"Yes, that's right," came the reply. "That'll allow us to buy the supplies we need to get cracking."

Ben could be forgiven for having a spring in his step, virtually dancing through his reception area as he was. From being plagued by seemingly insurmountable adversity only a short time ago, here he was now, thrown a lifeline by two burly construction workers and a crucial cash advance from his new-best-friend Austin.

"I won't be a moment, gents," Ben said by way of a placeholder, counting out the cash that Austin had dropped around earlier that morning. "There we go," he added a moment later, handing over a chunky pile of notes. "I won't be offended if you want to check it's all there."

"Don't worry, Ben. We know where you work," one of the men joked. "Right, then," he said, clapping his hands in a *let's-get-this-show-on-the-road* manner. "We'll be back this afternoon to get stuck in."

The builders' final quote for the remedial works, give or take a few quid for contingency, was around the 8k mark. To allow work to commence, Austin provided the crucial funding of the initial deposit, with the promise of more to come once the works had been completed. The fact that the work needed doing in the first place was galling, but Ben knew he couldn't allow himself to dwell on what had happened before and who had done what. His primary focus was now on the future. And with Austin's timely support, he was thrilled there was even a future to consider. Yes, it would take a little longer for the business to recover from this temporary setback, maybe even a year or two to completely pay back all of the money, Ben figured. But that was okay.

One small mercy was that most of the campsite's current guests were reasonably happy to continue with their stay. Taking the short walk to the nearby local swimming pool for a shower was, for most, only a minor inconvenience and an excuse to stretch their legs. Ben had also arranged for several portaloos to be dropped off at short notice while the shower block remained closed. It was an unwanted additional expense but one that couldn't be helped, really, as when you needed to go, you needed to go.

Of course, there were some campers who'd chosen not to stay, and Ben couldn't say he blamed them, but the volume of people requesting refunds was nowhere near what he'd initially feared. And now, with light shining at the end of the tunnel, he could once again reopen the reservations book to get a much-needed infusion of cash into the bank account so he could begin repaying Austin's generous loan and generally keep the wolf from the door.

Later in the day, Ruby dropped by the campsite on the way home from school, weighed down with several bulging shopping bags and her cheeks puce from exertion. "Hello!" she shouted over, the moment she clapped eyes on her dad.

Ben glanced up from the BBQ he was attending to, snapping his tongs like a lobster's claw. "Heya, Ruby!" he said, waving away some of the smoke getting in his eyes. "Hold on, I'll give you a hand," he said, setting down his utensil and sprinting over. "Here, let me take those bags," he said upon arrival, taking a peek inside one of them. "Bloody hell," he said with a laugh. "That's a *lot* of sausages."

"You're telling me?" Ruby said, wiping her brow now her hands were free. "I nearly emptied the shelves at The Chop Shop."

"Wait, you've not walked all the way, have you?" Ben asked. "I told you to take a taxi," he said, worried, as they headed back to his outdoor fire pit.

"I did. They dropped me off at the bottom of the lane, but still..." Ruby answered, flexing her fingers, hoping to restore blood flow to her throbbing digits. "So how many have you invited to your impromptu BBQ?" she asked, moving the conversation along.

"Everyone," Ben replied brightly, looking at the tents erected in every direction.

"Everyone?"

"Yeah," Ben said, checking in on his glowing coals.

Ruby moved closer, conscious several hungry-looking campers had the BBQ in their crosshairs. "Dad..." she said gently. "Dad, can we afford to do this?" she asked, placing a gentle hand on his back.

"Nope, not really," Ben replied. "But if all of our guests had requested a refund, we'd probably be hanging up the 'closed' sign, so it's a nice way to thank them for hanging in there. Plus, the money from Austin helped pay for all these lovely sausages and burgers." Then, sensing the genuine concern in her tone, he turned to face his daughter. "Ruby, it'll all be fine," he assured her, placing a peck on her cheek. "We're the dream team, yeah? We may get knocked down from time to time, but we come through it, and we'll come through this. Nothing can stop the Rubster and me." Ben curled his hand into a motivational fist, shaking it like he was about to throw a pair of lucky dice. "We've got this, Ruby. You, me, and Life's a Pitch. It's our future."

"I s'pose," Ruby said, perking up a bit. "But..." she started to say, before veering away.

"Go on," Ben pressed. "No secrets in our dream team."

"It's just, well, the whole Austin situation. Dad, do you not think he's, ehm... a bit of a knob?"

"Ruby Parker!" Ben admonished her, though he couldn't help laughing at her description just the same. "Ruby, he's actually quite a nice guy once you scrape away the arrogant, abrasive layers," he maintained. "Besides, without Austin's generous assistance, I don't know what I'd have done."

"Just keep an eye on him, Pops, will you?" Ruby offered. "You know how we trusted that churlish lout, Cecil, and look what he did to us."

"Fair enough. I will, Ruby," Ben replied, reaching for a bag of sausages. "I promise," he promised. Then, turning his attention to the campers milling around the vicinity. "Grab yourselves a beer from the chiller box!" he said, using his tongs to point the way. "And I hope you're hungry, folks, because there'll soon be plenty to go around!"

One of the many benefits of operating a campsite in the middle of the delightful Manx countryside was that there weren't too many neighbours to complain about the excessive noise levels. Only the occasional cow offered an inquisitive snout over the perimeter gate, perhaps concerned by the sound of off-key singing emanating from around the fire pit. Or it might have been the wafting aroma from the BBQ, scents that may have offered a sense of impending doom in the adjacent field packed with beef cattle.

But one thing that was for sure was that even though the communal buildings at Life's a Pitch were closed down, for now, the campsite felt very much alive and open for business. And in what felt like no time at all, the quality goods supplied by The Chop Shop were demolished in short order, as were the contents of the chiller box. Fortunate, then, that most campers had their own supply of alcohol secured in their tents, a supply they were only too happy to dip into, and share if need be, if it meant the party could continue.

Later that evening, just as the sun was setting, a contented and slightly tipsy Ben strolled around the campsite, exchanging pleasantries with his guests and making sure they'd had enough to eat. "Ruby?" he said, spotting his daughter whilst on his rounds. She'd separated from him earlier, and he now found her waiting outside a portaloo. "What's this? Are you drinking a beer?" Ben asked, noticing as she hastily concealed something behind her back.

Ruby shuffled awkwardly in place, as if she needed to pee, which was fortuitous given where she was presently standing. "Ehm, no... it's just... I was holding it for..." she fumbled.

"It's fine," a grinning Ben said. "But just the one," he advised, wagging a sensible finger towards her. Then, taking up a position next to her, he draped an arm across her shoulders. "What a fabulous night," he said reflectively, appreciating the image of a vibrant campsite stuffed with punters enjoying themselves. "You know, Ruby," he said, surveying the throng through glazed eyes. "Ruby, when I fell asleep at night, imagining what this business could be, this is exactly what I saw in my mind's eye," he told her, raising an arm like a preacher taking mass.

"Full of soused campers singing loudly?" Ruby joked.

"Full of happy campers having a wonderful time," Ben corrected her, along with a friendly squeeze. "I know it's not perfect, Ruby, but we're nearly there, aren't we?"

"We sure are, Pops."

Ben stood motionless for some time, enjoying a lovely moment with his beautiful daughter. "It ain't so bad, Ruby," he suggested with a sigh, just as his phone rang, snapping him back into the present. "Oh, that could be another customer," he mused, reaching into his pocket. "Life's a Pitch!" Ben said, cheerily answering his mobile.

Then, releasing Ruby from his side hug, Ben paced in a circle with the phone pressed to his ear. "I'm sorry to hear you've been let down," Ben offered sympathetically, in response to what he was being told. "Oh," he said, running a hand through his hair. "Next week...?" he asked, with uncertainty in his voice. "I'm not really sure that we—" he started to say, before stopping himself short. He briefly glanced skyward, as if he were consulting a higher power, which maybe he was. Finally, he cleared his throat, returning his attention to the caller. "In fact, strike that. I'm *sure* we can do that for you, no problem," he advised, his confidence returning. "How about I give you a call first thing tomorrow, and we can finalise the details for you?" he offered.

"Marvellous, I'll speak to you then."

"What was that about?" Ruby enquired, instinctively hiding the beer bottle she'd just taken a swig from, even though her father had already told her it was okay.

"That," Ben said, dancing a little jig. "Was the chairman of the local Aston Martin Appreciation Society hoping to use our campsite for a show they had planned. Apparently he knows Austin, who suggested he give me a call after his previous venue just cancelled, leaving him right in the shi... er, I mean, in a spot of bother."

"A show?" Ruby asked. "What, for people to gawp at cars they can't afford?" she added, the prospect not particularly appealing to a teenage girl with no particular interest in automobiles.

"Yeah," Ben said, his mind racing with the possibilities. "Don't knock it, Ruby. Those car meets can be extremely popular, and it could also be quite lucrative for us."

"How, exactly?"

"Well," Ben said, considering the options. "Well, we can charge a fee to use the back field, which is empty at the moment. Plus, he's asked if we can cater the event as well, which could be a good little earner."

Ruby had nodded along, liking what she was hearing, but then a thought jumped into her head. "Hang on," she said. "What if the toilet block and the guest area aren't open by then?"

"It'll be fine," Ben offered, buoyed by optimism or alcohol, and possibly both. "The builder reckons it'll only take a few days to get everything fixed, so there's more than enough leeway there. Plenty of time," he said, staring off dreamily into the distance. "Ah, Ruby. This is just the lift I needed, and once again, it's all down to Austin. Honestly, I could just kiss him the next time I see him! So, Ruby. Whaddya think?"

"About the kissing? Not on the lips," Ruby advised. "But other than that, I'm thinking I need to go for a pee, before I burst!" she said, darting towards one of the now-vacant portaloos. "I'll see you in a minute!"

Chapter Fifteen

Having a campsite on the grounds of a working farm was a perfect match, a hand-in-glove relationship that, for the campsite, meant easy access to delicious, fresh farm produce including eggs and milk. And for the farmer, it was another source of much-needed income in what was a challenging sector to scrape a living.

And even though Farmer Gerry was effectively Ben's landlord, he'd also become something of a friend in the relatively short period of time the two had known each other. In his sixty-three years on planet earth, Ben had learned, Farmer Gerry hadn't once left the Isle of Man. Not even for a day trip. Never. It was a fact that Ben found remarkable. Admittedly, he was no Judith Chalmers himself, but Ben thought it incredible that one could live their days without once stepping off this little rock in the middle of the Irish Sea, as charming a place to live as it was.

Ben enjoyed their talks, and each morning, just after six a.m., Ben looked forward to stopping in at the farmhouse to collect his daily shopping list in order to cater to his guests' hungry tums. Initially, with the temporary closure of the Guest Entertainment Centre, Ben had worried that serving food to his patrons was a lucrative sideline he'd have to curtail for the time being. But, as Farmer Gerry had been quick to point out, Ben could continue cooking a good number of items for his guests; he'd simply need to set up his base of operations in the outdoors as opposed to the indoors. Which Ben did. And it was on Gerry's borrowed BBQ that Ben had cooked up his delicious breakfast offerings these last few mornings. Indeed, one of the advantages of cooking al fresco was the enticing aromas wafting around the campsite, attracting sleepy campers like moths to the flame. In fact, his breakfasts had proved so popular the previous few mornings that Ben was seriously considering continuing it outdoors even when normal service resumed, weather permitting of course.

Today, having texted his order through the previous evening, Ben exited his car, strolling through the farm courtyard with the dawn chorus for company and a broad smile on his face. It was at moments such as this that the idea of being hunched over a desk for eight hours seemed very unpleasant by comparison. Instead, Ben had the distinct pleasure of calling these stunning surroundings his office, and for that, he was genuinely grateful. The reason, then, the spring in his step was particularly springy this fine morning.

Reaching the farmhouse, he tapped lightly on the weathered oak door, letting himself in, as he knew Gerry was expecting him. Once inside, Ben was greeted by Gerry's cheery face staring back at him as he enjoyed a nice cuppa. "Morning, Gerry," Ben said with a grin.

"There's fresh tea in the pot," Gerry advised, inviting Ben to join him at the kitchen table.

"I don't mind if I do," Ben said, placing two small bags he'd been carrying in front of Gerry, with one of the bags being a bit lighter than the other.

"What's this?" Gerry asked, looking at the bags and then at Ben.

"That?" Ben said, pulling out a chair from under the table. "That is a batch of fresh croissants I baked back at the house, for both you and your lovely wife. Plus, four bottles of that IPA you told me you liked, for later this afternoon."

"You can come around more often," Gerry suggested, peering into the better smelling of the two bags. "But why, exactly? Not that I'm complaining, mind you."

Ben reached over, removing the knitted cockerel tea cosy from the teapot that was placed there at the centre of the table.

"Because you kindly gave me the loan of your fire pit," he told Gerry. "And it's also an apology for the situation with the rent arrears."

"I know you've had a run of bad luck," Gerry answered. "The entire Cecil situation has been awful for us both, to be honest, and I told you not to—"

"And I do sincerely appreciate it, Gerry," Ben gently cut in. "But that investor I told you about has come good with his offer. He's advanced me the cash to put the builders to work, and by the end of the week I'll be able to catch up on any overdue rent."

"If I was a wealthy man, Ben, and money was no object, I'd give you all the time in the world, of course. But the costs of running a farm are extortionate."

"Gerry, you've already been so kind to me that I just didn't want you thinking I was taking advantage."

Gerry waved away Ben's concerns, rummaging in the bag for a croissant. "These smell terrific, Ben," he said, giving one a furious sniff. "Can I tempt you?"

"Not after it's been stuck up your hooter," Ben joked. And then, patting his tum, "No, I'm good, Gerry, thanks. I had two before I left the house, and I'll be sweating butter if I indulge in another."

While Gerry helped himself to several of the croissants, Ben sipped his tea, taking the opportunity to share his plans for the campsite, in which, of course, they both had a collective financial interest. For Ben, he enjoyed the chance to share his thoughts with someone in addition to Ruby, and he valued any feedback Gerry might have to offer. After all, Farmer Gerry was a wise old owl, Ben observed — aside from hiring Cecil, that is — and someone whose opinion he respected.

And it was for that reason Ben was delighted to receive Gerry's seal of approval for the upcoming car show, especially as the vehicles onsite might cause something of a disturbance. However, Ben needn't have worried, as being a bit of an auto enthusiast himself, Gerry was quite taken with the car show idea. Indeed, it was while talking through the details of the car show that Gerry's mind drifted to other related possibilities as well.

"There's no reason you couldn't approach the other car clubs on the island," Gerry proposed, applying a generous dollop of strawberry jam to the latest of his croissants. "You could make it a regular feature through the summer months. And, who knows, as long as they're already there, you might encourage people to camp out overnight," he added, thinking out loud. "In fact, what about approaching sports clubs to hire the land? Or children's groups such as the Scouts?"

"I was *in* the Scouts," Ben proudly advised, a nostalgic twinkle in his eye. "You're in the company of a knot-tying champion, as it should happen."

"Well, you could have a whole meadow full of Scouts filling that spare field," Gerry suggested. "A right captive audience to buy your fine baked goods," he added, wiping away a stray crumb that'd fixed itself to his chin. "And if I ever get stuck with my knots, I'll know where to come," he added with a wry smile.

"So, you don't mind if I use that field for such things, then?" Ben asked, seeking confirmation though already having it.

Gerry shook his head. "Of course not," he said. "As long as they don't mind sharing it with the sheep from time to time, then go for it. Anything to bring a few more people to your campsite is fine by me, Ben." And with that, Gerry drained the content of his mug, casting his eye to the wall-mounted clock. "Anyway, as much as I'd like to chat all morning, I need to go and attend to the other ladies in my life, who'll be mooing away in the cowshed waiting for me."

"Thanks, Gerry," Ben replied, taking the less-than-subtle hint that it was time to clear off. "You really are the best."

"I know," Gerry said with a sniff. "Oh, and that's your milk and eggs by the door. Don't forget it on the way out."

"Not on your Nellie," Ben happily promised.

In the Guest Entertainment Centre — which had by this time been scrubbed, bleached, and polished to within an inch of its life — Ben shuffled behind the clipboard-wielding chap from Environmental Health & Safety as he neared the conclusion of his inspection.

"So..." Ben offered, searching for an icebreaker, something to connect with Geoffrey, whose cold exterior provided no clues to what was being written on his inspection notes. As Geoffrey slowed, running a diligent eye over the interior of the fridge, Ben took a step closer, pushing himself up on his tiptoes, hoping to catch a glimpse over Geoffrey's shoulder.

"What are you doing?" Geoffrey asked frostily, pressing the clipboard into his chest like he was protecting his homework from the classroom cheat.

Ben shifted his weight from one foot to the other, still elevated on tippy toes. "Me?" he asked with a nervous laugh. "I was just..." he started to say, lowering himself to normal height. "I, ehm... I couldn't help notice you'd arrived by car today, Geoffrey," Ben said, changing subject and spouting the first thing that came to mind.

"Eh?" Geoffrey said, taking a step forward to restore some of his personal space. "Well, that's what one does, when travelling over roadways...?" he answered, unsure what Ben was getting at.

"So, you must like cars, then?" Ben pressed on, ploughing ahead. "What with you driving here in one today and everything?"

Geoffrey shrugged his shoulders, returning his attention to the cleanliness of the fridge, for the most part. "I suppose I like them well enough," he offered noncommittally, uncertain what else to say after such an unusual query.

Apparently not content with the awkward silence that followed, Ben continued on with his peculiar line of questioning. "Do you happen to like Aston Martins, Geoffrey?"

Geoffrey glanced over his shoulder, likely wondering if he should be phoning HQ for backup. "Do I like Aston Martins...?" he asked, repeating what he thought he'd just heard. "Well, I suppose I like them, yes."

"Would you like to sit in one?" Ben suggested immediately, jiggling his eyebrows like he was a man who had the power to make such dreams a reality. And in fact, "Because that's something I can arrange," he declared.

Geoffrey observed Ben's eyebrows until they finally settled down, several jiggles later. "Mr Parker," he said, his expression severe. "Mr Parker, are you attempting to bribe a government official? Because we take a very dim view of such approaches."

Ben stared without blinking. *"Bribe?* What?" he asked, laughing at what he assumed was some joke he wasn't really getting. But unfortunately, he was the only one laughing.

He'd only been trying to make some innocent — if very awkward — conversation, but it suddenly dawned on him what he must have sounded like.

"Oh, my goodness, no! No, I'm not trying to bribe you, I swear!" he added a moment later, fully appreciating the gravity of the present accusation. "I was just– You see, we're hosting the Aston Martin owner's club next week, Geoffrey. I just wondered if you'd like to come along, is all. Honestly. I swear."

Geoffrey tut-tutted. "I don't know, Mr Parker. That sounded awfully like a bribe to me. I believe I just may need to report this to my superiors," he advised.

"To your superiors?" Ben asked, his voice starting to shake. "But they could come to the event as well...?" he added for no reason, looking for a rope to climb out of the hole he was digging and ignoring the fact that this was only furthering the suspected bribe. "I'll be serving hot food on the day!"

But Geoffrey's solemn expression gave way to an emerging smile. "Ah, relax, Ben," he said. "I'm just pulling your leg."

"You are?"

"It's something we field operatives like to do to pass the time," Geoffrey revealed. "We all have a good laugh about it back at the office."

"So you're not actually going to report me to your superiors?"

Geoffrey shook his head in the negative. "Nah. I could see

you were just making chit-chat," he said with a chuckle, slapping Ben's arm. "But if you could arrange a sit in the Aston Martin, Ben, I'll bring my young fella along for the day."

"Consider it done," Ben said, his chest rising and falling as normal breathing slowly resumed. "So, ehm..." he added, attempting to steal a glimpse at the all-important clipboard.

"Oh, yes," Geoffrey said, offering the kitchen another once-over. "Yes, all clear," he said matter-of-factly, signing his name on the official-looking document secured under the metallic clip. "In fact, this is one of the cleanest establishments I've visited," he remarked, much to Ben's delight. "There's no sign of vermin infestation that I can see. None at all. So how the droppings ended up there in the first place, I couldn't even say."

"Oh, I could," Ben muttered to himself through gritted teeth, imagining his knuckles making contact with Cecil's jaw. "So, once building control is happy, I'm cleared to reopen?" he asked.

"There are no objections from me," Geoffrey said, ripping off a copy of his report and handing it to Ben. "Just make sure there are no more hazardous chemicals stored inside the building, and you'll be just fine."

"And, hopefully, our paths won't cross again," Ben offered.

Geoffrey's face hardened once more. "There's no need for that sort of talk," he said sternly. "We might be professional agents, but we've got feelings too, you know."

"What? I– that is– I never..." Ben stammered. "Wait. Are you pulling my leg again...?"

"I sure am," Geoffrey confirmed with a playful wink, after which he retrieved his suit jacket from the back of one of the chairs, where he'd left it. "Right-ho, I must get a move on. I'm off to close down a kebab shop. Anyway, I'll see you soon, yeah?"

"You will?" Ben asked, hoping this was the end of the inspection.

"Sure. For a sit in that Aston Martin, remember?"

"Oh, yes. Yes, of course!" a relieved Ben answered, standing in the doorway as his guest departed. "Have fun at the kebab shop!" he added for no apparent reason, waving like he was saying goodbye to an old friend.

With the Guest Entertainment Centre to himself and Geoffrey's signature on the report, Ben pulled up a seat and parked himself down, a wave of relief washing over him. He knew he wasn't home and dry just yet, but he was a step closer. With the builders confident of soon completing their work, Ben felt like he could now see the light at the end of the tunnel.

And then, completely catching himself off guard, a tear fell down Ben's cheek. "Silly bugger," he said, as the droplet landed on Geoffrey's report laid out on the table. It may have been the challenges of the last few weeks catching up with him, Farmer Gerry's words of support earlier, or it may have been simply reading Geoffrey's favourable summary detailed in the document. Probably a combination of all of it. But whatever it was, they definitely weren't tears of sadness he wiped away now. They were tears of optimism. Things were on the up, Ben reckoned, and his run of bad luck was now, hopefully, only visible in the rear-view mirror.

Chapter Sixteen

On first impressions, Sebastian Reeder wouldn't have looked out of place dressed in a fine tweed suit, shotgun in hand, hunting for grouse before quaffing a fine wine and a plate of truffles. Indeed, with his impeccable sense of elegant fashion and upmarket drawl, Sebastian was the epitome of English landed gentry. Fortunate, then, that he owned vast swathes of acreage thanks to his standing as the leading property developer on the Isle of Man, with additional interests in the UK and beyond.

But he was also nobody's fool, with many observers suggesting he could easily sniff out when something was off. A valuable trait, perhaps, in what was a cutthroat industry with vultures, snakes, and hyenas involved at every turn. It was no surprise, then, that old Sebastian demanded an audience with Austin Fletcher when progress on his prestigious Castletown development appeared to be faltering before it'd even begun.

"Excuse me, Mr Reeder," Trudy, his executive PA, said from the doorway. "Your two o'clock appointment, Austin Fletcher, is here to see you. Should I show him in?"

"That smarmy little dullard," Sebastian remarked, rolling his eyes as he laid his pen down on the hardwood surface of his desk.

Trudy offered a discreet smirk, offering no opinion one way or the other. "Would you like me to show him in, Mr Reeder?"

"Yes, please, Trudy. Could I trouble you for—"

"Two coffees," Trudy politely cut in. "Of course. Not a problem, Mr Reeder."

Sebastian eased back in his chair, massaging the tension

away on the bridge of his nose.

"And there he is!" Austin said, appearing a short moment later. "How's the island's most successful property developer?" he asked, showing himself in and promptly helping himself to a chair.

"I'd ask you to take a seat, Austin. But you already appear to have done as much," Sebastian replied. "Anyway..." he said, unable to take his eyes off Austin's garish pink shirt, open at the collar. "Was it a little bit too warm out for a tie?"

Austin chuckled in response, the barbed comment flying right over his head. "I understand from Miles that you're looking for an update on the Castletown situation?" Austin offered, moving the conversation directly to business. And then, without waiting for a reply, he pressed on. "I'm delighted to report that noteworthy progress is being made, Sebastian. And I expect to have the papers for you to sign imminently," he said.

Sebastian narrowed one eye, looking Austin over and considering him carefully. "There's something about you, Austin, which reminds me of myself when I was a young man," he observed.

"That's very kind of you to say, Sebastian."

"Not really, Austin, no. I was a pompous ass who'd say or do anything to get what I wanted. Fortunately, it was a character trait I've since grown out of."

"Coffee for two," Trudy announced, laying a tray down on the desk, the interruption serving to prevent Austin from responding to Sebastian's comment. "Would you like cream, Mr Fletcher?" Trudy asked, receiving a polite nod from Sebastian in response. "And can I get you gentlemen anything else?"

Using the sugar tongs, Sebastian sweetened his coffee, and then took a brief sip. "Thank you, Trudy. That'll be all for now," he said, waiting until she closed the door behind her before continuing his conversation with Austin. "Austin, do you know how many estate agents I currently have fighting to secure my business?" he asked.

Austin pursed his lips, as if he were giving this question

some serious thought, even though he already knew the exact answer on account of having an insider in the form of Miles on his payroll. "I can't say that I do, Sebastian," he answered, trying his best to sound convincing. "Quite a few, I imagine. Which is why I sincerely appreciate every—"

"Don't try and butter my bread, Austin. I've heard it all before," Sebastian told him, tapping his finger down on a pile of documents resting in front of him. "You know what this is?"

Austin tilted his head, attempting to read the page on top, which was difficult because of his upside-down perspective.

"This is a proposal to purchase a parcel of land in Jurby, Austin," Sebastian said, eventually answering his own question. "It wasn't my desire to shift my attention to the north of the island, but with the situation in Castletown..." he added, looking pointedly down the rim of his nose.

"Austin, I'd spoken with the landowner previously," Sebastian continued. "He made it quite clear that his intention was to retain that portion of land as an ongoing campsite. And because of that, I was ready to walk away from the project. But Miles from my sales team insisted to me that you were the man who could make it happen. Absolutely insisted. *'Austin's got the farmer in his back pocket,'* were his exact words, if I recall the conversation correctly."

"And that's still the case. I'm very nearly there!" Austin pleaded, likely imagining his new Sunseeker vessel sailing off over the horizon without him. "Sebastian," he said, smiling awkwardly, "Sebastian, I just need another day or two. I give you my assurances the farmer is ready to sign, as the current situation with the campsite is, quite simply, untenable. You have my word."

"Another day or two?"

"A week, maximum," Austin countered, hoping to buy himself a bit of breathing space, if needed.

"A week and no more, Austin. Otherwise, I'm shelving the Castletown development as well as your agency," Sebastian answered. "Understood?"

"Understood," replied Austin.

With the meeting soon concluded and Austin's coffee never having been touched, he returned to his car, nursing a dinted ego and sporting a generous sweat patch up the back of his gaudy pink shirt. "Stuck-up old fart," Austin muttered, reaching for his mobile and mashing numbers on the screen. "Cecil, it's me," Austin announced once the call connected. "What do you mean, *who's me*, Cecil? Why don't you take a wild guess?" he said, forming his free hand into a fist. "Yes, well done, Cecil," he added, once his identity had been correctly established. "Right, listen up, Cecil. I'm bringing the next stage of the operation forward to this afternoon, yeah?" he said, waiting for a moment to hear the reaction. "What? I don't care if you're getting your back waxed, Cecil! Unfortunately, time is no longer a luxury. So be ready to move when I text you, all right? And Cecil, don't muck this up, or a hairy back will be the least of your troubles."

Austin ended the call with the vein running through his temple now throbbing. He drummed his fingers against the top of his steering wheel, formulating the next phase of his master plan, a plan which was, thanks to Sebastian, moving forward with a little more urgency than expected. "Right. You've *got* this, Austin," he said, talking to himself. "Who's number one?" he asked, continuing on with his little motivational pep talk. "*You're* number one," he answered, flashing a smile into the rear-view mirror. With that sorted, he returned his attention to his phone, this time typing a message.

> Austin: Hey, neighbour! How's it all going over at the dream factory? Anyway good news, buddy. I've got the rest of your cash, so you can get the builders paid 😊

Austin hit the send button, which, to his delight, resulted in a series of ellipses indicating that Ben was already typing a response.

Ben: Amazing news, Austin! Builders finishing up today 😊 I'm at the campsite all day if you want to swing by. The kettle will be on, and there's a Danish pastry with your name on it. See you soon, and thank you so much!

Austin: Can you pop by my office instead? I'm back-to-back this afternoon. Bring pastry, though. Sounds lovely.

Ben: You got it, buddy 😊

After his meet-up at Austin's office, Ben happily made his way back to his campsite HQ, glancing periodically as he went along to the small rucksack resting on the passenger seat, offering it one adoring smile after another. Indeed, any casual observer would be forgiven for thinking he was a new father ferrying precious cargo home from the maternity ward as opposed to simply heading back to work. But, for Ben, the contents of that bag truly were a miracle and wouldn't have been made more welcome if a giant stork had delivered them in person. Because there, snoozing quietly inside that bag were eight thousand smackers that, for Ben, secured his immediate future.

Thanks to Austin's timely intervention, the cash injection meant he now had the money to settle the remaining invoice with the builders and pay Farmer Gerry the outstanding rent he owed. And, if his calculator had been working as it should, he reckoned there should be just enough left over to buy a marquee, offering an additional outdoor venue that would hopefully make its debut at the car show.

Ben sang merrily along to the radio that wasn't even turned on, taking a mental note to phone building control when he returned to the office. True to their word, the contractors he'd hired were on schedule to complete the works within the agreed timescale, correcting the horrid mess Cecil had left behind. As such, Ben hoped the building control inspectors would sign off the job in time for the weekend, meaning he'd finally be able to reopen the communal buildings. He'd also make arrangements to drop off a large box of chocolates to the staff at the swimming pool for kindly allowing his guests to make use of their shower facilities, he reckoned.

"The sun has got his hat on," Ben sang happily to himself, navigating the narrow Manx country roads. *"Hip-hip-hip hooray,"* he continued, taking an appreciative glance at the glorious rural landscape passing by through the window. Yes, life for Ben was pretty bloody marvellous at the moment, and nothing, not even the cyclist up ahead, delaying his progress on the narrow lane, would hamper his joyous mood.

"Come on, then," Ben said with a chuckle, slowing to match the cyclist's dawdling effort. He was no Bradley Wiggins himself, but the lady weaving on the road was moving so slowly that she was in danger of losing her balance. Ben virtually drew to a halt as a precaution, not wishing to pressure her, as she appeared to be having enough trouble on her own.

And it appeared gravity itself had seen enough of this spectacle, as the amply padded woman wobbled precariously before then tipping over, falling from her trusty metal-framed steed and crumpling to a heap beside the grassy verge.

"Bloody Nora!" Ben exclaimed, bringing his car to a quick halt and pulling up on the handbrake. Ben exited the car without delay, hurrying to the boot to fetch his emergency first aid kit that was always kept there for just such an instance. "Don't move!" he called out, slipping his arms inside his high-vis vest, designed for situations precisely like this.

Ben checked that the road was clear of traffic and then shot over, dropping to one knee so he could attend to his patient. "Hello. I'm with you," he said, trying to sound as calm and reassuring as possible. "Can you hear me, madam? Are you hurt?"

The woman lying on her back slowly opened one eye, appearing dazed. "I'm— I'm fine, I think...?" she replied, despite looking the exact opposite. "That's the benefit of having a bit of stuffing around the middle," she managed to say, joking despite the circumstance. But her subsequent laugh was followed immediately by a noticeable wince of pain.

"Do you know what day it is?" Ben asked, continuing his role as paramedic, which he'd assumed quite effectively. "Can you tell me your name?" he added, enunciating each word and syllable to be clearly understood.

"What? Do I look like a calendar?" the supine lady asked with another laugh, and then a grimace. "And the name's Fenella."

"No, Fenella. I was just making sure you hadn't suffered a brain injury," Ben explained, rapidly exhausting the limited extent of his first aid training. "Should I phone an ambulance?"

"Is anything broken?" Fenella asked.

Ben screwed up his face, almost afraid to look. "Well," he said, after a brief inspection, "the spokes on your front wheel look to be buckled, and I'm certain your bell is beyond repair."

"No, with me, you soppy sod," Fenella admonished him. "Does anything look broken on *me*?"

"Oh," Ben said, running his eyes up and down her like he knew what he was looking for. "No, I don't think so, Fenella. Would you like me to help you up?"

With Fenella's permission, Ben hooked a hand under her arm. "Ready?" he asked, before attempting to help the dear to her feet. Well, that had been the plan, at least. Because Fenella, being as kind as possible, could best be described as something of a unit. "You're going to have to work with me," Ben suggested under strain. "I can't do this on my own."

Fortunately, Fenella took up the challenge, and before too long, she was sitting on the grass bank, picking blades of grass from her hair. "Thank you," she said, looking up to her saviour.

"Can I give you a lift anywhere?" Ben asked, uncomfortable at the idea of leaving her unattended. "It's not a problem," he assured her.

"You're fine, but thank you," Fenella answered. "I only live over there," she advised, pointing to a spot somewhere in the distance. "I'm sure I can walk the rest of the way. And if I have too much trouble, I'll just phone the husband to come gather me up."

"Well, only if you're sure, Fenella," Ben offered. "And assuming you are sure, and you're certain there's no other way I can possibly help you, I suppose I'll be on my way...?"

Ben moved the bike completely off the road, resting it close to its owner. Then, he walked back over to his vehicle, returning his first aid supplies to the boot. "See you, Fenella," Ben called over as he climbed back into his car. Ben waved, put the car in gear, and then eased slowly away from the accident scene, taking great care not to clip either the bike or his patient as he pulled away from where he'd parked. He glanced in the rear-view mirror to make sure all was well, and then gradually got himself back up to speed, continuing his journey, albeit a journey delayed and slightly behind schedule by this point.

Fenella offered a grateful wave as she watched Ben's car set off and disappear through the tree-lined road, happy to still be in one piece even if the same couldn't be said for her bicycle. She inspected her knees, uncertain if she'd picked up a graze during her tumble.

"Oh, Fenella!" a cheerful voice called out from the other side of the road. "That was a performance worthy of an Oscar!" the voice's owner suggested, with him now appearing into view from behind the hedgerow that had just been concealing him.

Fenella shot him a look, pointing to her stricken bike. "You owe me a new bell, Cecil. And the front wheel looks like it's knackered."

"Oh, Fenella. Honestly, that couldn't have gone any better if we'd tried," Cecil said, skipping across the road and turning his attention to the bike, as instructed, but then with little apparent regard for his stricken wife.

Fenella helped herself up, as her husband showed no signs of doing so. "Well..." she said, dusting herself down. "Did you manage to swap the bags around?"

"Yes!" Cecil confirmed. "While you were playing the dying swan, I snuck into his car like a cat burglar," he announced, holding up the bag in question, held tightly in his grubby mitt. "Oh, Fenella. Now I know why I married you," he said, clutching the bag tenderly against his chest.

"It's a shame, because he appeared to be a nice guy. Even offering me a lift," Fenella remarked. "I actually feel quite bad, now I think about it."

"Yes, yes. He's one of a kind," Cecil replied dismissively. He then unzipped the bag and presented its contents for his wife's inspection. "Do you feel so bad now?" he asked with a cackle.

"I think I'm slowly getting over it, Cecil, now you come to mention it," Fenella answered with a laugh. "So, does this mean we can book the flights to Spain?"

"We sure can, my little lemon drop," Cecil confirmed, reaching for his phone and dialling a number. "In fact, book us those posh seats up the front of the plane," he added, before pressing the phone to his ear. "Yes, hello," Cecil said once the call connected. "This is Agent C," he added tersely, offering his wife a playful wink as he spoke. "I can verify the operation has been a success, with the bag currently held in my possession," he advised, before ending the call.

Fenella moved in close to Cecil. "Oh, I do love it when you talk like a spy," she said, scooping him into her ample bosom. "Give us a kiss, my tubby little James Bond."

Chapter Seventeen

N o, I completely understand where you're coming from," Cynthia advised over the phone, secretly chewing her lower lip in frustration. Indeed, it was fortunate it wasn't a video call, as she might well offend with the expletives she was presently mouthing as well. "And I certainly appreciate the call, Calvin, but I can assure you that nothing is untoward. The large cash withdrawals were simply to settle several invoices relating to building renovations we're currently working on. However, if you need anything else, you only need to ask, okay? Great, well, it was lovely to speak and let's meet up for that coffee soon."

Cynthia placed the phone back on its cradle, seething.

"Everything okay, Cynthia?" her colleague Carol enquired, setting down her coffee, and having been earwigging to Cynthia's half of her phone conversation in its entirety.

Cynthia continued gnawing on her lip, looking straight through Carol in the direction of Austin's office behind her.

"Cynthia?" Carol pressed, eager to restock her office gossip locker, it would appear. "That sounded like it was..." she started to say, but Cynthia was off before she could finish with her observation.

"Fake-tan-wearing, teeth-bleached, odious little twerp," Cynthia muttered, stomping the length of the office.

"Heads-up. Incoming," Barry whispered to Ricky nearby, noting a seething Cynthia approaching at speed. "This should be good," he added, rotating his chair for maximum view of the unfolding drama.

"That's bloody it, Austin!" Cynthia shouted, throwing open

Austin's office door. "I'm finished with all your bullshit and out of here for good!" she said, shooting him an icy glare.

"Uhm... I need to go, baby cakes," Austin said softly into his mobile phone. "Yes, something's just cropped up," he said, removing his feet from his desk and ending his call. He crossed his arms casually across his chest, offering Cynthia a sickeningly sweet smile. "What's up?" he asked nonchalantly, as if Cynthia's ire was not at all apparent.

"What's up?" Cynthia replied, unable to hide her contempt. "I'll tell you *what's up*, Austin. I've just finished talking to Calvin, our relationship manager from the bank."

"Oh? How is that old devil? Did he get those football tickets I sent him?"

"It didn't come up in conversation, Austin," Cynthia responded, narrowing her eyes. "You see, he was too busy quizzing me about the various large cash withdrawals you've taken from the business bank account over the last few weeks."

"Ah," said Austin.

"*Ah?* Is that all you've got to say on the subject?" Cynthia fumed. "Austin, he didn't come straight out and say it, but I could tell from Calvin's tone that he thinks we're up to something dodgy. And, as a result, I've just told him a complete pack of lies because I didn't have the faintest idea as to why you've withdrawn all of that cash." Cynthia moved closer, directing a stiffened finger in his direction. "Austin, I'm a director of this company, and I'm lying to the *bank manager* on your behalf! It's not on. It's bloody *not on*."

"Cynthia, I can see that you're—"

"Do you have a drug habit?"

"What?"

"Or a gambling addiction?" Cynthia went on, running through imagined possibilities. "Because I'm sincerely hoping it's something like that, rather than bribery and corruption."

The corner of Austin's lip curled, giving the impression he was about to start laughing. However, the steam presently coming out of Cynthia's ears may have convinced him this wasn't his smartest move. "Cynthia, what on earth are you talking about?"

"*You*," Cynthia shot back. "You're up to something, Austin, and don't deny it. You've been so very happy lately, which usually means you're up to no good. First, you make several large cash withdrawals, and next, you're having secretive meetings with Miles Frampton. Miles, who just so happens to be involved with this Castletown development you're so desperate to secure. This smacks of bribery and corruption to me."

Austin's expression hardened. "Miles Frampton?" he said, leaning forward and resting his elbows on his desk.

"You're going to deny it?"

Austin reached for his pen, twirling it between his fingers like a majorette. He didn't immediately reply, instead staring intently at the spinning pen. "You know..." he said a few long moments later. "You're absolutely spot on, Cynthia."

"I am? About which bit, exactly? Drugs or gambling?"

"Bribery and corruption," Austin admitted, along with a sinister grin, the only thing missing being an impressive crack of thunder. "It's a fair cop, Cynthia. You've got me bang to rights."

Cynthia's jaw fell slowly open, his frank admission catching her completely off guard. "You mean it's true? Oh, this is a nightmare," she said. "Why couldn't it have been a drug habit?" she moaned, running a hand through her hair and taking several deep breaths in an effort to compose herself. "So, you're bribing Miles to help you obtain the contract for the new development?"

"Yep," Austin readily agreed. "That's exactly what I'm doing."

"Right, and who's Cecil the Chubster?"

Austin set down his pen and began clapping, his smile now re-emerging. "Oh, Cynthia, bravo," he said. "And how on earth did you find out about—"

"I went through your desk," Cynthia revealed, unconcerned by the ramifications of this disclosure. "So, what's this Cecil person got to do with this mess?"

"Cecil the Chubster, as I like to call him, is helping me convince the landowner that there's no other option but to sell that portion of his property."

"By running the campsite into the ground?" Cynthia offered, the lightbulb shining brightly above her head.

"Bingo!"

"Austin, you're a devious, conniving, two-faced little wretch who—"

"Okay, enough with the sweet-talking, Cynthia," Austin cut in. "And don't make out like you're pure as the driven snow, either, yeah? I know you'd do nearly anything to seal a deal if the commission was large enough. So, that leaves us in something of a predicament about your future at this company."

"There's *no* predicament, Austin. I'm out of this bloody cesspit and resigning as a director."

"You could do that, or..."

"Or?"

Austin climbed up from his seat, wandering around the desk and casually perching himself on the front corner. "Cynthia," he said, cosying up to her like the sleazy salesman that he was. "Cynthia, once this deal goes through, I'm opening an additional office to handle the increased business, and I want you to run it for me."

"You've got to be kidding me, right? Austin, you'll be in a prison cell before that happens."

Austin shook his head, brimming with confidence. "That won't happen, Cynthia. I've covered my tracks, which means we'll come out of this smelling of roses. And just imagine it, Cynthia. You'll be heading up the new business on double your current salary."

"Double my current salary?" Cynthia repeated back.

"At least. And that's not including an annual bonus."

"And there's no way anything illegal can be traced back to us?"

Austin feigned shock at the suggestion. "Cynthia, how long have you known me? Of *course* they can't trace anything back to us," he told her. "So," he continued, extending his hand. "So what do you say? Can I call you partner?"

Cynthia uncurled her fingers from the fist she'd just made. "No more scurrying around like a rodent," she insisted, eyeing him with suspicion. "You keep me in the loop on everything, all right?"

"I promise," Austin promised.

"In that case," Cynthia replied, accepting his handshake with a wink, "I'd better get some business cards printed with my new job title."

There was a particular character trait predominantly shared by the male of the species, although not exclusively, of course. It was one that Ruby observed in her father from time to time and one that raised a smile each instance. And that particular hallmark was what she jokingly referred to as 'Builder Bromance' — the act of shadowing tradesmen, watching them like a hawk while they toiled and generally giving the impression that your tradesman abilities were on a par with theirs. Which, of course, in Ben's case, couldn't be further from the truth, as the half-built brick BBQ languishing in their garden at home would attest to.

But Ben's builders at the campsite were accustomed to this sort of attention, if their personable nature was anything to go by. Not only that, they'd embraced Ben peering over their shoulder at every chance, and utilised his enthusiasm as their unofficial labourer. As such, they'd allowed Ben to hammer this or fix that, offering some pearls of building wisdom to him in the process. It was an arrangement Ben was delighted to go along with, even proudly commenting to Ruby that he'd developed a callus on his right palm because of the considerable effort he was putting in.

For this reason, Ben was glum to finally bid farewell to his fellow tradesmen, although of course delighted to see the fruits of their collective labour. The boys had completed the work slightly ahead of schedule and had absolutely no concerns that building control would sign off their works without much delay, and as they assured Ben, they were only a phone call away if anything else did crop up.

And so, all that remained was a final inspection of the completed job to ensure Ben was delighted...

Ben ran a hand over a plastered wall the lads had patched up in the toilet block. "Yes, that's some excellent workmanship," Ben suggested, as if he were quite the authority on such matters. Then, to fully satisfy himself, he rapped a knuckle on some exposed pipework for reasons known only to himself. But whatever the resulting sound that was produced meant, Ben appeared pleased with the results. "Very good," Ben added, and then repeated these words periodically, pointing at this and prodding at that as he continued along with his inspection. "Ah," he said, once outside, coming to a halt in front of a recently laid retaining wall. "Do you remember how efficiently I carried these bricks for you?" Ben asked nostalgically, holding out his palm with swollen callus visible. "I put a shift in that day," he recalled, pointing to his irritated hand.

"Yes, you absolutely did," George the builder said with a smile. "Good times, Ben. And as I said then, if the camping gig comes to an end, we're always looking for another labourer. Aren't we, Ted?"

"Indeed," Ted agreed, and it was a sentiment delivered with complete sincerity.

Ben looked to them each in turn. "Aww, thanks, guys," he said, slightly embarrassed, yet bursting with pride. He gazed off into the distance for a moment, dreaming of himself as a builder. "Anyway," he added, once his giddy shiver subsided. "Now you're all finished, how about we get you paid up and squared away?"

"Wow," Ted remarked, turning to face his buddy. "We're often chasing the customer for payment after a job, so this makes for a pleasant change."

"And I just may have whipped up a few of those chocolate mud cupcakes the pair of you like so much," Ben revealed.

George rubbed his hands at the promise of this, following Ben towards the Guest Entertainment Centre. "Oh, yes! I'm actually tempted to damage something else, Ben, just so you'll need to keep us on for another few weeks," he joked.

"I reckon I've put on half a stone eating your cakes this past week," Ted confessed, patting his protruding belly and leaving a few dusty handprints on his t-shirt in the process. "And I don't regret a single calorie," he asserted.

Once inside, the two builders tucked into their cupcakes, washing them down with a nice cuppa that Ben graciously provided. "If I don't pay you now, lads, the money will only disappear on something else," Ben remarked, moving over and unlocking the drawer where he'd secured Austin's bag of cash earlier.

"You take your time. No rush," Ted suggested, reaching for another of the chocolate cupcakes. "We're perfectly fine as we are."

Ben offered a raised thumb, before laying down the navy-blue rucksack on his side of the reception desk. "There's more as well, and what you don't eat, you can take with you!" Ben called over, easing open the zip.

"Oh, I doubt there'll be anything left behind," Ted replied with a chuckle, dusting away a crumb from his lap. "Any chance of the recipe, so me or the wife can try making these at home?" he added, looking towards the reception desk. "Ben…?" he said a moment later, when no response was offered. "Earth to Ben?"

Noting the concern in his mate's voice, George looked over the rim of his cup, following Ted's eyeline. "Ehm, Ben?" he said, flashing a worried glance at Ted, and then back to their host. "Ben, are you feeling okay?" George asked, observing Ben's sudden anaemic complexion. "Ben?" he repeated, his tone more urgent this time.

Again, with no response offered, the two builders got up and approached the reception desk. "You've not had a seizure, have you, old boy?" Ted gently enquired, but then peered over the desk as it became obvious that there was something that had captured Ben's attention, and thus the explanation for Ben behaving strangely. There, behind the desk, Ted could see the opened rucksack stuffed with what appeared to be rumpled stacks of periodicals of one sort or another.

"Here, now's not really the best time to flick through your dirty magazines," George joked, hoping to snap Ben from his glassy-eyed stupor. But Ben didn't flinch, his attention unwavering.

"Ben!" Ted shouted, slapping a hand down on the countertop.

"What– who– yes– how can I help...?" Ben replied instinctively, appearing as if he'd just woken from a nap.

George looked Ben up and down. "You sure you're okay, Ben?" he asked. "Your hands are shaking."

Ben laughed an uneasy laugh, zipping up the rucksack. "Me? Oh, I'm fine," he assured them, even though it was fairly obvious he wasn't. "Isn't it lovely weather for the time of year," he added, eye twitching. "Anyway," he went on, shifting the conversation back to the matter at hand, as there didn't seem to be any way to entirely avoid it. "I know I invited you in to settle things up, but there's been a bit of a glitch in that particular department."

"Okay," George said, and then, "Look, don't stress about it, Ben, yeah? It's not like we've even given you the final invoice yet."

"Yeah, it's fine, Ben, we know you're good for it," Ted chimed in. "And if you're not, we know where you work," he added with a grin, hoping to put Ben at ease. "So long as you're okay...?"

Ben smiled like a man crippled with a nasty bout of wind. "I'm absolutely tip-top," Ben assured them both, raising a spirited thumb in the air to highlight just how marvellous he was. "In fact, I couldn't be better," he added, along with a drawn-out sigh.

"Right-ho, then," George said, although sounding unconvinced and still a bit worried. "In that case, we'll pack up our tools."

"Don't forget to dig out the recipe for those cupcakes before we go," a hopeful Ted added, running a tongue over his top lip.

Following a further series of waffling observations on Ben's part, he bid his fellow tradesman a fond farewell, waving from the doorway for longer than was reasonably comfortable. Then, the moment they disappeared from view, Ben sprinted back over to the reception desk again, clutching the rucksack so tightly in his hands that his knuckles turned whiter than his cheeks. "Please," he said, offering a prayer to whatever higher power might listen, hoping against hope that what he had seen earlier was not actually what he had seen, or that perhaps if he wished hard enough he could transform it into the money that was supposed to be there. Gently, he teased open the zip, holding his breath, eyes dry from being unable to blink.

But, sadly, the contents hadn't changed.

Ben staggered back, until his progress was impeded by the wall. He slid slowly down the vertical surface, legs buckling, until his bottom eventually settled to the floor.

"I don't believe this," he whispered, placing a hand against his forehead. "What's going on?" he asked. *"Where's the money?"*

Chapter Eighteen

Ben glanced down to the visible tan lines on his wrist, a white patch where the area of his watchstrap used to be, wondering how things had ended up at such an all-time low in what'd been a fairly miserable chapter in his life. He'd not slept a wink the previous evening, and neither had a single piece of food or drop of drink passed his lips since yesterday afternoon.

Even though he knew it was very likely a fruitless exercise, he'd retraced his steps from the previous day in his mind, hoping something might miraculously present itself and explain how he'd somehow ended up with a rucksack full of old magazines rather than Austin's cash. But there was nothing. How he'd left Austin's office, then, with a bag of money and ended up with what he had now was nothing short of a mystery.

He'd replayed the scenario in his head, more times than he could count, but unfortunately the outcome always remained the same — he was up shit creek without a paddle. There was the outstanding invoice for the building work that was due imminently, the arrears to Farmer Gerry were growing by the week, and as if that weren't bad enough in itself, Ben would eventually need to repay Austin for the loan of the thousands of pounds he'd borrowed. Thousands of pounds Ben had *never even had an opportunity to make use of*, as it had inexplicably gone missing and, just as mysteriously, been replaced by worthless paper. Naturally, he wanted to phone Austin to see if he might have any possible answers. But losing his money on the same day he'd handed it over wasn't a positive impression to present your new business partner.

But what cut Ben up the most was that he didn't feel able to share his worries with the one person that mattered most to him: Ruby. She knew instantly that something was off, simply by his general demeanour. But every time she asked, Ben had gently dismissed her concerns, insisting that things were finally on the up. Of course, he didn't like lying to his daughter, but the last thing he wanted to do was lay his business troubles on her young shoulders.

And so, following a visit to the bank and a whistlestop tour of the island's cash machines, Ben had already emptied his paltry savings account and maxed out his various credit cards through cash advances, and, in addition to that, he was currently standing in the absolute last place he wanted to be.

"I'd expected to get a little more, if I'm honest," Ben said to the emotionless face staring back at him from behind the glass countertop. "You know, what with it being a TAG Heuer and in excellent condition...?" Ben added, hopeful this would in some way improve things.

"Take it or leave it," the surly owner of the pawnshop said in reply, nudging Ben's watch back towards him. "Makes no difference to me," he added with an indifferent sniff, giving the impression he had somewhere else to be, or that there was little actual demand for fine, precision Swiss watches.

"And you say you'll give me thirty days to repay the loan and take it back?" Ben asked, seeking confirmation of the details he'd just been provided a moment or two ago.

"Sure, if you pay the full amount and the interest, yeah. It'll be all yours again."

Ben reached for his watch, hand wavering, uncertain if he should go through with the transaction. Eventually, he pushed it towards the pawnshop owner again. "Okay," he said, the pain dripping from his words. "And you can give me the money today?"

"I'll count the cash out for you now," the man advised.

"All right," said Ben, turning his back as the fellow proceeded, with Ben unwilling or unable to witness his prized watch heading towards an unremarkable-looking steel cabinet where the hopes and dreams of others in a similar situation to his own likely went to slowly die.

With the matter soon concluded, Ben made his exit, carrying a pocketful of notes and an unshakable feeling of shame. Unfortunately, the amount of cash he'd managed to gather today was nowhere near enough to resolve all of his debts, but it was enough to make a good dent in the arrears he'd amassed with Farmer Gerry, along with a few other things, which was a start.

Ben was, at present, spinning plates, financially speaking. Of course he wanted to settle all of his bills, but that simply wasn't possible, not with Austin's cash injection having vanished from the face of the earth. And to have any chance of paying the builders what he owed them and repay Austin when the time arrived, Ben had to have a viable business bringing in much-needed income. Ben's logical choice was to first pay Farmer Gerry what he could, for the simple reason that if there was no operational business, then the inevitable outcome was that *nobody* would get paid. At least this way, Ben reckoned, he'd still have a fighting chance of keeping his head above water even if the waves were somewhat perilous.

Moreover, the campsite was shortly due to host the Aston Martin Appreciation Society, which would, hopefully, be the first of many such events bringing in an extra stream of income. Indeed, desperate to make a memorable first impression, Ben had ordered a new catering marquee and was not cutting any corners in the kitchen supplies he was picking up for the event. With the event organisers expecting anywhere between fifty to a hundred people in attendance, Ben could turn a tidy profit if he played his cards right. And while he was acutely aware money was tight to non-existent, he felt confident that by going the extra mile, the word would soon spread around this little island he called home and the phone would soon be ringing off the hook. And fortunately, Ben was on the receiving end of some good news on his drive back from the supermarket...

"You mean you're happy with the building work?" Ben asked, speaking hands-free as he pulled into the Life's a Pitch carpark. "You've signed everything off, and I can fully re-open?"

"You're now free to do as you like, Mr Parker," the cheery voice over the phone replied. "The inspectors were completely satisfied with the remedial work and will confirm in writing over the next seven to ten working days."

"Seven to ten days?" Ben shrieked. "But that's—"

"Don't panic, Mr Parker," the woman cut in, sensing the stress in his shrill voice. "That's the very reason for the phone call," she explained. "We know how urgent it was for your business to start operating again, so I thought you'd appreciate a phone call in advance of receiving the letter."

"So I can re-open the communal buildings now?"

"Absolutely, Mr Parker."

Ben pulled into a parking spot, slapping the steering wheel in delight. "I can't thank you enough!" Ben told her. "And if you ever fancy a night sleeping under the stars, just give me a call."

The woman laughed a friendly laugh. "You're lucky I know you operate a campsite, Mr Parker," she advised. "Otherwise, a girl might take that offer of yours the wrong way."

Ben blushed, deciding to nip any further conversation in the bud before talking himself into trouble as he so often did. "I sincerely appreciate the call," he said simply.

Ben released a contented sigh. It was a pleasure to receive some positive news for a change after being kicked in every direction for the past few weeks. And it was just in the nick of time, too. The car club was scheduled to arrive the following morning after eight a.m. to set up ahead of an eleven o'clock start. And what better way to begin the day for those early arrivals than one of Ben's legendary breakfast baps on his own freshly baked bread? Then, at the event's conclusion, around five p.m., it was into the Guest Entertainment Centre for his selection of delectable homemade pies served with mash and onion gravy.

The only challenge for Ben at this stage was how many portions to cater for. But with the organisers not providing re-freshments as part of the entry price, it was up to Ben to serve up something so delicious that those in attendance couldn't possibly refuse his delightful offerings. He had no concerns about the breakfast menu, because after all who doesn't adore a bacon or sausage bap to start off the day. However, his choice for the evening meal was a calculated gamble on Ben's part. Everyone could simply choose to clear off as soon as the show concluded, so it was up to him to put in the hard yards and convince them otherwise. He knew he'd be burning the midnight oil to have everything prepared on time, but it was a burden he was more than happy to assume. Especially as a busy day could make significant inroads into the money he owed.

Later that afternoon, Ben offered a passable impression of Casper the Friendly Ghost due to him being covered head to foot in flour. Indeed, the casual observer might conclude that there'd been an explosion in the kitchen, with dishes strewn everywhere as well and not an inch of available workspace un-used. But the casual observer would be wrong, because this was a master baker plying his trade — organised chaos, if you will — pulling out one tray of delicious goods from the oven after another.

To Ben's immense delight, he wasn't alone in his Guest En-tertainment Centre, either, as he was now officially permitted to welcome campers inside for the first time in what felt like ages. Soon enough, a steady stream of guests were making full use of the facility, chatting merrily away, with many of them intrigued by Ben's current endeavours and likely drawn in by the variety of enticing aromas. For a time, he'd even attracted a couple of sous chefs in the form of Billy, aged eight, and Billy's sister Abigail, aged four. But what the pair lacked in experience, they more than made up for in enthusiasm, and before too long they were as caked in flour as their teacher, meaning Ben could tick off a few more items on his considerable 'to-do' list.

"Right. That's us all set up, Ben," Nigel from the marquee company announced through the opened window.

"Wonderful," Ben said, sliding another tray of lovely pies into the oven. "How does it look?" he asked as he stood up, clapping his hands and releasing a cloud of flour.

"I'll give you a guided tour?" Nigel suggested. "And, crucially, I'll show you how to take it back down again," he added.

Ben couldn't remove his apron fast enough. "Lead on, my good man, lead on."

Once outside, Ben's eyes were immediately drawn to the new structure, standing there tall and proud in the spare field. "Good lord, it looks bloody massive," Ben remarked, wiping his hands on his chef's trousers.

"Six metres by twelve," Nigel remarked, nodding proudly. "You could have a tennis court in there," he added, for no special reason.

As they approached the marquee, Ben's eyes widened even more than they'd been already. "Oh my, Nigel," he said, stepping in close and placing a loving hand on the sturdy canvas wall. "Yes, I can *easily* cater for a hundred people in there," he said, peering through one of the plastic windows. Ben strolled around his new wonder, his mind racing with the structure's business possibilities. "I could host weddings," he suggested. "Oh, and christenings."

"The world's your oyster with this bad boy," Nigel advised. "So, I can either talk you through how to take it down just now, or..."

"Or?"

"Or, I could pop along to the car show tomorrow, have a slice of that delicious-smelling steak and kidney pie afterwards, and then take her down with a hands-on tutorial."

Ben ran his eyes over the mammoth structure, contemplating the two options proposed. "Well, on the basis that I struggled with a small tent in my garden, I reckon the hands-on approach tomorrow would be greatly appreciated, Nigel," he decided, whilst removing the vibrating phone from his trouser pocket as he spoke. "Ah. That's the timer I'd set for my current batch of bread rolls. Let's head back, and I'll get you paid for this magnificent beast."

With the bread rolls soon evacuated from the oven in the nick of time, Ben headed behind his reception desk to square things up with Nigel. "I presume cash is okay?" he asked, taking the invoice handed over to him.

"Cash, cheque, or transfer," Nigel replied with a friendly smile. "Sadly, no matter the method of payment, it all gets spent just as quickly as it arrives," he said with a laugh.

"Cash it is, then," Ben answered, unlocking the drawer where his money was securely nestled. Then, with one eye still fixed on the invoice, Ben's shoulders began to drop. "Is this, ehm... correct?" he asked, now giving the document his complete attention.

"I think so," Nigel said, taking a step closer. "Does something not look right?"

"It's just that..." Ben started to say, until the answer became obvious. Because there, written near the bottom of the page, was the amount they'd agreed on, sure enough, but Ben had completely forgotten to factor in the VAT, which inflated the final total. "Oh, never mind. My mistake," Ben added, forcing a smile but crying on the inside. Ben counted out the banknotes, realising that his stupid error now meant he had even less cash to pay Farmer Gerry than he'd planned.

"You're sure everything's okay?" Nigel enquired. "Only you look a bit green around the gills," he observed.

Ben handed over the cash, cursing himself for his stupidity. "No, no. I'm fine," he replied, lying. "It's probably being covered in flour that's making me look a bit pale," he offered.

"Well, much obliged," Nigel said, tucking the collection of notes into his pocket. "And I'll pop by tomorrow near the close of your event, and then I'll show you how to take the old girl back down after everyone's left."

With Nigel on his way, Ben returned his attention to the invoice. "You bloody idiot," he admonished himself, shaking his head and thoroughly frustrated. Fortunately, he still had some cash remaining for Farmer Gerry, but the amount was seriously depleted owing to his oversight. "Oh, Ben. You absolute plonker," he added, lowering his head until his cheek was resting on the desk's surface like naptime at nursery school. And there he remained for the next few minutes, chuntering away and generally giving himself a right royal bollocking.

"Ben!" one of his campers suddenly called out. "Ben!" she said again.

"Yes? What? How can I help?" a startled Ben replied, lifting his cheek from where it'd been resting and positioning himself upright.

"I thought I smelled something burning! Is that– is that smoke coming from your oven...?"

Ben was making considerable progress with his preparations despite the unfortunate loss of several slightly charred steak & kidney pies, pies that he was happy to save for his own dinner at home but were in no way presentable enough for the upcoming event. However, it was only a minor setback, and he was soon happily back on schedule, thanks in large part to the arrival of his glamorous assistant Ruby, who was helpful enough to attend to other matters while Ben continued to man the kitchen.

Ruby was tasked with dressing the new marquee ahead of the car show, placing out tables and chairs, stocking their chiller cabinet with an array of drinks, and ensuring everything was just so for their motoring enthusiasts. Her efforts were very much appreciated, and after a herculean final push on his part as well, Ben was finally able to turn his new oven off before the sun had completely escaped from the sky.

"Cheers, Ruby," Ben said, slumped in a chair with a cold beer in his hand, his aching feet resting on the coffee table. "Is that you all finished in the marquee?"

Ruby raised her own drink — a ginger ale, in her case — toasting their collective efforts. "Sure is, Pops. And I've got to say, that tent is flippin' impressive."

"Isn't it. And just think... think about... about all the events we can..." Ben attempted to say, eyelids heavy and drooping.

"Dad?" Ruby asked.

"What? Oh. Yes, I'd love one, thanks," Ben replied, unsure what he'd just asked for.

"You just fell asleep. *Mid-sentence*," Ruby informed him with a grin. "I think we can take that as a sign you've been working too hard, yeah?"

"Nothing that an early night won't sort out," Ben suggested, along with a stretchy yawn. "Shall we head home?"

But before Ruby could offer a response, Ben's phone started to ring. "Well, at least, we'll head home once I take this call, that is," Ben added, looking at the phone's display. Then, shooting a concerned glance up at Ruby, "It's the chairman of the Aston Martin Appreciation Society," he advised gravely.

"And that's a problem?" Ruby asked, confused by her father's reaction.

"What if he's phoning to cancel? Why else would he be calling me this late, the very evening before the event?" Ben replied, clutching the phone to his chest as it continued to ring. "Oh god, Ruby, what if he—"

"Just answer the phone, Dad!"

"Hi, this is Ben," Ben offered weakly, sitting upright after doing as Ruby commanded. "No, it's fine," Ben offered through clenched teeth. "You're not disturbing me, no. So, what can I do for you?"

Ruby watched on, reading every line on her dad's face, searching for any clue as to what was being said, be it good, bad, or indifferent. But despite her best efforts, she soon realised that she was fairly rubbish at guessing. "Well?" she asked, after the call had concluded. "What were they phoning for? It wasn't unwelcome news, was it? It didn't sound like bad news, I don't think...?"

"It's fine," said Ben, running a relieved hand through his flour-encrusted hair and relaxing his jaw. "He was just calling to let me know, for catering purposes, that we could expect several vegetarians to be attending," Ben explained. "And..." he added, the corners of his mouth twitching.

"And?"

"And that they've sold another thirty tickets!" he advised, unable to contain his cheesy grin. "I'll need to whip up another few pies. Hmm, what kind to make for the vegetarians...? Potato, leek, and cheese? Vegetable curry?"

"Dad, you're absolutely shattered as it is!"

"I know, but just think of the extra money if they all sell!" Ben pointed out. "We need to make hay while the sun shines, as they say," Ben added, even though the sun outside was starting to go down, actually. Ben began patting his trousers, looking like he was searching for something.

"Fine," Ruby said. "But I insist on helping out, okay?"

"I wouldn't have it any other way, Ruby," Ben answered, rising from his seat and reaching for his nearby apron. "Oh, this is terrific news," he said, slipping the apron loop over his head. "Here, do me a quick favour, Ruby? I can't seem to find my notebook. Will you see if it's in my jacket, there over the back of your chair? I want to jot down what I'll need to prepare for the additional guests."

Ben skipped over to the kitchen, whistling a merry tune. For many, the thought of resuming work after a gruelling shift had already come and gone was the last idea they'd ever wish to entertain. But for Ben, every extra pie he baked was the opportunity to drum up some extra cash, plus make people happy at the same time. "Did you have any joy?" Ben asked, digging out his rolling pin. "Ruby...?" he asked, glancing over his shoulder.

Ruby didn't respond, but came and placed the notebook she'd retrieved down onto the worktop beside him.

"Thank you, my assistant chef," Ben offered, continuing on with the whistling of his cheery tune. "Would you mind passing me over a bag of flour?" he asked. But when Ruby made no move, one way or the other, he started to turn in her direction. "What's up? Are you just observing for now?" he asked.

But Ben's jolly demeanour collapsed as soon as he got a good look at his daughter. "Ruby?" he said, in response to the tears flowing down her cheeks. "Ruby, whatever is the matter?" he asked, placing his hand against her face.

Ruby was barely able to speak, her shoulders heaving with emotion. "I... I found this in one of your jacket pockets," she finally managed to say, holding up a receipt with some scribbled writing on it. "Dad, this is from the pawnbroker."

"Ah," Ben offered, lowering his head.

"This is a receipt for your watch, Dad," she said, telling Ben what he already knew. "Your father left you that watch. You *love* that watch," she said between sobs. "Are things really that bad?"

Ben was devastated that his actions had upset her. "Oh, Ruby," he said, taking her in his arms. "It'll all work out," he assured her, giving her a gentle squeeze. "I had some cashflow issues and needed to raise a few pounds," he explained. "But if tomorrow is half the success I hope it will be, we'll be back on track, I promise," he added brightly, hoping to allay Ruby's fears.

"But you've had to pawn your dad's watch, and you're working all hours," Ruby answered. "Dad, I hate to say this, but I'm not sure if this is worth it. I don't like what this is doing to you."

Ben wiped a tear away from his own cheek now. "I know, Ruby, I know," he said, giving her a kiss on the top of her head. "But I'm only going through a temporary rough patch, I swear."

"But your dad's watch?"

"I didn't give it up permanently. It's only pawned for now. And if we have a good result tomorrow, I might be able to go and get it straight back. So, it'll be fine, Ruby."

"I just don't want this place making you unhappy, Dad. Promise me it won't get to that stage?"

"I promise, Ruby," Ben said, releasing her from his grip. "And before I start on the other pies, how about we take a walk up to the marquee, and you can show me what you've done?"

Ruby took her dad's hand, running a finger over the light patch of skin on his arm that was once covered by the watch. "You'll get it back, won't you, Dad?"

"I will, Ruby," Ben insisted. "And after that phone call I've just had, I've got a sneaking suspicion that things are on the up for us."

Chapter Nineteen

"You know something, Cecil?" Austin said, peeking into the rucksack at the nice, tidy pile of cash inside. "If you weren't such an unpleasant little fellow, I could come over there and give you a big, sloppy kiss."

"Thank you very much," Cecil replied, the barbed compliment causing no offence at all. "Although, I'm not sure I like being out of bed this early in the day, and what's with these eggs?" he asked, jabbing his breakfast with his fork.

"Those?" Austin replied. "They're what's known as *poached* eggs, Cecil. Surely you've seen them before? They're similar to fried eggs, only not dripping in fat, and much less likely to clog up your arteries. And that bowl to your left? It contains something called *fruit*. It's nice. You should maybe try it."

Cecil's yolk burst, releasing a golden river over his smashed avocado. "Yeah, well I dunno about this place," he said, running his eyes around the interior of Austin's health club, where they were both currently sat. "It all feels a little bit sterile, you know what I mean?"

Austin drained the contents of his glass before responding, enjoying the last of his freshly squeezed orange juice. "That's because the floor's been mopped and there's not a choking cloud of tobacco in the air like the usual haunts you bring me to."

"Yeah. But still..."

"Anyway," Austin said, moving the conversation along. "Tell me about the heist," he asked, stroking the rucksack like it was an adorable little pussycat.

Cecil's face lit up in response. He liked talking about himself and his accomplishments. "It was poetry in motion, boss," he explained. "Honestly, 'er indoors put in a belting performance. I'm half expecting her to win best supporting actor at the Oscars or summat. One minute she's snaking up the road on her bike, and the next, she's slumped in a heap, calling out like a bloody dying swan. She gets on my nerves from time to time, it's true, but watching on from behind the bushes, I couldn't have been prouder of my old girl."

"She sounds like a keeper," Austin agreed. "And our target didn't suspect a thing?" he asked with a cackle, enjoying this anecdote.

"Nah, of course not. He was too busy attending to my injured wife, and was all, *'Should I call you an ambulance?'* and, *'Do you think you've broken anything?'* and suchlike, rather than keeping an eye on the cash as I would've done. So I slipped in unnoticed, swapped the bags over, and Bob's yer uncle, back behind the hedges before the poor bastard was finished playing Florence Nightingale."

"Marvellous. So, she had no lasting injuries?"

"Who?"

"Ehm... your *wife*, Cecil."

"Oh," Cecil replied with a chuckle. "You know, I really couldn't say. I suppose I should ask her."

Austin rolled his eyes. "I'm sure she might appreciate it," he suggested nonchalantly, as if they were talking about nothing more than buying her a bunch of roses. "Poor old Benjamin," Austin said with a laugh. "I'll bet he's wracking his brains wondering where all that money went."

"And the best part is that you're now sat there with the cash he has to pay you back for, boss. So, it's actually quite genius when you think about it."

"Well, I certainly do try, Cecil," Austin answered, although momentarily distracted by the ladies walking towards the gym area. "Morning, girls!" he said, flashing them his finest smile while looking over the rim of his Ray-Bans. "I'll bet you don't get to see anything like *that* in your grubby little hangouts," he told Cecil, fanning himself with one of the menus. "Anyway, what was I saying?" he asked. "Oh, yes. I'd love to be a fly on the wall when the builders come looking for the cash that Ben no longer has," he said, drifting off and imagining that exact scenario. "Do you know the poor chap hasn't even admitted yet that he's lost my money?"

"Oh, I think that's a bit rude of him, boss," Cecil commented.

"It is, isn't it? Especially when you consider that we're business partners," Austin replied, a remark which resulted in some serious laughter around the breakfast table. Then, once they'd both settled down, "So, you're sure you're leaving, then, Cecil?" Austin asked. "We may have had our differences over the years, but we've had some remarkable results when you think about it, along with some jolly good fun."

"Happy times, boss. But no," Cecil answered. "The flight tickets are booked, and I'm off for a new life in sunny Spain. My days of ruining people's lives are well and truly over, I'm afraid."

"Apart from your new neighbours in Spain?" Austin asked with a wry smile, but his impeccable wit again sailed straight over Cecil's head. "Right, then I must bid you farewell," he advised, reaching for his jacket. "We're about to sign a monster of a deal, so I need to view some new retail space for my expanding business empire," he said, loudly enough so as to annoy and/or impress those seated at any of the adjacent tables. "Oh," he added, addressing Cecil directly again. "You sorted that other bit of business for me, didn't you, Cecil?"

"Of course, boss," Cecil replied, as if the answer was never in doubt. "When old Cecil says he'll do something, it gets done!" he said, loudly enough to also annoy and/or impress those sitting at any of the adjacent tables, same as Austin had just done.

"Splendid, Cecil. Simply marvellous. Safe travels, then, and don't forget to send me a postcard."

"Ehm, what about the bill for this lot?" Cecil asked, motioning towards the empty plates on the table. "Boss...?" he called after the figure already rapidly heading to the door. "Boss, what about this lot...?"

That same morning, Ben was up with the lark over at Life's a Pitch, enjoying an early morning stroll around the campsite, completing his morning inspection as he did each day. But for Ben, this wasn't a chore. Instead, it was thinking time. An opportunity to collect his thoughts while wandering around the picturesque Isle of Man countryside, listening to the wildlife stirring, and a time he felt at one with nature. And even though he'd not operated the campsite for too long, giving all of this up was impossible to contemplate. Yes, there were some challenges and times he wanted to rip his hair out, but moments like this, taking in the fresh country air, more than made up for the negatives. And, bizarrely, the sound of campers snoring in their tents often raised a smile as well. Perhaps he'd finally found his ideal vocation, he reckoned. The reason, then, that he was happy to work all the hours God sent to make a success of the business.

"Nice," Ben said to himself, nodding his approval after casting his critical eye over the interior of the new marquee. Of course he'd seen it the previous evening, although that was in partial darkness and with tired eyes after slogging away for most of the day. And even though he was still in deficit on the sleep front, he could now, in full daylight, properly appreciate Ruby's hard work. In front of each seat, she'd folded napkins in the shape of a lotus flower. It must have taken her an age, Ben considered, and seeing the effort she'd invested choked him up for a brief moment. "Oh, Ruby," he said, moved by her unwavering support. She even went to the trouble of rolling up the menus like an ancient scroll, each secured by a hand-tied ribbon. It was little touches like this that might go unnoticed by some. But Ben noticed. And he was certain others would as well, appreciating her attention to detail just as he did.

Ruby had been Ben's rock of late, keeping him anchored. Wise beyond her years, it was easy to forget that she was still a teenager. And being the weekend now, he knew what she really ought to be doing was enjoying herself with her mates. But that wouldn't be the case, as knowing how vital the money from the car show was for the business, she'd insisted upon providing her services as his waiting staff for the day. Not only that, but she'd also recruited two of her friends to keep her company and also lend a hand.

These unselfish acts on her part melted Ben's heart, and he was determined to treat her to a little surprise as a result. She wasn't a particularly materialistic person, not even when she was very young. But after a bit of investigative work on his part, which consisted of asking her best mate Ella for any suggestions, Ben had settled on gifting her an upgrade of her mobile phone. It certainly wasn't the cheapest surprise he'd ever purchased for her, but the phone shop had a deal where he could spread the cost to worry about it later. And she was worth it, he reckoned, and couldn't wait to see the smile on her angelic face.

With his rounds completed without incident, fresh air in his lungs and a healthy appetite, Ben returned to the Guest Entertainment Centre to fire up the ovens. The first of the vehicle owners were expected just after eight a.m., giving them plenty of time to set up ahead of the event's official starting point at eleven, and Ben couldn't wait. Of course, it was unlikely he'd see much of the action as he'd likely remain chained to the kitchen throughout the better part of the day, but he didn't mind as long as the till was ringing. And it was a lucrative opportunity, as he'd have both his own hungry campers to cater for as well as a steady stream of car enthusiasts looking for a bite to eat. At least that was the hope. Otherwise, he, Ruby and her pals would be eating bacon, sausages, and homemade pies for at least the next month or two.

And fortunately, his guests didn't disappoint, with a ready queue forming before the bacon had even started sizzling. And soon...

"Here we are. That's two bacon butties, one with mushroom," Ben said brightly, handing the order to his latest hungry punters, a pair of campers. "Are we off anywhere nice today?" he asked by way of small talk.

The two women of a certain vintage looked at each other as if figuring out who would speak first.

"We're going to Douglas," one of the ladies advised.

"Then we're going to catch the steam train," the other chipped in, making the noise of a steam train for effect. "Then a few cheeky G-and-Ts in Port Erin before catching the train for the return leg."

"You'll love it," Ben suggested, handing them their change. "Be sure to wander down to the seafront, where you'll find a charming local bookshop and a pub, both within easy reach. You can sit on the seawall and take in the glorious beach."

"Oh, that sounds right up our street, doesn't it, Mavis?"

"Right up our street, Sue," Mavis was delighted to agree. "But we better get our strength up for a busy day," she suggested, running her tongue over her lips as she eyed their breakfast. "And we cannot wait to book in for another visit next year."

"You're coming back?" Ben asked, with hope-filled eyes. "To the campsite, I mean?"

"Oh, sure," Mavis confirmed. "And we're not coming alone."

"We're bringing the rest of the girls from our bingo club," Sue offered. "We've loved it here."

"Oh yes," Mavis added. "The views are to die for, and the location is perfect."

"Not far to stagger home from the pub," Sue said with a snigger.

Ben was chuffed to bits with the positive feedback. "Well, I look forward to welcoming you all next year. And if there's anything I can do for you, just ask."

"Oh," said Mavis, glancing over her shoulder. "Well, there was one thing," she whispered, stepping in close.

"Is there?" Ben asked, eager to please. "You just name it."

"Well, handsome," Mavis said. "After we've staggered home from that charming little pub down the road, if you wanted to tap on my tent and tuck me in, I'd definitely unzip my canvas for you."

Ben blushed, unsure what to say. "I– ehm– that is…" he stammered, quickly returning his attention to the frying pan.

"Oh, leave him alone, you saucy old goat," Sue admonished her friend, playfully slapping her arm. "Just you ignore her," Sue said to Ben. "That's how she got us both barred from the local café."

"I'm in the pink tent in the far corner," Mavis said with a wink and a grin, but she was only teasing. At least that's what Ben sincerely hoped, if his concerned expression was anything to go by.

Early morning proposals aside, Ben was thrilled to learn some of his campers were willing to return as it meant people enjoyed his facilities. Of course, he'd love to be able to take all of the credit, but he suspected the breathtaking scenery offered by this magical island might also have played a teensy-weensy part in their decision-making process. But the important thing for him was seeing names in the reservation book, whatever the overall reason.

Just before eight, Ruby and her two friends popped their heads into the Guest Entertainment Centre long enough to say hello and report that they were ready for duty. And they'd embraced their role for the day, with each of them dressed smartly in their school uniform, only swapping out their formal tie with a brightly coloured dickie bow.

"You all look the part," Ben proudly observed. "And guys," he said, addressing Ruby's two friends, "I can't thank you enough for stepping in to help."

"Our pleasure, Mr Parker," they both said together.

"Ruby, do you want to head up to the marquee to greet the early birds and give them the breakfast menu?"

"Sure thing, Dad," Ruby said, giving the notepad in her hand a jiggle. "You keep frying, and we'll keep them buying," she told him, immediately laughing at her poetic brilliance.

Fortunately, Ben could see the queue of famished campers was nearing an end, meaning he'd soon be able to focus all of his efforts on the car aficionados. Well, at least until the next wave of campers rose up from their tents.

But he adored being busy like this. It reminded him of the heyday of the bakery when hungry customers snaked back on themselves like holidaymakers queuing for the check-in desk. And every pound he received today was another towards what he owed, a realisation spurring him on if his energy levels should happen to fade.

"Right," Ben said, taking a generous slurp of his coffee. He then glanced down at his watch that wasn't there. "Damn," he said, having forgotten about his trip to the pawnbrokers for a moment. But the wall-mounted clock confirmed that it was now ten past eight. "Phase two," he said, talking out loud to himself as he pulled out a jumbo-sized packet of Cumberland sausages from the fridge.

Ben peered through the window, spotting Ruby heading across the campsite towards him, just as he'd expected. "Here we go, Ben. You can do this, my old son," he said, giving himself a quick little pep talk and arming himself with a pair of clean spatulas in preparation for all the breakfast orders surely coming his way. "What've you got for me, my darling daughter?" he asked once she was inside.

"Ehm, nothing," Ruby replied, holding out her blank notepad to illustrate the point.

"Nothing? Oh. Well, maybe they're going to get set up first and work up an appetite before—"

"No, no, Dad," Ruby cut in. "When I say *nothing*, I mean there's nothing there. No cars, no car nuts. Nothing!"

"Nothing? I don't understand," Ben said in answer, setting his dual spatulas down and wiping his hands on his apron. "Show me," he suggested, escorting his daughter out into the fresh morning air. "Ah, good morning, folks!" Ben offered to a family of four making their way inside just as he and Ruby were exiting. "If you're after something for breakfast, I'll be back in only a few minutes. So just make yourselves comfortable and help yourself to some orange juice from the pitchers on the table if you like."

Ben quickened his pace, walking through the maze of tents towards the spare field where the car show was being hosted. "Oh," he said, as he caught a glimpse of the empty grass through a break in the hedgerow. Ruby's two friends stood outside the marquee on sentry duty like guards outside Buckingham Palace, ready to leap into action. That is, if there was any action to be had, at least.

"Where are all the cars?" Ben asked, stomping over to the area he'd signposted for vehicular access. "There are no cars," he stated, a fact Ruby and her pals were already acutely aware of. Ben spun round, like Maria von Trapp atop a large Alpine hill, looking in every direction. Only there was no dress for him to twirl, and no joy to be had. "Where are they?"

"Perhaps they're just running late?" Ruby put forth, though her grim expression suggested she thought otherwise.

"What? All of them?" Ben moaned. "I could understand one of them, yes. Maybe two. But *all* of them?"

"Maybe there's been some mix-up or confusion as far as the day the event's meant to be held?" Ruby's friend Ella proposed, trying to be helpful, as unlikely a scenario as her suggestion might be.

Ben shook his head in the negative. "No, the club chairman had phoned me just yesterday, confirming all the details," he advised. "Perhaps there's been an accident of some kind? Something blocking the roads?" he thought aloud. "Anyway, I've got a family waiting for their breakfast I need to attend to," he told the girls. "But let me know when you hear the throb of Aston Martin engines, yeah?" he asked with a plucky raised thumb, hopeful that this was just a minor delay of some sort and nothing more.

Back in the kitchen, Ben checked his phone for any missed calls. But with none displayed, Ben started to question himself. "What if I *have* got the wrong day?" he asked himself, while attending to the sizzling egg on his skillet. "I suppose it's possible...?"

But his musings were disturbed by Ruby popping in once

more and quickly making her way over to him. "Dad," she said, breathless as if she'd run the whole way there. "Dad, a car just pulled up outside the marquee."

"Yes!" Ben shouted, excited about a subject that wouldn't, under normal circumstances, please him quite so much. "I *knew* I wasn't losing my marbles."

Ruby appeared as if she'd just sucked a particularly sour lemon. "Yeah, but Dad. It's not an Aston Martin. It's a taxi."

"What do you mean, a taxi?" Ben asked, just as he was handing over an order to another of the campers.

"A taxi, Dad. As in, it's a *taxi*. The driver is outside the marquee and insists that he speak to you and you alone."

Ben narrowed one eye, uncertain if he was being subjected to a teenaged practical joke. "Ruby, if this is—"

"Dad, I know how important this is. I wouldn't joke about this."

Ben followed Ruby back towards the marquee. If nothing else, at least he was getting his daily step count in. "It *is* a taxi," he remarked, spotting the solitary vehicle parked in his designated area. "Uhm... can I help?" Ben asked of the slovenly driver, who was slouched casually against the passenger door of an equally unwashed cab.

"Ben Parker?" the driver asked, peeling himself away from the bodywork.

"I'm Ben Parker."

"Then this is for you," the man said, handing over a sealed white envelope. *"To be viewed only by your eyes,"* he stressed, using his sinister voice. "This is like something from one of them Jason Bourne movies, isn't it?" he added with a grin.

Ben ignored him, taking hold of the envelope. He glanced over to Ruby with a shrug, before peeling the flap open and removing a note from inside.

"Dad?" Ruby asked, watching the expression on her father's face turn almost instantly from surprise to anger. "Dad, what's up?"

Ben tilted his head towards the heavens. "Here," he said, eyes closed, holding out the small piece of paper.

Ruby flicked her eyes over to the taxi driver, and then took hold of the note, reading what it said:

Dear Ben,

I hope you have a wonderful day. Fingers crossed, the weather is as lovely as has been forecast. I'm sorry I can't be there to share what's sure to be a memorable day. Memorable, that is, in that there won't be any cars there to greet you. Anyway, I must 'motor' as I've somewhere warm to be.

Best wishes,
Cecil (temporary Chairman of the 'Aston Martin Appreciation Society')

"Oh no, Dad," Ruby said, scrunching the note into a ball. "Dad," she said, throwing her arms around him. "Don't worry, Dad," she said, with panic evident in her voice. "We'll get through this, Dad, I promise," she vowed, much to the bewilderment of her friends, who still remained clueless as to what exactly was happening.

"Anyway..." the taxi driver entered back in, clearing his throat after a long, emotionally charged silence. "I was told you were paying my fare on delivery," he advised, holding out his hand like a young Oliver Twist asking for seconds. "And I was promised a *very* generous tip," he added. "So, if you'd like to settle up, then I'll be on my way?"

Chapter Twenty

And you can now relax for a moment," Bethany, the yoga instructor, said gently, using a voice so soothing it could likely send an insomniac into a deep sleep. "And don't forget to breathe," she advised, as she adjusted herself for their next position, the Triangle Pose. "When you're ready, class," she told them, smiling at the Lycra-clad figures mirroring her every move. Then, starting out with her hands on her hips, Bethany slowly raised her arms to shoulder height like she was trying to frighten crows away from a farmer's field. "Now remember to take your time, class, and don't force it. And above all, take time to breathe and relax as we—"

"Oh, bollocks!" a distinctly male voice called out, disturbing the entire class, along with his mobile that had just gone off as well, erupting into life with a lively rendition of Right Said Fred's classic hit from 1991.

Bethany's calm, soothing demeanour faltered slightly, the faintest hint of a scowl crossing over her face like a passing cloud on an otherwise sunny day. "Austin?" she said. "Austin, now what do we say at the start of every class?"

"Yeah, yeah, I know. No mobile phones during the class," Austin replied, unconcerned at breaking the rules, and retrieving his phone from his back pocket. Which wasn't an easy task, given just how tight his tight-fitting shorts were. "But this is important," he said, looking at the screen. "Vitally so," he insisted, as he made haste towards the exit, his "I'm Too Sexy" ringtone still at full volume.

Once outside the school sports hall, the venue of his weekly yoga class, Austin took Bethany's earlier advice of breathing deeply. After all, he'd been waiting for this call for days.

"Hiya, Ben!" Austin said into the phone, sickeningly sweet, once he finally answered. "How's my favourite business partner?"

Austin strolled up the deserted school corridor, listening intently to what was being said. And it was a good thing nobody was watching, too, because at one point he even started skipping gaily like a six-year-old girl on her way to spend her pocket money at the sweet shop. "You don't *say*," Austin said in response to what he was hearing. "Oh, no, Ben, that's terrible news. Shocking, even. But I don't understand why this horrible fellow — Cecil, you said his name was? — would wish to do that to you."

Austin continued with his convincing performance of being a trusted confidant listening to a dear friend pour his heart out. "Yes, Ben, that's awful," he said, chewing down on his knuckle to stifle a laugh. "Wait, you've lost *what*?" Austin then said, his raised voice echoing around the tiled corridor. "But how on earth do you lose a whole rucksack full of cash?" he asked, feigning astonishment. Austin then softened his tone in response to what sounded like sobbing coming from the other end. "There, there, buddy, don't get yourself upset over it, okay?" he said. "After all, it's only money, right?"

Austin struggled to contain his delight as he listened on. "What's that, Ben? You're finished with the campsite?" he asked. "But Ben, this is your *dream*, don't forget," he pointed out, though not laying it on too thick, for obvious reasons. "Oh, I'm not too worried about the money, Ben, I know you're good for it," Austin insisted. "I know you'll pay me back for it eventually, somehow or other," he added. "What's that?" Austin said. "Can I come over to talk about a repayment plan?" he asked, repeating Ben's words back to him. "Well, I *am* at a rather important meeting right now," he lied. "However, I wouldn't want to abandon a friend in his time of need, now would I? Right. Just give me a bit, Ben, and I'll be over shortly, yeah?"

Barely able to contain his delight, Austin ended his call with

Ben and then immediately placed another to a number he had on speed dial. "Cynthia," he said once the call connected. "Cynthia, it's me. Yes, I'm at my yoga class, but something—" he tried to explain, but struggled to get a word in edgeways. *"Cynthia,"* he pressed on, talking over her. "Cynthia, I have yacht-launching news," he said, raising his voice, which appeared to do the trick. "My car show plan has finally tipped that imbecile over the edge," he was thrilled to report. "I need to get straight over there before he changes his mind. So, Cynthia, I need to get hold of Miles at the developers and tell him that we're almost there, yeah? Then, ask him to get the lawyers working on the paperwork from his side." Austin took a breath for a moment, listening to Cynthia repeat his instructions. "Perfect," he said, keen to get this show on the road. "Oh, and Cynthia. Start thinking about the paint scheme for our new premises. Because we're opening a new office, baby!"

Austin was so pumped after his conversation with Ben that he could have easily made it over to the campsite in about three minutes. But not wishing to appear overly eager and make his motivations too glaringly obvious, he took a slightly scenic route, enjoying a short relaxing drive through the winding Manx countryside. He was on cloud nine. Although, rather than soaking up the delightful views, his mind was more occupied thinking of suitable names for the new yacht he was soon to be purchasing. He whittled down the list in his head, eventually settling on either *Seas the Day* or, as an even classier option, *The Dirty Oar*. But he might have to give the matter some more thought, he reasoned, as choosing a name for one's yacht was a significant decision and not one to be made lightly.

Driving up the lane towards Life's a Pitch, Austin slowed, winding the window down. One might have thought Austin was simply taking enjoyment from the warm temperatures on this magnificent sunny day. But, in reality, Austin was surveying the fields, calculating how many properties the developer might possibly squeeze in. The more the merrier, as far as he was concerned, as each one built would mean that much more commission in his pocket.

Once parked up, Austin climbed out of his car, making a concerted effort to sour his expression. Although it was potentially a joyous day for him, he didn't want to give himself away by sporting a huge grin. At least not until all of the paperwork was signed and the deal had gone through.

"Ben!" Austin called out, spotting his target placing bottles into one of the outdoor recycling bins. "Ben!" he called out again, finally attracting his victim's attention as he made his way up from the car park in Ben's direction. "Hey there, buddy," Austin offered, upon arrival, doing his very best to sound sombre. "It sounds like you're having an absolutely terrible week," he added, giving Ben a consoling pat on the back.

Ben released another bottle into the bin before finally turning to greet his visitor. It became obvious why Ben hadn't faced him immediately, as his eyes were puffy and raw. "Austin, thank you for coming around," he said. "Yes, I won't lie. It's been bloody awful."

"I can only imagine," Austin replied, tilting his head in a *tell-me-what's-on-your-mind* manner.

Ben ushered Austin towards the Guest Entertainment Centre, a short walk away. "I'll stick the kettle on and tell you all about it," he said.

Austin followed, giving the impression he was there to comfort and support a friend, which of course couldn't have been further from the truth. Instead, he was struggling to contain his delight at the prospect of this rural idyll morphing into a construction site.

Anybody not consumed with their own greed would've noticed that Ben appeared like a broken man. Gone was the goofy smile, the spirited expression, or even the penchant for happy, idle chit-chat. Instead, he dragged his feet along, shoulders sagging with the sorry demeanour of a punter leaving the bookies after a crippling losing streak.

With the kettle soon boiled and Austin accepting his tea, Ben pulled up a chair and began to regale Austin with his tales of woe. "... And then I opened the rucksack you gave me, and the cash was *gone*," Ben eventually concluded, holding his palms out.

"The cash was in there," Austin was quick to mention. "Remember, it was you that packed it yourself."

Ben nodded, appearing to be in full agreement. "Yes, I know," he said. "And that's what makes it even more of a mystery. Because once I left your office, I headed straight to the campsite, only stopping for a moment for a woman who'd fallen from..."

"Ben?" Austin asked, after a pause in which Ben didn't speak.

"Ah, never mind, it's probably nothing," Ben answered, shaking away his thoughts. "Anyway, it still doesn't change the situation that the money's all gone, Austin. And for that, I'm deeply sorry."

"I know you're good for it, Ben, as I said before," Austin replied, waving away his concerns. "I never would have lent it to you otherwise," he remarked, while reaching for a chocolate-covered HobNob and dipping it into his brew.

Ben placed his head in his hands. "It's not just that," he said, looking up again. "Because I've lost that money, I'm no longer able to pay the builders for the work they performed," he told Austin, slapping his hand down on the table. "Then, just when I think I've got a chance of raising a few quid from the car show, it turns out the entire event was concocted by that malicious sod, Cecil, putting on a fake voice over the phone, apparently. None of it was even real. Honestly, I was nothing but kind to that man, and how does he repay me? First, he steals my card reading machine, then locks me out of my computer system, then a whole drawer full of cash goes missing from the till. And now this with the car show. I mean, why? What did I ever do to Cecil that made me deserve all of this?"

Austin shrugged, reaching for another biscuit. He usually didn't indulge in biscuits, but today was such a lovely day that he was making a special exception. "Oh, he sounds like a horrible wretch, Ben," Austin said in mock commiseration. "I see it all the time in my line of work. Honestly, you think you're dealing with a man of integrity, and it turns out they're a wolf in sheep's clothing the whole time. It really does destroy your faith in humanity, doesn't it?"

But Ben didn't immediately respond. He was staring off into the distance, looking distracted. "What if it was him?" he said abruptly.

"How's that? If *what* was him?" Austin replied.

"What if it was Cecil who took the money you gave me?" Ben offered, but with nothing concrete to back up his hypothesis. "Although how could he, exactly?" he added, wracking his brains for an answer. But when nothing of use presented itself, Ben's thoughts returned to the present. "Anyway. After all that man's done to me, Austin, do you know what hurt me the most?"

Austin's sympathetic demeanour appeared to be waning if his bored expression was anything to go by. "Dunno?" he said in reply, feeling like the question required some kind of response from him. "Making you look stupid, maybe?"

"Exactly, Austin. It's like you're able to read my mind," Ben answered. "When that taxi turned up with Cecil's message, I was humiliated in front of my daughter and her friends."

Austin briefly perked up at this revelation. "That can't have been nice," he said, eyebrows raised.

"It wasn't. And seeing my daughter with tears in her eyes cut me up inside. And then, as if to rub salt into the wound, I had to pay for the bloody taxi as well! I could almost hear Cecil laughing when I pulled out my wallet."

"I know it's a..." Austin started to say, before trailing off, tiring, it would appear, of his role as grief counsellor. "*Anyway,*" he added, hoping to steer Ben more towards talk of business.

"Ah, yes. Sorry for waffling on like a negative Nellie."

"So, you mentioned on the phone that you'd reached the end of your camping adventure?" Austin reminded him.

"No," Ben replied brightly, perking up a bit.

"No? What do you mean, *no?*" Austin asked, scanning the face across the table.

"I've decided I need to push on," Ben admitted, a flicker of hope evident in his previously sad eyes. "It's the only solution to my financial troubles, I reckon."

Austin held himself back, resisting the urge to rip Ben's theory to pieces, as well as Ben himself. "Right. Okay. So the only way to save a business that's financially destroyed you is to press on regardless?" he asked, trying to remain calm.

Ben reached into his jacket pocket for his notebook. "I've done the sums," he said, tapping a finger down on his scribbled notes. "And if I walk away now, the honest truth is that I'll never have the money to pay you, the builders, or Farmer Gerry. But the campsite still has a healthy pipeline of reservations, so if I knuckle down, then there might be a chance to save the business and repay everybody what I owe them."

Ben then shuffled nervously in his seat. "There's just one thing, Austin," he added, his expression pained. "You'll absolutely get the money you're owed. But I'll just need quite a bit more time to pay you back than we'd originally discussed, if that's possible?"

Austin didn't seem as if he liked the direction this conversation was heading, and in an instant, his compassionate demeanour disappeared. "Oh, I don't think that'd be possible at *all,* buddy," he advised. "You see, I've got rather aggressive expansion plans for my estate agency, and that cash I lent you is earmarked for... for, em..." he said. "For, ah, office furniture," he eventually settled on.

"Oh," a deflated Ben offered weakly, his rescue strategy faltering before it'd started. "It's just that without—"

Austin leaned forward, elbows on the table. "Here, now. I've got an idea," he said, as if a thought had only just now presented itself to him and wasn't already a plan he'd been hatching for days.

"You have?" Ben asked.

Austin nodded. "Yes, I have," he replied cryptically. "Ben,

what if I told you there was a way to step away from this whole sordid mess without you owing a penny to anybody? Just imagine it, yeah? There would be no campsite to stress you out, and all of your debts are wiped away," Austin told him. "Just like *that*," he added, snapping his fingers, before pausing to allow Ben to imagine this new reality. "*And*," he continued, a moment later. "And there'd even be enough money left over for you and that lovely daughter of yours to have a nice little holiday. That'd be nice, wouldn't it?"

"Eh?" Ben offered, unsure what to say. "I don't understand," he said, not understanding. "How could that happen? Who'd do that for me?"

"*Moi*, Ben. That's who," Austin answered. "*I'd* do that for you. Your good friend Austin."

"You'd do that for me? But why? I mean, I certainly appreciate it... but why?"

"Oh, it's not entirely selfless on my part, Ben," Austin confessed. "If the campsite remained financially unviable, then the landowner would likely—"

"Sell that land to a property developer?" Ben entered in, putting some of the pieces of what Austin was saying together.

"Exactly, Ben. And if that were the ultimate outcome, the owner and developer would hopefully appoint my estate agency to sell and manage their properties once completed."

"Yes, but if I continued to run the campsite, there's still a chance I could possibly make a go of it, isn't there?" Ben said, although sounding more like he was trying to convince himself of this than Austin. He glanced down at his notebook, running a finger over the numbers he'd scribbled down. "If I could just get through the next month or two, there's still a chance I could succeed," he said, thinking out loud. "I'm sure I can use the new marquee for—"

"Ben," Austin interrupted, cutting him off mid-flow. He then pushed his chair back, giving the impression he had somewhere else he needed to be. "Ben, Farmer Gerry has a charge on your property to secure the lease on the campsite, correct?" he asked, even though he was already well aware of the answer.

"Yes, that's correct," Ben admitted.

Austin knew it was time to turn the thumbscrew, cutting off any romantic notions Ben might still have about turning the faltering business around. "The way I see it, Ben," Austin said, setting out his stall. "You *could* push on with the business. But remember that the end of the tourist season is rapidly approaching, yeah? And the old farmer won't mind if you continue racking up rent arrears because, ultimately, he can force you to sell your house to pay him back."

Austin could see the blood drain from Ben's face, and he knew he'd just delivered a fierce uppercut, with his opponent now floundering on the ropes, so to speak.

"Also, don't forget your builders, Ben," Austin continued. "I'm fairly sure they won't be able to pay their mortgages on your good intentions, waiting around for payment for who knows how long. But, you know, whatever..."

Austin rose to his feet, effectively drawing the meeting to a close. "Anyway, buddy," Austin said, turning to leave, "I've somewhere to be. But, whatever you decide, I hope it all works out for you." Austin then began walking towards the exit, confident his work here was done. "Oh, and let me know when you're planning on paying back my loan, yes?" he added for good measure, saying this last bit over his shoulder, along with a smirk unseen by Ben.

Once outside, Austin slowed his pace. Then, strolling leisurely across the grass, he started a countdown. "Three... two... one..." he whispered to himself.

"Austin!" Ben called out, jogging to catch up with him. "Austin, wait there a minute!"

Austin came to a halt, his smirk developing into a full-on smile. Turning on the spot, he shook away his obvious joy, transforming his face into a mask of innocence. "Oh? What's up?" he asked casually. "Did I leave something behind?" he said, certain his trout was about to land in his waiting net. And in fact...

"What you were just saying in there," Ben said, hooking a thumb over his shoulder. "So, if I heard you correctly, Austin, if I walk away from the campsite, you'll settle what I owe to Farmer Gerry, the builders, *and* the money I owe you?"

"I'll wipe all of that clean," Austin confirmed, waving his hand like he was cleaning a window. "You'll walk away completely debt-free, and with some money left to treat yourself on top of it. All I ask in return is that you point out to the farmer just how much of a challenge running this portion of his land as a campsite is. Help convince him that the easiest, most stress-free option is to sell it to the developer. If you can do that, then we have a deal."

Ben turned slowly, running his eyes around the campsite with great fondness. He smiled as he watched a group of young children chasing tirelessly after a football with the adults struggling to keep pace. This place was special to Ben. This place was his dream. But now, he had to face the reality of his situation, and he couldn't allow himself to be selfish. No matter how much it hurt, he didn't see that he really had any other choice but to give it all up. He had to think of his daughter and keep a roof over their heads.

"Austin, I'll do it," Ben decided, turning back to face him. "And I don't know what I'd have done without you," he added, stepping close and taking Austin into a grateful embrace, resting his cheek against his shoulder. "I can't thank you enough," he told him, giving him a gentle squeeze. "Truly, you've been a real friend throughout all of this, and I don't know how I'll ever be able to thank you enough."

Austin patted Ben's back as if he were burping a baby. "Oh, it's my pleasure, Ben," he said with a broad smile. "After all, what are friends and neighbours for if they can't help each other out?"

Chapter Twenty-One

Farmer Gerry already knew the writing was on the wall when Ben came round to the farmhouse. Spotting him in advance through the kitchen window, Gerry could tell from Ben's grave expression that it likely wasn't a simple social call he could expect.

Gerry was deeply disappointed that Ben had decided to throw the towel in, but completely understanding as to why. After all, he had also tried and failed to make the campsite a viable business himself, so he knew from experience what a challenge it was. But either way, this ultimately left Gerry with a decision he'd hoped he could avoid — namely, to find someone else to operate the campsite, or to sell it off, cashing in his chips and saying farewell to that huge portion of his rolling countryside views.

Gerry knew what his heart thought on the matter, but in the end, his head helped him reach the final decision to sell. Of course, someone else could have taken over the business and made it a roaring success, but it was a risk that neither he nor his bank balance could gamble on. The simple fact of the matter was that Gerry needed the rent payments to overcome the shortfall from his farm, and without that, there was only one viable outcome: sell the land. And it was a decision that weighed heavily on his shoulders.

Ben, for his part, was on the verge of tears relaying his decision to Farmer Gerry, who wasn't just his landlord but also a friend. But in good conscience, Ben couldn't continue on a wing and a prayer, hoping for a change in his fortunes. And following Austin's generous offer also meant that, at least this way, all parties would be paid what they were owed and could part on amicable terms.

Sitting around the kitchen table, Gerry listened intently as Ben filled him in on all the grim details, particularly in regard to Cecil's one-man mission to trip Ben up at every turn. It was especially galling to Gerry as this was somebody he had once trusted, so much so that he'd even made of point of offering his services to Ben. As such, not only did Gerry feel deeply betrayed, but he also felt largely responsible for what had befallen Ben (and, by extension, himself).

"We need to throw that idiot Cecil into the field with Sylvester, my prize bull," Gerry suggested.

Ben smiled, the mental image of Cecil stumbling through a field with an angry bovine in hot pursuit affording Ben a moment of light relief. "So, you're not too annoyed, Gerry?"

"No, son. Not at all. I'd have been more annoyed if you'd carried on with your head in the sand. I'm gutted that it didn't work out for you, Ben. For either of us, actually," Gerry answered. Gerry then stood, walking over to the window above his large Belfast sink and looking outside. "I don't mind admitting I'll miss that view when the diggers arrive," he added wistfully, admiring the unspoiled landscape. "I suppose it'll take some getting used to."

"So you'll sell to the developer my friend Austin is working with?" Ben asked.

"I suppose so, son," Gerry said. "In my experience, anyone working in the property business, well, they're slippery snakes, the lot of them, only interested in money. Even so, after what you've told me about this Austin fellow, I reckon it'd make sense to work with him and his developer. Better the devil you know than the devil you don't, and all that."

"He's a little bit brash," Ben offered. "And for some, I admit he's something of an acquired taste. But he's had my back, Gerry, and I don't think he'll let you down."

Then, distracted, Gerry reached into his pocket, cursing the not-altogether modern technology to be found there. "This bloody thing has not stopped vibrating," he said, removing the dated Nokia brick that had served him well enough through a number of harvests in recent years. "Twenty-eight missed calls," Gerry remarked, reading the phone's screen. "I don't think I've had twenty-eight missed calls in all the time I've *had* this flippin' phone."

"Ah, that might actually be my fault, Gerry," Ben confessed. "I mentioned to Austin that I was coming straight up to talk to you about the lease on the campsite. So, I suspect he's keen to start the ball rolling."

"Well, he's keen, all right," an incredulous Gerry suggested, reholstering the phone in his pocket and leaving the twenty-eight missed messages for later. Then, Gerry turned his attention to Ben once again, studying his face carefully.

"Don't mind me, Gerry," Ben advised, worried he'd perhaps outstayed his welcome. "I'll get out of your hair, and let you—"

"Ben," Gerry cut in. "Ben, before I speak with Austin, you're absolutely certain you're making the correct decision? You're positive you don't want to give it one final go...?"

At that moment, Ben recalled how happy he was that first day he'd brought Ruby to visit the campsite. He'd never forget the giddy excitement of being at the start of a thrilling new adventure, taking on a new business venture he felt sure would offer them both some financial security. But that dream had soured, and the debt he now found himself in meant that continuing on was an option he could simply no longer consider. And although it pained him to do so, he felt he had no alternative but to reply to Gerry in the negative.

"As much as I'd like to carry on, Gerry, I know I've no other choice but to walk away, for your sake as well as my own," Ben told him, a lump forming in his throat. "I have to walk away from Life's Pitch," he reluctantly conceded, head bowed.

"Yes, you absolute beauty!" Austin screamed from his office, startling his underlings sitting at their workstations on the other side of the glass. He fell to his knees, shaking his fists to the heavens like he'd just scored from an overhead kick in the last minute of the World Cup final. "Who's bloody number one?" Austin yelled out loud. *"You're* number one!" he answered himself.

"Ehm, everything okay there, boss?" an inquisitive Barry enquired, poking his head in through the door.

"Everything okay?" Austin said, repeating the words back to him. "Yes, you *could* say that, Bazza. In fact, everything's bloody tip-top!" he happily advised, now back up on his feet and shadowboxing with some unseen opponent. Oh, and do me a favour and send Cynthia in, yeah?"

"Roger that, boss. Roger that."

Austin didn't quite know what to do first. He was like a child who'd just received the keys to the toy store, the fireworks factory and the trampoline factory, all at once. Or, perhaps more apt where Austin was concerned, he was like a pig wallowing in some lovely filth. With Barry gone, Austin flashed a smile into his full-length mirror, falling in love with his own reflection like Narcissus, and mouthing the words *"Austin Fletcher, you're the man!"* at himself.

"I presume that screaming indicates good news?" Cynthia asked, appearing in the doorway. "So, I'm guessing you've either won the listing for that large-bosomed divorcée you were regaling us about ad nauseam, or the press will soon announce a gigantic new housing development springing up in Castletown?"

Austin bounded across his office like Tigger on a caffeine overload. "Castletown is in the bag!" he announced, raising his hand for an enthusiastic high-five. "The farmer just called me back and told me he's ready to sign the paperwork!"

"Breathe, Austin," Cynthia said with a smirk, though she could completely understand Austin's jubilation. "That really is superb news. So, would you like me to speak with the developer and the lawyers? Is that why you called me in?"

"No, no. I just wanted to share the good news," Austin answered, returning to his desk. "But thanks," he said, unlocking one of his drawers. "I'll take care of that now, as the farmer has agreed to meet and sign the paperwork this afternoon."

"Can the lawyers work that quickly?" Cynthia asked.

"Oh, yes," Austin was delighted to confirm. "And since I knew this day would come, I had my old mate Miles at the development company preparing the paperwork for weeks."

Austin may have had his faults, but Cynthia couldn't help but admire his efficiency. "I should never have doubted it, Austin," she said. "So, how can I help? Is there anything you'd like me to do?"

Austin placed a plump black holdall bag on his desk. "Well, let me see," he said, running a hand over his hair and composing his thoughts. "I'll arrange for the developer, legal team, and the farmer to sign the paperwork at four o'clock this afternoon. Oh, and I need to make sure that sad muppet Ben is available."

"Ben? The chap running the campsite?"

"*Formerly* running the campsite, yeah. Apparently, we need him to sign a cancellation of the lease or something like that," Austin explained, although more interested in the contents of the holdall bag just now. Austin had to think for a moment. "Okay, Cynthia... *partner*. Eh, how does that sound, do you think? *Par-ter-ner...?*"

Cynthia couldn't hide her apparent delight. "Sounds pretty good to me, Austin, now you mention it."

"You just may need to borrow one of the magazines from my bottom drawer very soon," Austin suggested.

"Eww, no," Cynthia responded.

"I mean the ones about sailing, Cynthia. Not the *other* ones," Austin said with a laugh. "Ah, I can just imagine your yacht berthed next to mine, the way things are going. Although, my yacht would be bigger, of course. Just to be clear."

"Of course," Cynthia was happy enough to agree.

"Anyway," Austin said, regaining his train of thought. "Okay, in this holdall are two bags of cash, Cynthia. The smaller one needs to be delivered to an associate of mine, Cecil, for an extra task he's recently performed for me. You can do that if you like."

"Cecil the Chubster?" Cynthia said, recalling the name from her previous forage through Austin's desk. "For what, exactly? Remember, you said you'd keep me completely in the loop, Austin."

"Oh, just a wee bit of sabotage," Austin replied. "Cecil the Chubster, living legend that he is, was pivotal in helping Ben realise that owning a campsite might not be the life for him. Previously, with his help, I was able to steal back the cash I'd loaned to Ben. Apparently, we've an Oscar-winning performance by his wife to thank for getting the money back without Ben knowing."

"Right, so, you had Cecil steal back the money you loaned to Ben that was supposed to bail him out of his financial troubles? Have I got that right?" Cynthia asked.

"Precisely!" Austin answered. "It's genius, isn't it?"

Cynthia couldn't argue with Austin's vindictive brilliance, much as she'd like to. "Remind me never to get on the wrong side of you," she said. "Anyway, that'll be Cecil taken care of. But what do you want done with the other amount? The larger bag?"

Austin handed Cynthia a note with two addresses written on it. "The other amount is for our friend Miles," he explained. "This cash shows our gratitude for winning the contract to sell the houses in the new development."

"Hmm, I think that's what's known in the trade as bribery and corruption," Cynthia suggested, now taking possession of the bag. "*Oof,* it's heavy," she remarked, using both hands to support it.

"A small price to pay for the loads and loads of cash we'll soon be rolling in, partner. So, can I leave the two deliveries to you while I meet at the farmer's house at four?"

Cynthia headed towards the door, loaded down from the weight of the bag she was carrying. "Sounds like a plan, Austin. Oh, and if I forget to say it later? Bloody well done."

"Oh, go on, stop it, now," Austin replied with a sniff and a grin. "I'm just doing what I do best."

Chapter Twenty-Two

Fortunately, Farmer Gerry's kitchen table was long enough to accommodate all of those who'd arrived to disturb his peace and quiet. Indeed, with the majority of those in attendance all suited and booted, offering furtive glances in every direction, one might have assumed they'd stumbled into a meeting of the local mafia.

But this wasn't a powwow to settle a beef or decide if someone was about to be 'clipped.' Instead, this was a rather more mundane group of lawyers and bankers congregated to finalise the sale of a parcel of agricultural land to a property developer.

However, to look at Farmer Gerry's despondent expression, you'd be forgiven for thinking he was about to be 'clipped' rather than receiving an impressive chunk of cash from the sale proceeds. Instead, Gerry remained distant throughout the proceedings and appeared uninterested as those in suits waffled on about this covenant, contract detail or what have you, with him mostly staring out the kitchen window instead. He watched on as a herd of cows wandered leisurely across the vista, stopping here and there to munch on grass and let out the occasional moo. It was a view he'd seen a thousand times previously, but only now did he realise how much he was going to miss it when it was gone. Of course, he would move the livestock to one of his other fields, but it didn't make his current decision any easier.

"Look, can we just get this business sorted?" Gerry asked politely but firmly, addressing the group. "It's just that I need to attend to the animals who'll be expecting their dinner soon."

Austin, standing in the corner, observed the gathering without saying a word. It was difficult to bite his tongue for a man often so brash, but the fear of hindering progress while so close to victory kept him tight-lipped.

"If you could just sign there, then," Emma, one of the impeccably dressed lawyers, requested, sliding the relevant document under Gerry's nose. Gerry, for his part, shot his own lawyer a glance, receiving a nod of approval for him to proceed.

Also willing Gerry to put pen to paper was Sebastian, the haughty property developer. "That's it, old bean," Sebastian offered across the table. "Nearly there, and we'll be on our way."

But Gerry hesitated, sitting there with his pen hovering above a sea of words, consumed in his own thoughts.

"Is there anything you're uncertain on?" Emma asked, noting the lack of pen-on-paper action. "I'm happy to clarify anything if you should have any questions."

Gerry snapped back to the present, conscious of several pairs of eyes boring into his skull. "What? Oh, no, I'm fine," he said. "Just sign here?"

"Yes, please," Emma confirmed, leaning closer to point to the section requiring his autograph.

But as Gerry's pen was readying itself to kiss the document, his lawyer was shuffling through his own stack of paperwork and noticed something of apparent concern. "Just a moment," he said, clearing his throat.

"Is everything in order?" Emma asked.

"Hold on, I just need to make sure…" said Gerry's lawyer, as he continued shuffling through his documents. "Right. It's as I thought. We don't seem to have a signature on the cessation of the lease at present," he commented, looking to Gerry for confirmation.

"No, you're right," Gerry agreed. "Ben's due to join us any minute and will have to sign it then."

"I'm afraid we'll need Ben's signature to conclude the lease before we can finalise the sale agreement," Gerry's lawyer advised the group.

Austin stepped forward, finger raised. "How about I scoot

out and give Ben a nudge?" he offered, helpful fellow that he was, and made an immediate beeline towards the door. After all, he wasn't prepared to let anything delay that document being signed.

Once outside, Austin picked up the pace, which wasn't easy considering he was wearing new Italian leather shoes he'd not yet broken in. "Where are you?" he asked, jogging along the gravel path leading towards the campsite. Austin's usual self-assured manner escaped him, knowing that every minute without a signature on the document was another minute for Gerry to potentially change his mind and walk away from the deal. However, Austin needn't have worried because there, walking across the campsite towards him, was the glum figure of Ben.

"Heya, buddy!" Austin greeted him, placing a firm arm around Ben's shoulders as the two met. "We're all in the farmhouse having a party without you," Austin advised, giving Ben a gentle push in the right direction.

"Sorry, I was just reading through the reservations book. Trying to figure out how many bookings I'll need to phone and cancel," Ben replied forlornly, struggling to keep pace with a rather more energetic Austin. "You know," Ben continued, "I'm absolutely gutted this place didn't work out, despite all of the effort I put into it, and—"

"Don't worry about that," Austin cut in, not really listening to what was being said anyway. "Just look at this as the start of a brand-new adventure, yeah? You and your daughter Rhiannon can dust yourselves down and reinvent yourselves," Austin added brightly, keen to offer a positive slant on the situation.

"Uhm, it's actually Ruby."

"That's the spirit, Ben!" Austin said, opening the farmhouse door for him, once again not really listening to what was being said.

Like two cowboys walking into a dimly lit saloon, all eyes inside the kitchen fell upon them.

"Ben, I presume?" Gerry's lawyer politely asked, sliding his chair to make space for the new arrival. "We just need your signature to confirm that the lease on the campsite will conclude with two weeks' notice," he explained, handing his pen to Ben for Ben's consideration.

Ben glanced over to Gerry, who seemed about as thrilled as he was about the situation. Then, like removing a plaster, Ben decided to just get it over and done with as quickly as possible. "Thank you," he said, taking hold of the offered pen. "Just here?" he asked, before scribbling his name on the legal document as directed.

In the corner of the kitchen, standing next to the AGA cooker oven, Austin gnawed on a finger as he observed, holding his breath like he was watching his favourite football team in a penalty shoot-out. "*Yeeesss,*" he murmured to himself, once Ben was finished.

"Excellent, thank you," Emma said. "I presume we're permitted to conclude the signing?" she asked, flicking her eyes over to Gerry's lawyer.

"I believe we are," the lawyer replied, casting one final eye over the lease agreement. "Yes. Yes, you're free to sign now, Gerry," he instructed, shuffling his papers into a neat pile. "And then that's the matter concluded."

Austin paused his breathing again, watching as Gerry took hold of the pen and slowly, carefully, advanced it towards the document. It was like slow motion, and if Gerry didn't hurry up about it, Austin was likely to keel over and die of asphyxiation from holding his breath for so long.

"Here we go," Gerry said, leaning over and preparing to put pen to paper. But then, with his pen agonisingly close, he suddenly glanced up, his attention diverted to a figure entering the room. "Hello there," Gerry said to the unexpected guest. "Are you with the legal advisors?" he asked of the woman he'd not previously met.

"Sorry about that," Austin offered, promptly stepping forward. "This is Cynthia, who works for..." he began. "Sorry, I should say this is Cynthia, my *business partner,*" he added, correcting himself. "Join me over here," he told Cynthia, waving his hand to shoo her over in his direction and out of the way.

"Hello, Austin," she said, as she stood beside him.

"What are you *doing?*" Austin furiously whispered, trying not to be heard by the others. "I don't need you here. I *told* you to—"

Cynthia smiled in response, as if she wasn't able to notice Austin's obvious distress. "I just wanted to be included at the signing of such an important deal," she explained, whispering back at him.

"Ah. Sorry, gentlemen," Austin said to the group, after noticing everyone was staring at them. "Please proceed. Don't let this minor interruption hinder you in any way."

"So, if we're not expecting anybody else?" Emma, the lawyer said, prompting Gerry with a polite smile.

Gerry appeared like a man about to sign his own death warrant. "Okay," he said, hunched over the contract. "The sooner we get this done, the sooner we can—"

But before ink could be applied to paper, Cynthia stepped forward abruptly, effectively separating herself from Austin. "STOP. *Don't* sign that contract," she advised, holding her hand aloft like a police officer directing traffic.

"What's all this nonsense?" Sebastian entered in with bluster, clearly annoyed by this disruption. "Austin, what the devil *is* this?" he demanded.

Cynthia marched forward, over to the kitchen table, inspecting the document below Gerry's poised hand. "You've not signed?" she asked, seeking confirmation that he had in fact not signed.

"Cynthia, can I, ehm... can I speak to you for a moment?" Austin asked, laughing uneasily as he bounded over and placed a hand on her back. "Something's just cropped up that requires your urgent attention," he lied. "Erm... back at the office?"

Austin tried to coax her towards the door, but Cynthia wasn't for budging. Instead, she turned so she was looking directly at Ben. "You're Ben, right?" she asked. And it was a logical guess, as Ben was the only one there besides Farmer Gerry who wasn't presently dressed in business attire. "Ben, I don't know how to tell you this other than to just come out and say it," she began. "I hate to be the bearer of bad news, but—"

"But...?" said Ben, looking around the room for answers. "I don't understand. What's the bad news?" he asked, wondering if this was the start of some sort of ill-timed joke at his expense.

"Your run of bad luck, Ben. It's all thanks to one man," Cynthia answered. "Your sabotaged renovations. That bag of money that was switched. Everything."

"You're talking about Cecil?" Ben asked, eyes narrowing. "You're saying Cecil was responsible for the money that was swapped with magazines? Because I already suspected that, but I wasn't—"

"We're just leaving!" Austin advised the room. "Cynthia, *we're leaving,*" he added, grabbing her arm.

"Get your hands *off* me, Austin," she shot back, shaking free of his grasp and giving him a long, lingering glare.

"She's clearly gone mad," Austin protested. "Stark raving mad. Mad as a hatter! Does somebody want to phone the police?"

Cynthia turned her back on Austin, ignoring every word that was coming out of his mouth. "Ben, you're correct that Cecil was involved in destroying your business," she said. "But he was only the dancing monkey, if you will. The organ grinder, however, the *real* architect of your misery, is none other than the overly suntanned buffoon standing behind me."

"Right, that's it, Cynthia. You're fired!" Austin yelled, stamping his foot on the stone tiles of the floor for good measure. "Get out of here and take your ludicrous slander with you!"

"Oh, button it, Austin. You can't fire me because I've already quit," Cynthia replied.

Farmer Gerry rose up from his chair, appearing completely bewildered. "Would someone mind telling me what's happening?" he asked.

"Go on, then," Cynthia prompted, looking to Austin with arms folded across her chest. "Why don't you tell everybody what you've been up to?" she asked. "No?" she pressed, after a few long seconds of silence. "What's up, Austin? At a loss for words? Well, how about I spell it all out, then."

First, Cynthia approached Ben, bringing him up to speed on Austin's master plan to destroy both him and his business, no matter the personal cost to Ben. She spoke of how Cecil was on Austin's payroll the whole time, tasked with the mucky job of doing whatever he could to damage Ben's fledgling enterprise. All the while, Ben listened on, slack-jawed and casting the occasional disgusted look at a squirming Austin. But it was when Cynthia began mentioning the recent heist — whereby Ben was relieved of the cash he'd only just borrowed from Austin — that Ben interjected.

"But how could Cecil have taken the money?" Ben asked. "How could he manage it? Because I packed it into the bag at Austin's office myself, and it hardly left my sight after that."

"*Yeah*," Austin chimed in with a sneer. "Try and explain *that* one, Cynthia," he said mockingly.

"Happily," Cynthia responded, reaching into her handbag. She removed her mobile phone, tapping away on the screen for a moment or two. "Do you recognise her?" she asked, holding the phone up for Ben's inspection.

Ben moved his face closer to the screen, squinting his eyes. "I'm not sure I do," he said, examining the image of a portly lady lying on a sun lounger next to a swimming pool. "Should I?"

Cynthia touched the screen, spreading her fingertips apart to expand the image. "What about now?"

"Uhm, I'm not..." Ben started to say, until a moment of realisation smashed him in the face. "Wait," he said, incredulous. "That's the woman I helped up when she fell off her bike!"

Cynthia nodded. "You mean when you'd just left Austin after picking up the money, correct?"

"That's right! On my way back to the campsite!"

"And what about the chap in the background of the image, walking along the edge of the pool?" Cynthia said, using her fingers to zoom in on another area of the picture.

"The man carrying the beer?" Ben asked, moving his nose

even closer to the screen. "I don't believe it," he said, not believing it. "It's that lowlife Cecil!"

"It is indeed," Cynthia confirmed, holding up her phone for all to see. "This is a lovely little snap I borrowed from Cecil's Facebook page, showing Cecil having a jolly old time on holiday. On holiday with his beloved wife, I should say. *'Practising for sunny Spain,'* the caption says."

"The lady I helped on her bike was Cecil's wife?" Ben asked, the penny finally dropping. "The absolute scumbag! So while I'm there helping his stricken wife, Cecil's diving into my car to swap out the bag with one filled with rubbish?"

"Bingo!" Cynthia said, addressing the room like she was a prosecutor in a murder trial. "But that's not all," she said, shifting her attention specifically over to Sebastian now, the property developer, whom she recognised.

"You're not going to listen to the ramblings of this obviously crazy person, are you, Sebastian?" Austin cut in. "She's clearly mad as a box of frogs, or drunk. Or possibly both."

Cynthia laughed off the suggestion. "Oh, I could certainly benefit from a large gin and tonic right about now, I don't mind admitting. But, no, I'm completely sober, I can assure you," she said. "Anyway, I've just left a meeting with your sales manager, Miles," she told Sebastian. "That's why I arrived late here."

"*And...?*" Sebastian puffed. "What's meeting Miles got to do with the price of fish?" he barked, appearing increasingly frustrated with the present situation.

"You may want to listen to this," Cynthia suggested, the corners of her mouth raising into a smile as she played the recording on her phone. "That's Miles' voice?" she asked of Sebastian.

"Of course," he replied, listening on.

Miles could be clearly heard in the recording thanking Cynthia for delivering to him Austin's slush money. Further, Cynthia deliberately turned the conversation towards matters of bribery and corruption — although avoiding the use of those exact words, of course — drawing out a proud confession from Miles about his involvement in helping Austin win the business from the new development. He couldn't shut up about himself, bragging about his future earnings potential and how he'd one day be taking over and running the company for the 'old man,' at which point he then attempted to turn on the charm with Cynthia, trying to steer the conversation in a more intimate direction.

"That's when I made my excuses and left," Cynthia explained, with a sickened expression. "So, Sebastian," she summarised, "now you know what your sales manager and Austin have been busy working on. Bribery, corruption, fraud, and theft. At the very least."

His demeanour changed, Sebastian now lowered his head in shame. "You have to know I wasn't aware of any of this," he said, looking up and glancing over to Ben, and then to Farmer Gerry. "Miles was operating outside my authority, and I'll bloody well make sure he's hauled over the coals for this," he insisted, pushing his chair back and taking to his feet. "Gerry, after what I've heard this afternoon, I regret I must step away from purchasing your land," he advised. "And rest assured, nobody makes a fool out of me," he added, addressing Austin now. "Mark my words, Fletcher, you've not heard the last of this, you snivelling little wretch."

Sebastian headed towards the exit with his group of legal advisors in tow, leaving Austin squirming in the corner. "For what it's worth," he said, turning to address Ben as he passed by, "I'm sorry you've been embroiled in this mess."

And at this point, Sebastian and his entourage finally took their leave.

"Oh, bravo. What a performance," said Austin, slowly clapping his hands, his voice dripping with contempt. "I believe I've heard enough of this claptrap," he declared, making his own way towards the door. "And Cynthia, make no mistake, you'll be hearing from my legal counsel over this. I'm going to bloody sue you for everything you've got."

Cynthia appeared unconcerned by Austin's threat, dismissing it with a flourish of her hand. "Yeah, yeah, do your worst," she told him. And then, ignoring Austin, she turned to speak to Ben. "Ben, do you mind if I ask you a personal question?" she said.

"A bit desperate, isn't it?" Austin scoffed. "Asking the man out on a date when he's just lost everything?"

Cynthia continued to ignore Austin, allowing his taunts to wash straight over her. "If you had the money to clear your debts, would you continue running the campsite?" she asked Ben.

"I suppose so, yes," Ben replied. "No, scrap that," he added. "In fact, I know I would. It was my dream job."

"*Pfft*," Austin remarked, still standing by the door. "The man's not got a pot to piss in. Good luck with that one."

"Haven't you gone yet?" Cynthia chided him. "Anyway, you're not entirely correct," Cynthia added, wagging her finger. "The thing is, Austin, I might have just accidentally forgotten to hand over the cash to Miles. Oh, and I didn't really fancy spending any time in the company of Cecil, either. So, you know, all of that money? It's still nestled safely in the holdall you gave me."

"That cash is mine!" Austin snapped, taking a step back inside the kitchen.

"No, Austin, my dear boy. That's dirty money," Cynthia replied. "And it's all going to Ben to settle the debts you helped him accrue. The way I see it, it's the least you can do. And think about how cleansed your soul will feel by helping out a fellow businessman?"

The vein in Austin's neck was nearly in danger of exploding. "You'll return my cash, Cynthia!" he said. "And, Ben," he added, extending a rigid finger. "Don't forget that loan you need to repay me! We've still got a signed agreement, so if you don't—"

"You'll do nothing," Cynthia abruptly cut in. "What you're going to do, Austin, is to jump in your flashy penis extension of a car and drive off to lick your wounds. You see, the conversation with Miles wasn't the *only* one I recorded."

Austin's cocksure manner ebbed as the meaning of Cynthia's statement began to register. "You recorded our conversations...?"

"Of course I did, Austin. After all, I didn't want to end up in the prison cell next door to yours, did I? And I'm sure the police would be just delighted to hear you chatting about all of your various and sundry criminal enterprises."

"Oh, bravo," Austin said again, his lips contorting into a smile. But it wasn't a happy sort of smile. It was more that he didn't know what else to do with his face. "And if I'm reading this situation correctly, if I conveniently forget about all of my cash being in your possession, then the recordings disappear? Is that it?"

"Oh, I wouldn't say disappear, necessarily," Cynthia advised. "More like stored safely in case they're required for future reference."

Austin went to speak, searching for a suitable scathing reply, but unfortunately for him, nothing presented itself. "Fine. Whatever. I'm bored of all this," he said instead. "I hope you're all very happy together," he added, stomping outside into the courtyard, kicking out at an innocent garden gnome on the way back to his motorised penis extension.

Farmer Gerry was first to break the silence as he watched Austin go. "He broke my gnome!" he commented, observing through the kitchen window as a ceramic head in a pointy hat rolled across the courtyard. "What an asshole."

Ben, for his part, appeared rather dazed, as if he'd been through a washing machine on the spin cycle. "Does this mean I can keep the campsite?" he asked of nobody in particular.

"Well, the money's there to completely catch up on what's owed to your builders," Cynthia answered. "And also to your landlord," she said, nodding at Farmer Gerry. "And Austin's generously written off the debt you owe him," she added, with an evil cackle that she enjoyed more than she probably should have. "So, I suppose it's all down to whether your friend Gerry here is happy for the campsite business to continue...?"

Ben and Cynthia's eyes both fell on Gerry now, who was still looking out the window, mourning the loss of his gnome. "Do I want you to continue with the campsite," he said, as a statement rather than a question. He gazed out at the rolling, verdant fields outside. "Well, I'm not sure about that," he mused, stroking his chin. "Having a load of diggers ripping up the land certainly *does* have its appeal," he said, though the smile on his face, as he turned around, told them he was only joking. Then, turning serious again, he said, "Ben, if you can make a go of it, and you're confident you can keep up with the rent, then what the hell. Let's do it."

"You mean I can stay?" Ben asked, fidgeting like he needed the loo, scarcely able to believe what he was hearing. "You're telling me that Life's a Pitch can continue?"

"That's what I'm saying," Gerry replied, a moment before Ben pounced on him.

"I can't believe this!" Ben yelled, spinning Farmer Gerry around like they were dancing the Viennese waltz. *"Life's a Pitch is back in business!"* he said, singing the words. "And the first thing I'm doing once I phone Ruby is to glue your garden gnome back together!"

Chapter Twenty-Three

L adies and gentlemen, may I have your attention," the chirpy tannoy announcer announced. "This is a final call for EasyJet flight E-Z-Y-eight-five-six to London Gatwick. Please, could passengers Mr and Mrs Crumpet kindly make their way to departure gate three where your aircraft is now boarding."

Meanwhile, plodding their way through the departure lounge, Cecil and his wife Fenella moved as fast as their undigested breakfast and inappropriate footwear permitted.

"I told you we didn't have time for a second helping," Fenella scolded her husband, who struggled to keep pace, his ill-fitting flip-flops slapping against his feet with every step. "And you've spilt egg yolk all down the front of your new shirt *again*, like you always do," she admonished.

"It's a breakfast buffet, Fenella," Cecil pointed out. "So you've got to get your money's worth," he told her, chomping down on the Cumberland sausage he'd managed to smuggle out for their long, arduous journey from the departure lounge to the departure gate.

If any of the other passengers in the airport were so inclined, it wouldn't have been too tricky to hazard a guess that Cecil and Fenella were heading for sunnier climes judging by their modest attire. Indeed, one could be forgiven for thinking they were ready for an afternoon lazing by the pool rather than merely embarking on the first leg of their journey from the Isle of Man. With Cecil's baggy denim shorts, flip-flops, and finest Jim Royle-style white vest, here was a man clearly ready to embrace his new life by the beach.

"They're starting to leave without us!" Fenella exclaimed, as she spotted the staff doing just that. "Yes, hello!" Fenella shouted out, waving her bag of duty-free Tanqueray gin to attract their attention. "Mister and Missus Crumpet are here!" she advised, long in advance of their ultimate arrival. "Don't close the gate because we're heading for sunny Spain!"

Fenella was the first to reach the gate. One of the airport ground staff, a smartly dressed lad who looked not long out of school, stepped forward to address her. "I'm sorry, madam. The gate is unfortunately closed," he told her, pointing to the door over his shoulder that was, as advised, now closed.

Fenella placed an angry hand on her hip, looking for her husband, who was still some distance behind her, finishing the last of his Cumberland sausage as he ran. "Thanks to your gluttony, the gate's closed!" she scolded.

"Ah, no matter. I think I know what's going on here," Cecil suggested, as soon as he caught up, unzipping the waist pouch secured around his ample middle. "There you go, my lad," he said with a wink, handing over a crisp note.

"You're giving me a five-pound note?" the lad asked, clipboard under his arm. "Seriously?"

"That's right," Cecil said. "And there's another fiver in it for you if you carry my hand luggage onto the plane for me."

The lad glanced down at the note in his hand and then back up to Cecil, unsure what to say. Perhaps it was the partially encrusted dollop of HP Sauce drying on Cecil's chin that distracted him, or the dried egg yolk on Cecil's sleeveless top (or "wifebeater," as the Americans would say). Or possibly the fact it was the first time anybody had ever attempted to bribe him. But whatever it was, this lad's integrity wasn't for sale, and a firm shake of the head confirmed as much to the Crumpets. "I'm sorry, sir," he added, handing the five-pound note back. "As much as it's *life-changing* money you're offering, I regret to say the gate is now closed."

Cecil's stomach started gurgling. It might have been from the damage he'd inflicted on the breakfast buffet, but more than likely, it was the thought of his Fenella's face when their plane took off without them on it. "Look, there must be something..." he started to say, desperately considering his options. And then, "Wait, hang on. I *know* you," Cecil said, staring at the boy for a long moment, just to be sure. "Yes. I knew I recognised that face. I *do* know you."

"I don't know about that, sir," the lad replied. "But regardless, the gate's still—"

"Your father is a vicar, yes?" Cecil cut in, as he rummaged through his memory banks and pulled out a file of particular interest. "He is, isn't he?"

"Uhm, yeah?" the lad replied, unsure where this was going.

Cecil leaned in very close, positioning himself so that the lad's colleague couldn't earwig. "You don't remember me, do you?" he whispered, breathing breakfast breath all over the left side of the lad's head. "Cecil Crumpet," Cecil said.

"No, sir," the lad said, taking a step to his right. "I don't think I've had the pleasure."

"Oh, we have," Cecil declared brightly. "Do you not remember? It took me a minute to place your face, but as I recall, I was around your house a couple of years back. It was when your dad, the vicar, needed some help in reclaiming a group of compromising photos that had fallen into the wrong hands. It was him doing something with his Dyson hoover, in fact. Something that wouldn't have been covered by the warranty."

At this, the blood drained from the lad's face. "A Henry Hoover, actually," he said, quickly reaching for Cecil's bag. "I'll carry this to the plane, sir," he said. "No need for an additional fiver. And I hope you both have a pleasant onward journey."

"Marvellous," Cecil said, following closely behind. "And don't forget to tell your father, the vicar, I said hello."

Eventually, finally aboard the aircraft and shuffling their way down the narrow aisle, the pair were oblivious to the audible tut-tuts from frustrated passengers annoyed that their departure had been delayed by at least ten minutes. "This is us," Cecil announced, drawing to a halt beside their row of seats.

"Room for two little ones?" Cecil said with a happy chuckle, speaking to the lady occupying the seat closest to the aisle.

In response, the woman smiled politely, though on the inside she'd probably been wishing the pair of them would continue walking down the aisle. "Oh, yes, of course," she said cordially, struggling to adjust herself to let the two of them take their seats.

"So sorry," Cecil offered, twisting this way and that, but unable to manoeuvre his portly frame through the limited available space.

However, the smiling lady likely figured getting Cecil successfully through was akin to slotting a round peg into a square hole. A *very* round peg, that is. "How about I just slide up to the window seat?" she offered.

Cecil shook his head. "No, no. My Fenella wanted to look out the window to say goodbye to the Isle of Man," he insisted.

Confused as to why Cecil was trying to squeeze in first if it was indeed his *wife* who wanted the window seat, the woman grew briefly annoyed, but then appeared to conclude that it wasn't worth the hassle of fighting over. "Fine. How about I just stand in the aisle for a moment?" she proposed, and then did exactly that, taking care not to make contact with Cecil's food-stained top as she and Cecil switched positions.

Following an impromptu game of Aircraft Twister, Cecil and Fenella were eventually seated. "This is us, my love," Cecil declared, reaching above his head and fumbling for the air conditioning nozzle. "Oh, bugger," he said a moment later.

"What have you done now?" Fenella asked, having just taken a sneaky swig from her gin bottle.

"I think I've pressed the button that—"

"Can I help you, sir?" the flight attendant asked, after hurrying over. "Is everything okay?"

"Sorry about that. I tried to turn the air conditioning on and hit the other button by mistake. But as you're over this way, I could murder a glass of red wine?"

"We just need to prepare the aircraft for departure, sir," the attendant advised. "We're already behind schedule, so if you could just bear with us a few more moments," she instructed politely, returning to her duties.

"And some peanuts?" Cecil called after her. "Or better yet, some cashews, if possible!"

Cecil reclined his seat, much to the annoyance of the passenger behind. "This time tomorrow, we'll be lounging around the pool in our new home, my love," he said, settling back. "*Y viva España*," he sang to himself, raising a smile from his wife.

"Ladies and gentlemen, your attention please," a voice crackled over the intercom system. "Ladies and gentlemen, this is your captain speaking. I regret to advise a delay of about fifteen additional minutes before we can push back from the stand. So, if you'd like to relax, we'll be on our way as soon as possible."

"Bloody typical," Cecil moaned, settling back and closing his eyes for a catnap. "Just when you're ready for the off, someone's always running late," he remarked, conveniently overlooking, of course, their own tardiness in boarding the flight. And before too long, Cecil was in the land of Nod, very likely dreaming about lazy days sipping something cool.

Well, that was until a firm finger tapped him on the shoulder. "Wake up, Mr Crumpet."

"Hmm? Was I snoring...?" Cecil asked, confused and disoriented. "Are we there yet?" he added, unsure what day it was. But unfortunately, for Cecil at least, the firm finger rousing him from his nap was a man dressed in uniform, flanked by another.

"Mr Crumpet?" the man asked.

"Ehm, yeah," Cecil said, assuming this uniformed man to be the captain, although why the captain should wish to speak with him like this, he couldn't say. Maybe he and his wife had earned some sort of reward for being the umpteenth passengers to fly with the airline? Anything was possible. "Everything okay, Captain?" Cecil asked, wondering what kind of prize they might have won.

"Cecil Crumpet, you need to collect your belongings and

leave the plane with us," the uniformed man responded, flashing his warrant card.

"Wait, what?" Cecil protested, looking across to his wife. "Is this because I pressed the call button by mistake?" he asked, wondering what was happening.

"No, Mr Crumpet, it's not because you pressed the call button by mistake," the man insisted. "Cecil Crumpet, you're under arrest for forgery, fraud by false representation, handling stolen goods, and theft. You need to come with us."

"You've *got* to be kidding me," Cecil answered, now sitting bolt upright. "We were just on our way to a new life in Spain!" he protested, pointing to his wife.

"Your new life in Spain might be on hold for a while longer," the police officer suggested. "Please. Collect your belongings, and we shall escort you from the plane."

"I don't believe this," Cecil said. "I'm supposed to be on my way to sunny Spain!"

Over at the campsite, Benjamin Parker was sitting under a magnificent oak tree, listening to the birdsong ringing out over the Manx countryside. This elevated farm area offered enviable views of the rolling hills and a complete panorama of his business empire. A business empire that had, just recently, come so perilously close to slipping through his fingers.

He could easily have sat there for hours, lost in his thoughts, wondering what was next for him and his daughter going forward, and what was next for Life's a Pitch. And it would have been too easy to become bitter, analysing the abhorrent actions of sleazeballs who valued money above all else, with little care for how such greed might destroy people's lives in the process. But Ben was a bigger man than that. He had grand plans for the future of the business, and toxic thoughts were something he didn't need in his life.

Unfortunately, Ben couldn't completely avoid Austin, what with him being a neighbour. But he was happy to ignore him as best as he could. And in no way did he condone the actions of his daughter and her friends, who'd apparently taken great delight in peppering Austin's property with eggs. Although he did permit himself a wry smile at witnessing the results, even though he didn't know with a hundred percent certainty it was them.

And while there were some 'rotten eggs' out there that could quickly destroy one's faith in your fellow man, Ben chose to focus on the positives. Including the other business owners who'd so graciously steered customers his way, helping out his fledgling enterprise, the patient and understanding builders who'd done such outstanding work for him, Cynthia (who'd ultimately saved his business), and Farmer Gerry, who Ben was proud to class as a friend.

It was a sobering thought for Ben, sitting there at that moment, knowing just how close this magnificent, lush green aspect came to being ripped apart by modern machinery with little concern for its natural beauty. But he was determined that this outcome would never happen under his watch. And yes, there'd been a few bumps (and a few boulders, even) along the way, but he wouldn't let them deter him. Instead, he'd learn from them, emerging bigger, better, and stronger, with a fierce determination to build an improved life for himself and his daughter.

"I thought I'd find you up here," Ruby said, parking herself on the grass beside him. "What's going on?" she asked, draping an arm around her father's shoulders.

"Nothing, really," Ben answered. "I'm just taking it all in, Ruby, and realising how fortunate I am."

"It's pretty special, isn't it?"

"Hang on, did I just hear clinking glasses?" Ben asked, looking over to see Ruby foraging through a bag she'd set down at her feet.

"Did you?" Ruby teased, liberating the bottle of Prosecco she'd procured from the campsite fridge. "I thought you might appreciate a glass," she told him. "It seemed like a good time to toast the new business, as well as the occasion of that tosspot Cecil finally getting what he deserves."

"Yeah, but I thought I heard *two* glasses?" Ben joked.

"I am nearly sixteen," Ruby felt the need to point out. "And I couldn't really let you toast to the future on your own, now could I?" she said. "That'd just be rude."

Ben laughed. "It would indeed be rude, Ruby," he happily conceded. "And I can't think of anybody I'd rather raise a toast with. Just don't tell your mother, okay?"

"Ah. There's little chance of that," Ruby promised.

"Oh," Ben added with a smirk, a thought occurring to him now that his daughter was there with him. "Remind me to pick up some eggs on the way home, as we appear to be running very low for some strange reason," he said, giving her a sideways glance.

"Uhm… yeah, okay. Sure," she said, grinning back, though without any overt admission of guilt. "Anyway," she said, handing her dad the bottle, "I'll let you do the honours."

Ben peeled away the foil, loosening the muselet securing the cork. With the sun setting, casting a warm glow over those campers preparing for another night under the Isle of Man's starry sky, there wasn't a place on earth that Ben would rather be. And nobody else he'd rather share the moment with.

"Wait!" Ruby said suddenly, before Ben could remove the cork. "Dad, what time is it?" she asked.

"The time? Why?" Ben answered. "Have you got somewhere you need to be?"

"No, no. I just need to know the time," Ruby told him.

"Ah," Ben replied, instinctively flicking his arm forward in response to the request. "Oh," he said, when his eyes fell on the pale patch of skin on his wrist. "Sorry. I guess I don't really know for certain what time it—"

"Here, this may help," Ruby cut in, handing him a walnut box.

"What's this, then?" Ben asked, temporarily stowing the bottle of Prosecco against his thigh.

"Look inside," she instructed.

Ben extended the lid of the hinged box, staring open-mouthed at its contents. "I don't believe it. Ruby, this is my watch," he told her, telling her what she already knew. "But why? I mean, *how?*"

Ruby offered a wink in return. "You just have to know the right people," she replied cryptically.

Ben removed the watch from the box, returning the time-piece to its rightful home on the end of his arm. "I don't know what to say," he said, not really knowing what to say. "Ruby...?"

Witnessing her dad's reaction melted Ruby's heart. "I went to see that woman Cynthia," Ruby explained. "I told her about how you'd had to pawn your watch because of what those scuzzballs did to you, and I wondered if there was enough money left over, from what she took from Austin, to get it back. And then she told me she'd sort it, and sort it she did."

"Oh, Ruby. I can't tell you how happy I am to have it back."

"She seems nice, Dad," Ruby went on. "Apparently, she's setting up an estate agency of her own. And her first client is the property developer who nearly bought this place."

But Ben wasn't listening right at the moment, instead fixated on the seconds hand of his watch as it slowly swept round in a circle.

"And she's pretty, as well," Ruby continued. "Dad? Dad, are you listening...?"

"Hmm?"

"I was saying that Cynthia is pretty."

"What? Oh, yes. Yes, I suppose she is," Ben answered. Then, spotting the smirk on his daughter's face that wasn't going away and was in real danger of becoming permanent, Ben eyed her with suspicion. "Ruby?" he said. "Ruby, what've you done?"

"Nothing," Ruby answered, twirling a strand of hair between her fingers. "Except, maybe... I might have mentioned to Cynthia that you like her?"

"Ruby Parker! You didn't!"

"Uh-huh."

"Ruby, that's really not..." Ben started to say, but then gave up on protesting any further. "So?" he asked.

"What?"

"So what did she say?" Ben pressed.

"Oh, I dunno," Ruby offered with a shrug. "It was a while ago, and you know what my memory is like," she teased.

"Ruby!"

"Okay, okay. Cynthia told me she wouldn't mind at all if you wanted to take her out for a drink," Ruby was pleased to convey. "She also said– Wait, Dad, are you blushing...?"

"How should I know? I can't see my face," Ben replied, pleasantly flustered. "I can't believe I'm at the stage of my life where my own daughter is arranging a date for me," he marvelled. "But thank you," he said, leaning over to plant a kiss on her head. Then, returning to the matter at hand, he gripped the Prosecco bottle, popping the cork with the skill of a sommelier. "Hold out those glasses, will you?"

"All the way to the top," Ruby instructed, ensuring there were no half measures at this fine outdoor establishment.

With their glasses full to the brim, Ben and Ruby leaned into each other, watching the sun setting on another glorious day on the Isle of Man.

"Here's to Life's a Pitch," Ben said, raising his glass.

"To Life's a Pitch," Ruby agreed, chinking her glass against her father's. "And you know what, Dad?" Ruby added. "We're the dream team, and we'll totally smash this!"

The End

For a complete list of the author's other books and to subscribe to his newsletter, please visit:

www.authorjcwilliams.com

You can also find all of his books on Amazon globally in Kindle, paperback, and audiobook formats.

Printed in Great Britain
by Amazon

85237115R00144